the scarlet gang of asakusa

浅草紅團

クレナヰダン

川端康成著

the scarlet gang of asakusa
yasunari kawabata

translated with preface and notes by **alisa freedman**
foreword and afterword by **donald richie**
illustrated by **ōta saburō**

university of california press *berkeley   los angeles   london*

F/C

University of California Press
Berkeley and Los Angeles, California

University of California Press, Ltd.
London, England

Originally published as *Asakusa kurenaidan* in 1930 by Senshinsha.
Chapters 1 through 37 were serialized in *Tokyo Asahi* from December
20, 1929, to February 16, 1930.

The 42 illustrations by Ōta Saburō that appear in this translation of
The Scarlet Gang of Asakusa (Asakusa kurenaidan) appear courtesy of his
estate. For these and the other illustrations, see the credits that begin
on page 229.

Library of Congress Cataloging-in-Publication Data
Kawabata, Yasunari, 1899–1972.
[Asakusa kurenaidan. English]
The Scarlet gang of Asakusa / Yasunari Kawabata ; translated by
Alisa Freedman ; with a foreword and afterword by Donald Richie ;
illustrated by Ōta Saburō.
p.   cm.
Includes bibliographical references.
ISBN 0-520-24181-9 (cloth : alk. paper)
ISBN 0-520-24182-7 (pbk. : alk. paper)
I. Freedman, Alisa.   II. Richie, Donald, 1924–   III. Samurō, Ōta,
1884–1969.   IV. Title.

PL832.A9A8913   2005
895.6′344—dc22   2004051614

Manufactured in Canada

14   13   12   11   10   09   08   07   06   05
10   9   8   7   6   5   4   3   2   1

The paper used in this publication meets the minimum requirements of
ANSI/NISO Z39.48–1992 (R 1997) *(Permanence of Paper).*

The publisher gratefully acknowledges the generous contribution to this book provided by the Literature in Translation Endowment Fund of the University of California Press Associates, which is supported by a major gift from Joan Palevsky.

contents

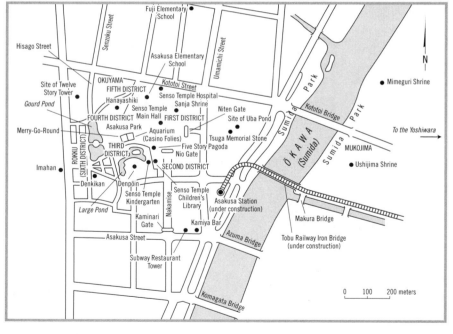

Asakusa, 1929. Adapted from A. M. Yori.

Fuji Elementary School

Senzoku Street

Hisago Street

Asakusa Elementary School

Umamichi Street

Park

N

Mimeguri Shrine

Site of Twelve Story Tower

OKUYAMA

FIFTH DISTRICT

Kototoi Street

Gourd Pond

Hanayashiki

Senso Temple Hospital

Sanja Shrine

FOURTH DISTRICT Main Hall FIRST DISTRICT

Senso Temple

Niten Gate

Kototoi Bridge

Sumida

Merry-Go-Round

Asakusa Park

Site of Uba Pond

To the Yoshiwara

Aquarium (Casino Folies)

Tsuga Memorial Stone

Ō K A W A (Sumida)

Sumida

Imahan

ROKU (SIXTH DISTRICT)

THIRD DISTRICT

Five Story Pagoda

MUKOJIMA

Nio Gate

SECOND DISTRICT

Ushijima Shrine

Denkikan

Denpōin

Senso Temple Kindergarten

Nakamise

Senso Temple Children's Library

Asakusa Station (under construction)

Large Pond

Kaminari Gate

Makura Bridge

Kamiya Bar

Asakusa Street

Azuma Bridge

Tobu Railway Iron Bridge (under construction)

Subway Restaurant Tower

Komagata Bridge

0   100   200 meters

foreword
donald richie

DURING THE FINAL decades of the nineteenth century and the first half of the twentieth, Asakusa was the major entertainment center of Tokyo. From the 1840s to the 1940s, it was to Japan's capital as Montmartre was to Paris, as the Alexanderplatz was to Berlin.

A place of mercantile pleasure, it at the same time retained a neighborhood vitality. It was perhaps this combination of brazen pleasure-mongering and downtown-district virtues that attracted the crowds. Tanizaki Jun'ichirō wrote of the "innumerable classes of visitor and types of entertainment and its constant and peerless richness preserved even as it furiously changes . . . swelling and clashing in confusion and then fusing into harmony."[1]

It was certainly this blending that was mourned when, after the 1923 earthquake, Akutagawa Ryūnosuke wrote of "the little pleasure stalls, all of them reduced to cinders . . . tiled roofs after a rain, unlighted votive lanterns, pots of morning glories, now withered. This too, all of it, was left a charred waste."[2]

Yet Asakusa recovered and, to the end, managed to retain something of its earlier charm. The novelist Takami Jun wrote in 1939 that Asakusa still had a "peculiar kind of warmth." Though it was like "a jazz record blaring forth in an alien tongue," it was also "all shyness and awkwardness as of a girl with an old-fashioned coiffeur and an advanced bathing suit."[3]

In a city that saw its pleasures and freedoms curtailed as Japan left behind the liberties of the 1920s and 1930s and marched into the wartime austerities of the 1940s, Asakusa remained to indicate that there was more to life than serving the country. It might be mercantile, but it was also acceptingly human. As observed in a popular song of the day by Soeda Azenbō, "Asakusa is Tokyo's heart / Asakusa is a human market."

ORIGINALLY ASAKUSA was not a part of Edo, the original name of the city of Tokyo. The district was beyond one of the city's checkpoints and was initially merely a community serving the needs of Sensō-ji, the big Kannon Temple, which drew hordes of both the pious and profiteers. During most of the Tokugawa period (1600–1868), Asakusa was just a place to go through. After the sumptuary edicts of the 1840s, which banned theaters and bordellos in Edo itself, however, Asakusa and the government-licensed prostitution quarter of Yoshiwara, to its north, were designated places of pleasure— tolerated retreats from the rigors of the samurai sternness of other parts of the city.

It was only during the Meiji period (1868–1912) that Asakusa developed its own identity. The novelist Saitō Ryōkū compared it to Ueno, a neighboring downtown district, and found that "Ueno is for the eyes, a park with a view, but Asakusa is for the mouth, a park for eating and drinking. . . . When you go to Ueno you feel the day's work isn't yet finished. When you go to Asakusa you feel that you have shaken off tomorrow's work."[4]

The great Asakusa Kannon Temple still brought the crowds to

the district, but it was the great pleasure city, Asakusa itself, that entertained them. Even the foreigners knew about it and went there. The widely read 1891 guidebook by Basil Hall Chamberlain and W. B. Mason finds that "the grounds of Asakusa are the quaintest and liveliest place in Tokyo . . . performing monkeys, cheap photographers, street artists, jugglers, wrestlers, life-sized figures in clay, venders of toys and lollipops of every sort, and, circulating amidst all these cheap attractions, a seething crowd of busy holiday-makers."[5]

There were other kinds of liveliness as well. An early foreign observer, W. E. Griffis, noted that near the temple were ranged the archery galleries, "presided over by pretty black-eyed Dianas, in paint, powder and shining coiffure. They bring you tea, smile, talk nonsense, and giggle . . . and then ask you leading and very personal questions without blushing. . . . Full-grown able-bodied men . . . can find amusement for hours at such play."[6] And later, in the back of the stalls, able-bodied men could take further advantage of these black-eyed Dianas.

With its attractions of sensationalism and sexuality, Asakusa prospered. One of Tanizaki's characters indicated the protean joys of Asakusa in 1911:

Changing my costume every night so as not to be noticed, I plunged into the crowd in Asakusa Park. . . . One night I'd tie a scarf over my head, don a short cotton coat with vertical stripes, apply red polish to the nails of my carefully scrubbed bare feet, and slip on leather-soled sandals. Another night I might go out wearing gold-rimmed dark glasses and an Inverness with the collar turned up. I enjoyed using a false beard, a mole, or a birthmark to alter my features. But one night, at a second-hand clothing shop . . . I saw a woman's lined kimono with a delicate check pattern against a blue ground, and was seized with a desire to try it on.[7]

Visitors to the Sensō Temple in the 1920s.

The Nakamise and the Nio Gate, 1924.

Later, in an unfinished novel, *The Mermaid (Kōjin)*, Tanizaki tells what Asakusa was like in 1918. Its attractions were "plays of the old style, operettas, plays in the new style, comedies, movies—movies from the West and Japanese productions, Douglas Fairbanks and Onoe Matsunosuke—acrobats balancing on balls, bareback riders, *Naniwa bushi* singers, girl *gidayū* chanters, the merry-go-round, the Hanayashiki Amusement Park, the Twelve Story Tower, shooting galleries, whores, Japanese restaurants, Chinese restaurants, and Western restaurants—the Rairaiken, won ton mein, oysters over rice, horsemeat, snapping turtles, eels, and the Café Paulista."[8]

There was also the Asakusa Opera, where originally some opera was actually sung. An early attraction was *Rigoletto,* and "La donna é mobile" became a local hit, although, no tenor being available, the Duke was sung by a soprano. Shortly, however, the attractions became more varied. Tanizaki's hero here discovered "caricatures of Charlie Chaplin, [and] living reproductions of such stars as Pearl White, Ruth Roland, Doris Kenyon, Billie Burke, and Dustin Farnum. The reproductions were, of course, crude knock-offs . . . but paradoxically they charmed the audience precisely because they were crude."[9]

The Asakusa Opera also meant flesh on view, the firm thighs of the chorus line. In a 1942 story, "The Decoration" ("Kunshō"), novelist Nagai Kafū remembers what it was like. Backstage

was given over to clutter, such a clutter that you wondered how anything more could possibly be added. An indescribable disorder . . . what first caught the eye, however, was not the violent jumble of colors, or even the faces of the girls as they sprawled about on the floor and then sat up again. It was the powerful flesh of the arms and legs . . . it called to mind the earthen hallway of a florist's shop, where a litter of torn-off petals and withering leaves is left unswept and trampled into shapelessness.[10]

Crudity became an Asakusa commodity. The hero of Tanizaki's unfinished novel is simultaneously repelled and attracted by it. He confides that he is drawn to Asakusa because, finding Tokyo ugly, he wants to "experience this ugliness in its purest state." He suggests that "since seeking beauty in this city of Tokyo is useless, can it not be said that the most agreeable place to live is Asakusa, where ugliness bares its essential form?"[11]

This crude and ugly but vibrant and sexy Asakusa was soon after destroyed. The 1923 Kanto earthquake demolished it, as it demolished much of Tokyo and Yokohama. Among the more famed calamities was the collapse of the Asakusa Twelve Story Tower (the Ryōunkaku, or Cloud-Surpassing Pavilion), a brick structure that had become synonymous with Asakusa. Also gone was the old neighborhood structure of the place. The sense of community, raffish but real, that had appealed to many (Akutagawa Ryūnosuke among them) was never entirely recovered.

Because it was a pleasure city, an entertainment capital, one of the great night towns of the world, however, reconstruction began at once. And now, symbolizing the new Asakusa, instead of the Twelve Story Tower there was the Subway Tower building, with its observation platform. Kawabata said it was in the Osaka style, all the floors except the top being eating places. This influence of Osaka, known for commerce rather than culture, upon what was left of old Edo was commonly lamented. "Why, it's gotten just like Osaka," complains a character in one Kawabata story.

Actually, it was like no place else on earth. In commenting on *The Scarlet Gang of Asakusa*, Kataoka Yoshikaze, writing in 1939, described the new Asakusa as that "human market" where

the pleasure resort of the Edo period, the vestiges of the crude, semi-enlightened curiosity of the Meiji era, and the over-ripeness . . . of the present era of capitalist corruption, are thrown together in a

The Rokku, the cinema and theater district of Asakusa Park, in the late 1920s.

The Rokku and its cinemas and revue halls, 1933.

Movie theaters in Asakusa Park around 1930.

Movie theaters in the Rokku in the second half of the 1920s.

forever disordered state. Or organized in a manner peculiarly like the place itself. Eroticism and frivolity and speed and comic-strip humor; the bare legs of dancing girls and jazzy revues; kiss-dances, foreign girls, ground-cherries and popular songs; the movie, the circus, the fake, dilapidated aquarium and insectarium. Here the girls bob their hair and "Bobbed-hair" so-and-so, wearing a red dress, plays the piano, deep in a narrow backstreet lane, with her knees exposed. Her rendezvous notes are scribbled on the back of the Goddess Kannon's written oracles.[12]

Like Montmartre in the 1890s, like New York's Times Square in the 1940s, the place was license itself. In *The Scarlet Gang of Asakusa,* Kawabata quotes Soeda Azenbō's heightened description: "In Asakusa, everything is flung out in the raw. Desires dance naked. All races, all classes, all jumbled together forming a bottomless, endless current, flowing day and night, no beginning, no end. Asakusa is alive."

AMONG ALL THESE varied attractions, one of the most popular was the cinema, a form of entertainment early associated with Asakusa because the first Tokyo movie house, the Denkikan, had opened there in 1903. Here one could see the wonders of the West; after 1932, one could even hear them—Marlene Dietrich and Gary Cooper talking to each other in *Morocco,* one of the first films subtitled for Japanese audiences.

Kawabata noted that by 1930, Asakusa had fourteen movie houses. He also stated, however, that it had even more live theaters. (In addition, his survey counted half a dozen vaudeville, or *yose,* halls, one kabuki theater, the largest number of pawnshops in the city, and the most beggars: in the summer of 1930, some eight hundred were living in Asakusa Park, though Kawabata did not trust this official estimate and maintained that there were far more.)

Kawabata himself eschewed the screen in favor of the stage, in particular the Asakusa revue, a dance and comedy show with erotic undertones first performed in 1929 by the Casino Folies (Kashino Fori). He described this performance as composed of "eroticism and nonsense and speed, and humor in the vein of the topical cartoon, the jazz song, legs."[13] *Ero guro* was the spirit of the age. This combination of the first syllables of "erotic" and "grotesque" typified that combination of the sexy and the absurd and characterized the many entertainments of Asakusa: on the one hand, the firm-thighed chorines, and on the other (since Meiji times, it was said), the man who smoked through his navel.

Kawabata's novel made the Casino Folies famous, though the revue's leading comedian, Enoken, said that its popularity was based only on the false rumor that on Fridays the chorus girls dropped their panties. In any case, the novelist also gave us our only real record of what the place was like.

Kawabata shows us Asakusa at its prewar prime. *The Scarlet Gang of Asakusa* captures the area at its most Asakusa-like, a hundred million people a year, a human wave, money spilled into shows, eateries, geisha houses, a world frivolous, frenetic, and filled with flesh. "Asakusa is like a specimen in the Bug House," says the narrator of the novel, "something completely different from today's world, like a remote island or some African village."

Soon after that, the place began its decline. Exotic bloom that it was, in increasingly illiberal Japan, Asakusa began to fade. Takami Jun wrote that by 1938, "The famous old places of Asakusa had been abandoned. . . . The birthplace of the Asakusa revues was in a state of advanced neglect, the subject of weird stories. Late at night, it was said, you could hear the sound of tap dancing on the roof. It has since been torn down, and so those who loved the Casino Folies have lost all trace of their dream."[14]

The military takeovers of the 1940s subdued even more the Asakusa spirit. Nagai Kafū, one cold night in 1944, recorded the closing of the Opera House, his favorite. "As I passed the lane of shops . . . on my way to the subway, I found myself weeping again. . . . I have been witness to it all, Tokyo going to ruin."[15]

It went completely to ruin in 1945. In the U.S. incendiary raids of March 9 and 10, between 70,000 and 80,000 people were killed, and some two-fifths of the city was destroyed—Asakusa, too. The Kannon Temple was hit at one-thirty in the morning and was consumed by flames in just two hours.

After the conclusion of the Pacific war, the Allied Occupation authorities gave much of the land in Asakusa to the Kannon Temple, which, having no money of its own, sold it. Thus, Asakusa Park, with its famous pond, disappeared. The area behind the temple was turned into a parking lot for tourist buses; another portion went to a motion-picture company, which built a theater and an amusement hall.

That postwar innovation, the strip show, was visible from 1948—more flesh than ever before seen, with variations as well: the bath strip, the tightrope strip, etc. But all this activity was illusory. Tokyo was moving west; Shinjuku was the new night town, and Asakusa was forgotten. By 1966 one newspaper headlined, "Deserted Place, Thy Name Is Asakusa."[16]

ASAKUSA EARLY HELD a fascination for Kawabata. He once said that for three years during his high school days, he commuted daily, rain or shine, between two popular Asakusa gathering places, the Café Paris and the Café Elban. One day he glimpsed Tanizaki, some thirteen years his senior and already a well-known writer, at the nearby Nihonkan, surrounded by pretty girls, and thought that this would someday be he.

After graduating from high school in 1920, the twenty-one-year-

The Twelve Story Tower. Built in 1890, the tower was Tokyo's tallest building.
It was destroyed in the 1923 Great Kanto Earthquake. This photo
was taken sometime between 1910 and 1923.

old Kawabata, though nominally a Tokyo Imperial University student, rented his own place in Asakusa, on the second floor of a hat repair shop, and started to write.

He was in his room when the 1923 earthquake hit, but the building stood and he escaped unhurt. His first reaction, as soon as the tremors stopped, was to round up fellow writers Kon Tōkō and Akutagawa Ryūnosuke and make a walking tour of the ruins. He continued taking long walks every day, carrying with him a jug of water and something to eat in his knapsack. Later he wrote that there couldn't have been many who saw so plainly what the earthquake had done.

He was also neglecting his Imperial University studies. A contemporary noted that the student Kawabata was "more fond of soaking in the public bath than of attending classes."[17] He was writing, however, and later he became the editor of a new magazine,

The Age of Literary Arts (Bungei Jidai). In it, he said his ambition was to view every incident of the human condition through new eyes. The critics dutifully labeled his group the New Perception School (Shinkankaku-ha).

Viewing every incident through new eyes was one of the tenets of the new aesthetic movement, modernism. This is a loose label, indeed, but it may be at least provisionally defined. According to Malcolm Bradbury, it is experimental, formally complex, and elliptical. The language is often awry, cultural cohesion is lost, perception is pluralized. It "tends to associate notions of the artist's freedom from realism, materialism, traditional genre and form, with notions of cultural apocalypse and disaster."[18]

A body of writers illustrates the concept. Among them are Proust, Mann, Gide, Kafka, and Joyce in fiction; Strindberg, Pirandello, Wedekind, and Brecht in drama; Mallarmé, Eliot, and Rilke in poetry. Their works are often aesthetically radical and technically innovative, often emphasize spatial as opposed to chronological forms, tend toward irony, and involve what Ortega y Gasset (who did not like modernism) called a certain "dehumanization of art."[19]

Kawabata knew modernist narrative—indeed, he had already created some. In 1926 he wrote the scenario for *A Page Out of Order (Kurutta ichipeji),* Kinugasa Teisuke's modernist film (produced by the New Perceptionist School Motion Picture Federation). Like everyone else, Kawabata had seen Robert Wiene's *Das Kabinett des Dr. Caligari,* a modernist landmark and another film set in an insane asylum.

In addition, though he understood English only with difficulty, he had attempted to read *Ulysses.* One wonders if he also knew about the other big-city modernist novels of the period, Bely's 1916 *Petersburg* and Döblin's 1929 *Berlin Alexanderplatz.* He certainly knew *Shanghai* (1928–1931), then being written by his best friend and fel-

Poster for the Casino Folies revue, June 9, 1930.

low New Perceptionist, Yokomitsu Riichi. Indeed, Kawabata stated that *Shanghai* was the "grand summation of the methods" of the New Perceptionist School.[20] And he had early had some knowledge of the aims of modernism. Marinetti's 1909 *Declaration of the Futurists* had been translated by prominent literary figure (and Japan's surgeon general) Mori Ogai and published in Japan the same year it came out in Italy.

He would also have been familiar with Nagai Kafū's *Geisha in Rivalry (Udekurabe)*, published in 1916. In it, one of the characters, having visited an Asakusa prostitute, walks back past the Kannon Temple and stops to look at it, then recalls that "he had once read, in some magazine or other, a review of a novel by Blasco Ibáñez called *La Catedral* . . . [which] had used the cathedral of Toledo as a focus for sketching the lives of those who lived in its environs. It had immediately occurred to [him] to write a novel applying this idea to the Kannon Temple of Asakusa."[21] Nothing came of this, but four years later Tanizaki set out to write just this sort of book, *The Mermaid*. Nothing came of this either—the author abandoned it after two hundred pages. It was Kawabata who finally wrote the novel you are about to begin.

The author would also have known that Asakusa had already been singled out as the best place to study the popular culture that formed the basis of the kind of modernism that interested him. In 1921, Gonda Yasunosuke, scholar of Japanese popular culture, told his students, "Go to Asakusa—Asakusa's your text."[22] His advice became famous, and a number of students did their fieldwork there.

Kawabata moved to Asakusa in 1929. He already knew it well from his high school days and its post-earthquake days. Now he began to frequent the Casino Folies, which had just opened, taking notes about the dancers and the lives of the demimonde. It was these notes that were made into the novel *The Scarlet Gang of Asakusa*, its sequel, and his other Asakusa writings.

In this way, Kawabata later said, he made use of his three years of research walking around Asakusa. "All I did was walk. I never became acquainted with any of the young delinquents. I never addressed a word to the vagrants either . . . but I took my notes."[23] He was not interested in journalism, or in reportage. He wanted to write down what he saw and to display it in modernist form.

In 1930, when Kawabata was still living in Asakusa, Gonda Yasunosuke completed a study of the area, in which he wrote that in Asakusa, the differences were all visible—that he could show, as though in relief, what restaurants sold what and who ate or drank it, which different classes went to the movies, the vaudeville halls, the stage shows. He included the sizes of the businesses, distinguished the employees by sex and age, and counted the different sorts of enterprise native only to that place.[24]

This is, in a way, what Kawabata was attempting as well, except that he was creating not a work of advanced sociology, but a modernist novel. Gonda contended that the excesses of Asakusa were not intended as escapes from the economic recession then gripping Japan, but as resistance to the social conventions reinforced by monopoly capital. Kawabata had much the same aim, to show the vitality of the place and the people, but his means were artistic.

In this he was somewhat like Virginia Woolf, another writer he had tried to read. His Tokyo is like Mrs. Dalloway's London. It is composed of a collection of seemingly random perceptions unattached to social issues. A difference is that Kawabata's novel is also (another modernist strategy) a commentary on itself. To begin with, it is a pop novel, complete with two-dimensional *manga* or comic-book characters and a gag title—*Asakusa kurenaidan* sounds just as jokey in Japanese as *The Scarlet Gang of Asakusa* does in English. It employs a comic deflation of the past, as when Prince Genji and Lord Narihira caper together on the same stage. There is purposely hokey melodrama, as in the boat scenes, which feature Yumiko's panther leaps and her notorious arsenic kiss. There are pop tag lines, such as "Follow those bikes!"

At the same time, there is serious dislocation. The story is often broken into and is at one point abandoned and not rediscovered until the final page. There are "cubist" catalogues, such as the various views from the Subway Tower, so timed as to disturb any idea of continuity. And there is much questioning of the narrative itself, as in the pretense that events influenced its composition: "By the way, dear reader, as for Yumiko . . . When I'd reached this point in my story, I met Yumiko in a strange way, and so my novel must also suddenly change course."

Insisting upon artificiality, Kawabata maintains throughout that, as he says at the beginning, "in the end, this is just a novel." And at the end, he indicates it. Suddenly, Yumiko reappears, this time dressed up as a young peddler from the island of Oshima and is selling its local product, camellia oil for the hair. Kawabata knows that his readers will be aware that "selling oil" *(abura o uru)* is a colloquialism for pulling a fast one and getting away with it. This then, he now indicates, is just what he has done with his novel—getting away with it becomes a metaphor for his book and his method.

Recondite as all this is, the book was intended for a popular audience and was originally serialized in the widely read *Asahi* newspaper. It was as though *Ulysses,* hot from Joyce's pen, had appeared weekly in the *London Times.* This was possible because in Japan, then as now, the avant-garde is at once incorporated into the taste of the masses, so strong is the lure of the new. Also, in Kawabata's novel, the brand new came sandwiched between the tried and true.

In it, the reader savors

> the curious inebriation induced by a cocktail made, as it were, from [Asakusa's] tradition and its modernism. Hence, as a story, it is not aimed at a consistently integrated delineation of characters and incidents, the latter having been treated merely as bubbles of all sorts and shapes that give form to the swirling currents of Asakusa, leaving them to rise and vanish at will, and thus creating numerous focal points in the narrative and rendering its sensation both intricate

and many-sided. . . . Cutting, linking, superimposing, unraveling, the story is plotted out on a bewildering scale which is at once variable and involved and which, in short, is very like the cinema.[25]

Certainly, the narrative is very unlike that of the ordinary novel. Seiji M. Lippit, in his masterly exegesis of *The Scarlet Gang of Asakusa,* has identified many of the differences. There is a multiplicity of writing styles and genres, along with aggregated language and much slang. The literary mixes with the non-literary, resulting in a fragmentary style, that of reportage and descriptive poetry. The narrative moves from image to image, a progression Kawabata said was like "the succession of images in a newsreel" and that insisted upon a "free and reckless association."[26]

The conventional novelistic structure is, in the process, dismantled, and there is a willful confusion of tenses and persons. Amid all this Lippit has identified three narrative voices: first, the narrator, the one addressing the "dear reader"; second, this narrator as character in the novel itself; and third, another voice, objective, in the third person, recounting things the first two voices could not know.[27]

All of this accounts for the famous difficulty of the text. Critic Maeda Ai has said that when he first tried to read it, as a college student, he couldn't make it to the end. The famous opening—one long, many-claused sentence, beginning with confusing particulars and only widening into its subject at the end—all but defies translation.

The structure is equally unexpected. The book stops in the middle while new protagonists take over, and it is not until the final pages that the story we began with suddenly returns. In the meantime, the work turns self-referential, with asides referring to its own popularity, even to the stage and screen versions of it. *The Scarlet Gang of Asakusa,* Edward Seidensticker has said, is like Asakusa itself:

"mannered, diffuse, obscure, and inconclusive even as Kawabata novels go . . . but it is interesting."[28] Certainly, some of this is due to the author's becoming a modernist. Kawabata was familiar with the foreign models, and his idea of what the new perception and new art ought to consist of precluded much that might have been expected.

Van C. Gessel has written that "the attempt to adopt some of the techniques of European modernism and the struggle to break away from the flat, overly realistic and autobiographical tendencies that dominated the first two decades of the twentieth century in Japan are noteworthy achievements. Much that seems surprising, elliptical and sometimes even odd in Kawabata's writing can be traced to his days as a New Perceptionist."[29] It can also be attributed to his membership (and he was one of the founding members) in the New Art School (Shinkōgeijutsu-ha), that short-lived organization formed in opposition both to old-fashioned naturalist literature and newfangled proletarian tracts. The New Art School shared many aims with the New Perceptionists, but there were many differences as well.

The New Art School certainly emphasized an affiliation with that subgenre that Alisa Freedman has identified as the laconic "urban sketch," which she characterizes thus: "The urban gaze is not a meditative one and instead is a fleeting look at the barrage of spectacles that pass before the eyes of the viewer like the landscape seen from the window of a moving train."[30]

At the same time, one can also say, as Edward Seidensticker has, that "the influence of Edo literature [on *The Scarlet Gang of Asakusa*] is so strong as to make it seem almost imitative. It is not typical Kawabata. The investigation of lonely lives on the edge of the Asakusa demimonde is, however, close to the central preoccupation of Kawabata's writing."[31]

The role of observer was one Kawabata felt fit not only the aspirations of the New Perception School but also his own nature. Many critics have noticed how the role of observer seems to define or limit his fiction. The detachment and distancing he showed in all of his work was the dominant theme of his own life—the loss of both parents when he was four, then, one by one, the demise of the rest of the family, and unhappy love affairs, one with a fellow student, later one with a girl. Isolated, he chose to maintain this separation between self and others both in his work and in his life.

The detached, watching narrator communicating elliptical fragments of his vision also has some precedents in Japanese literature. The protagonists of that genre known as the *shishōsetsu (watakushi shōsetsu,* the first-person-singular novel) share this regard, though it is more often self-regard.

Kawabata was, however, at least in his Asakusa writings, a special kind of spectator. He was a flâneur, one who strolled about, committing himself to nothing and no one. An often ironic observer, he turned perception itself into a kind of judgment. Like Baudelaire on the boulevard, Kawabata in Asakusa was a literary dandy whose gaze was his only comment.

When Kawabata went to study Asakusa, he was, at the same time turning against the respectable life of a university student with an assured social position. His first popular success, *The Izu Dancer (Izu no Odoriko),* is about a student who, rather than studying, wanders the countryside of Izu and encounters an itinerant performing group and the very young dancer who excites his regard. In one of his last books, *The House of the Sleeping Beauties (Nemureru Bijo),* the narrator is an old man who pays to sleep with heavily drugged young girls who are unaware of his loving, critical, intrusive, accepting gaze. The young girls of *The Scarlet Gang of Asakusa*—Yumiko, Haruko, and all the rest—are members of this crew that so attracted the author all his life.

The elegant stroller is also slumming—the regard of the flâneur is also the open stare of the voyeur. Kawabata in this novel says he is afraid of being like the Edo poet Ōta Nanpo, also known as Shokusanjin and characterized as "a debauched man of letters." Yet his apparent fears invite our speculations.

"That's Asakusa," he proclaims at each new revelation, apparently not noticing his own condescension or that he is reveling in "this world-of-nothingness garbage-can of Asakusa." The lower classes, as they would be called, seem to invite this regard. And the lower classes at play seem to make it mandatory. Asakusa thus strongly appealed to those with a *nostalgie de la boue* or, as Kawabata phrased it, a "taste for back streets."[32]

This savoring of the lower classes is often aligned to a taste for control. Not only is the "mud" found more "authentic" than anything upper class, it is also found to be more malleable. Paul Morand in Montmartre, Carl Van Vechten in Harlem, Paul Bowles in Tangier—all are examples of men who found their métier in becoming purposely, if temporarily, déclassé. They found a new (sometimes finer, more admirable) authenticity, they found a container for their own feelings, and, though often powerless in their own social spheres, they found something they could control. It was not a question of patronization, however, or of venting simple superiority. This "taste for back streets" contains a sincere admiration coupled with an equally deeply felt need to manipulate. It is this combination that lends such a sense of conviction in this literature.

The Scarlet Gang of Asakusa was written swiftly. By December 1929, it was already being serialized in Japan's most-read newspaper. *The Izu Dancer* had made the writer famous, and here was a new work that promised even more. It proved quite popular, created a kind of Asakusa vogue, and made a sensation of the Casino Folies. Having read the novel, people started to come to see the place, and for a time it commanded the attention of what Kawabata disdainfully called the "Ginza people." Perhaps it was in scorn of such success (though he was slumming no less than they) that Kawabata said that in his work he had used only a hundredth of his material and that even so, he was ashamed of the results.

Or perhaps it was that modernism as a technique no longer expressed his needs. A number of writers during this period—Yokomitsu Riichi, Itō Sei, Hori Tatsuo, Satō Haruo—were experimenting with the style. All of them, including Kawabata, abandoned it. Stephen Snyder speaks of "the general consensus that the attempt to find a Japanese idiom in which to render the verbal pyrotechnics of the European brand of modernism was by and large a failure."[33]

If Kawabata was truly ashamed, he shouldn't have been. *The Scarlet Gang of Asakusa* may have been one-shot modernism, but it effortlessly captures a remarkable era and a fascinating place, both now gone. It also was the theater where Kawabata could create a persona for his first-person singular, for a narrator who was not himself, one who had no authorial validity but without whom he could not express observations, justifications, reflections of the place as he really found it. Both personality and place are joined, face to face, in this evocation of somewhere that never existed and somewhere that did.

NOTES

1. Paul Waley, *Tokyo Now and Then: An Explorer's Guide* (New York: Weatherhill, 1984), 176.
2. Edward Seidensticker, *Low City, High City: Tokyo from Edo to the Earthquake* (Cambridge, MA: Harvard University Press, 1983), 208–209.
3. Edward Seidensticker, *Tokyo Rising: The City Since the Great Earthquake* (Cambridge, MA: Harvard University Press, 1990), 113.
4. Seidensticker, *Low City, High City*, 119.
5. Ibid., 158.
6. Ibid., 207.

7. Jun'ichirō Tanizaki, "The Secret," trans. Anthony Hood Chambers, in Aileen Gatten and Anthony Hood Chambers, eds., *New Leaves: Studies and Translations of Japanese Literature in Honor of Edward Seidensticker* (Ann Arbor: Center for Japanese Studies, University of Michigan, 1993), 161–162.

8. Ken K. Ito, *Visions of Desire: Tanizaki's Fictional Worlds* (Stanford, CA: Stanford University Press, 1991), 69–70.

9. Ibid., 73.

10. Edward Seidensticker, *Kafū the Scribbler: The Life and Writings of Nagai Kafū* (Stanford, CA: Stanford University Press, 1965), 331.

11. Ito, *Visions of Desire*, 67.

12. Yoshikazu Kataoka, "*Asakusa kurenaidan*," in *Introduction to Contemporary Japanese Literature* (Tokyo: Kokusai Bunka Shinkokai, 1939), 339.

13. Ibid., 73.

14. Seidensticker, *Tokyo Rising*, 112.

15. Seidensticker, *Kafū the Scribbler*, 166.

16. Seidensticker, *Tokyo Rising*, 184.

17. Van C. Gessel, *Three Modern Novelists: Sōseki, Tanizaki, Kawabata* (Tokyo: Kodansha International, 1993), 155.

18. Malcolm Bradbury, "Modernism," in *A Dictionary of Modern Critical Terms*, ed. Roger Fowler (London: Routledge & Kegan Paul, 1987), 151–152.

19. Ibid., 152.

20. Donald Keene, *Dawn to the West: Japanese Literature of the Modern Era*, vol. 3 (New York: Holt, Rinehart, and Winston, 1984), 656.

21. Ito, *Visions of Desire*, 65.

22. Miriam Silverberg, "Constructing the Japanese Ethnography of Modernity," *Journal of Asian Studies* 51, no. 1 (February 1992): 30.

23. Keene, *Dawn to the West*, 795.

24. Silverberg, "Constructing the Japanese Ethnography of Modernity," 44–49.

25. Kataoka, "*Asakusa kurenaidan*," 341.

26. Seiji Mizuta Lippit, *Topographies of Japanese Modernism* (New York: Columbia University Press, 2002), 126–127.

27. Ibid., 131.

28. Seidensticker, *Tokyo Rising*, 71.

29. Gessel, *Three Modern Novelists*, 158–159.

30. Alisa Freedman, "Tracking Japanese Modernity: Commuter Trains, Streetcars, and Passengers in Tokyo Literature, 1905–1935" (PhD diss., University of Chicago, 2002), 172.

31. Edward Seidensticker, "Kawabata Yasunari," in *Kodansha Encyclopedia of Japan*, vol. 4 (Tokyo: Kodansha International, 1983), 175–177.

32. Keene, *Dawn to the West*, 796.

33. Stephen Snyder, *Fictions of Desire: Narrative Form in the Novels of Nagai Kafū* (Honolulu: University of Hawaii Press, 2000), 127.

translator's preface

AS DONALD RICHIE discusses in his foreword, *The Scarlet Gang of Asakusa (Asakusa kurenaidan)* by Yasunari Kawabata (1899–1972) is an important piece of Japanese modernism that captures a fascinating period of Tokyo history and culture. Straddling the border between fiction and nonfiction, the novel focuses on a group of delinquent Asakusa youth who guide the narrator through this burgeoning commercial and entertainment area in 1929 and 1930. During these years of economic recession, Asakusa, with its mystique of old Edo, or Tokyo before the mid-nineteenth century, became the center of new popular entertainments, including the Casino Folies dance revue that Kawabata helped make popular. Asakusa was also the place where increasing numbers of homeless people sought shelter. In this playful yet highly complex work, Kawabata strives to create a mode of expression that conveys both the sensory perceptions of rapidly modernizing Tokyo and the aspects of social relations and material culture that he believed best represented the allure and anxieties of early-twentieth-century urban life. As a result, *The Scarlet Gang of Asakusa* differs markedly from Kawabata's later work on

Japanese aesthetics and introduces another side of this 1968 Nobel Prize winner. To better enjoy the novel and more fully understand its place in Japanese literature, some background information on its publication and explanation of the formal idiosyncrasies in the original are necessary.

The first thirty-seven chapters of *The Scarlet Gang of Asakusa* were serialized in the evening edition of the popular daily newspaper *Tokyo Asahi* between December 20, 1929, and February 16, 1930. Installments appeared toward the bottom of the first page, with breaks every couple of days to alleviate some of the pressure on Kawabata. Publication was suspended when there were many news stories to report.[1] From the latter part of the nineteenth century, literature by both new and established writers was commonly serialized in Japanese daily newspapers. At the time of *The Scarlet Gang of Asakusa,* up-and-coming authors were published in the *Tokyo Asahi* evening edition; Kawabata's novel immediately followed the serialization of *City Hyperbola (Tokai sōkyokusen)* by then-Marxist and modernist Hayashi Fusao. The morning edition contained works by better-known, often older writers; while *The Scarlet Gang of Asakusa* was put in print, *Yuri Hatae* by Kishida Kunio finished, and *Spring of Truth (Shinri no haru)* by Hosoda Tamiki began. Although Kawabata had published short pieces in newspapers— the Asakusa story "Japanese Anna" ("Nihonjin Anna") appeared in the January 9, 1929, issue of *Tokyo Asahi*—this was his first serialized novel.

In September 1930, the remaining sections of *The Scarlet Gang of Asakusa* were published concurrently in two intellectual literary journals. While chapters 38 through 51 appeared under the title "The Scarlet Gang of Asakusa" in *Reconstruction (Kaizō,* volume 12, number 9), chapters 52 through 61 were printed as "The Red Sash Society" ("Akaobikai") in *New Currents (Shinchō,* volume 27, number 9). The story was left unfinished after chapter 61. The entire novel and five works of short fiction—"Japanese Anna," "Whitening Powder and Gasoline" ("Oshiroi to gasorin"), "The Fettered Husband" ("Shibarareta otto"), "Asakusa Diary" ("Asakusa nikki"), and "The Aquarium Dancer" ("Suizokkan no odoriko")—were published as a book in December 1930 by the Senshin company.[2] In the early 1930s, book versions of *The Scarlet Gang of Asakusa* were also published by the Kaizō and Shun'yōdō companies. As mentioned in chapter 39, a no longer extant film version of *The Scarlet Gang of Asakusa* was produced in 1930, while the story was still being serialized and the fates of the characters were yet unknown to readers.[3] A Casino Folies revue based on the novel was first performed on July 10, 1930, and starred dancers described in the book.

In addition, *The Scarlet Gang of Asakusa* was included in anthologies of New Art School (Shinkōgeijutsu-ha) writing. The New Art School was a short-lived literary club that essentially lasted from 1930 to 1931. Most of the approximately thirty members had earlier been affiliated with the New Perceptionist movement (Shinkankaku-ha) discussed in Donald Richie's foreword. They were young men who experimented with American and European modernist forms, which they abandoned in the 1930s and 1940s either as a conservative reaction to what they saw as too much alienating and superficial Westernization or because of the control of the Japanese state over literary production.[4] Although possessing diverse literary backgrounds and aesthetic ideals, these authors were united in their advocation of "art for art's sake" *(geijutsushijō shugi)* and in their desire to create a means of expression that did not narrate or internalize urban sensations but instead presented a more unmediated experience of the power of the city. Similar to the New Perceptionists, who have received more attention from both Japanese and Western scholars, members of the New Art School—frequently socially conscious but rarely Marxist—were vehemently opposed to the proletarian literature being written from the early 1920s to the first years of the 1930s, which they criticized for advancing political ideologies at the expense of aesthetics and for being old-fashioned in its literary form and focusing solely on despair.[5] They believed that the patterns and problems of the city could be revealed through depictions of the especially erotic and grotesque *(ero guro)* aspects of urban everyday life. Although sometimes unintentionally, through their choice of literary content and form, New Art School writers tended to exoticize the Tokyo underworld, to uncritically celebrate consumer culture, and to turn social problems into alluring urban myths. The group dissolved in part owing to differing literary concerns among its members and increasing censorship of their stories. Slightly less than one-third of *The Scarlet Gang of Asakusa* was included in the 1930 *Modern Tokyo Rondo (Modan TOKIO Rondo)*, a collection of urban sketches and stories by twelve New Art School authors edited by Kuno Toyohiko. As the musical title indicates, the selections depicted the fast-paced rhythms of city life and focused on the decadence and complexity of Tokyo, its glamour and grime.[6] *The Scarlet Gang of Asakusa* was also published in *The Collected Works of New Art School Writers (Shinkōgeijutsu-ha bungaku shū)*, the sixty-first volume in the series of modern Japanese literature *(Gendai Nihon bungaku zenshū)* published by the left-leaning Kaizō company.

As with many novels serialized in daily newspapers, *The Scarlet Gang of Asakusa* was illustrated, and a different line drawing by Ōta Saburō (1884–1969) appeared with each of the first thirty-seven installments.[7] (These thirty-seven drawings, the originals of which were lost during the Second World War, have been reproduced here.) In each episode, Ōta's name was printed right after Kawabata's, showing that these illustrations were an important component of this very visual novel. (Notably, the narrator is not depicted in any of them.)

Five additional drawings by Ōta that were published in the Senshin version and in *Modern Tokyo Rondo* are also found in this volume. Both fictional and factual texts about Tokyo published around the same time as *The Scarlet Gang of Asakusa* featured line drawings, photographs, and collages of bridges, streets, transportation, women wearing Western hairstyles and clothing, and other images characterizing the modern metropolis. The cover of the Senshin edition of *The Scarlet Gang of Asakusa,* used as the frontispiece in this volume, is strikingly similar to that of "ethnographer of Japanese modernity" Kon Wajirō's illustrated guidebook and essay collection *The New Edition to the Guide to Greater Tokyo (Shinpan dai Tokyo annai),* published by the Chuō kōron company.[8] Both covers were drawn by Kon's research partner Yoshida Kenkichi. Western-style painter Koga Harue (1895–1933), whose 1930 *Makeup Out of Doors (Sogai no keshō)* has been selected for the cover of this English translation, created covers for such works as Ryūtanji Yū's immensely popular 1930 novel *The Age of Wandering (Hōrō jidai)* and Kataoka Teppei's 1930 *In Praise of Women (Joseisan).*[9]

Although Kawabata remarked that rereading *The Scarlet Gang of Asakusa* made him feel nauseous, he wrote a sequel.[10] *Asakusa Festival (Asakusa matsuri)* was serialized in the monthly journal *Literature (Bungei)* from September 1934 to February 1935. Like its precursor, *Asakusa Festival* was left unfinished, and publication ceased after twenty-four chapters. As in *The Scarlet Gang of Asakusa,* the narrator strolls through Asakusa, describes what he sees, and reminisces about the women and places once found there. Asakusa, however, is not the same, in part owing to increased police control, changing Tokyo demographics and consumer trends, and socioeconomic conditions. Characters from *The Scarlet Gang of Asakusa* appear, but they have changed for the worse. For example, Haruko, now called Oharu, is the madam of a struggling house of assignation. She no longer seems as coy and cheerful as she did in the novel a few years before and goes so far as to offer to sell the narrator information about Asakusa. Although she is not a major character in *Asakusa Festival,* Yumiko, now age twenty-five, is spotted playing the old-fashioned koto with Utasaburō, the boy actor whom she had helped with his socks in *The Scarlet Gang of Asakusa.*

IN TRANSLATING *The Scarlet Gang of Asakusa,* I faced the challenge of making this novel, which demands a broad knowledge of Japanese literature, history, and popular culture and a familiarity with Western literary modernism, accessible to English-speaking readers. Although it is impossible to replicate *Asakusa kurenaidan* in English, my goal has been to create a translation that does justice to the original and conveys the experience of reading this vibrant story.

Translation is not a dry, mechanical process of transliterating words and substituting sentences, nor is it a free and unrestricted act of ignoring the text as it exists and producing a mere re-creation in another language. Instead, the translator is forced to make choices and compromises and to constantly negotiate between literalness and readability. Aspects of form and accuracy are inevitably sacrificed, and jokes often lose something in the translation. Yet the process allows a certain amount of creativity and interpretation, and translators enjoy a rare opportunity to engage in a dialogue with a text they come to know very well. Every translator unavoidably brings his or her own background into the work. As experienced Japanese translator Jay Rubin has remarked, "The Japanese language is *so* different from English . . . that true literal translation is impossible, and the translator's subjective processing is inevitably going to play a large part. That processing is a *good thing;* it involves a continual critical questioning of the meaning of the text. The last thing you want is a translator who believes he or she is a totally passive medium for transferring one set of grammatical structures into another: then you're going to get mindless garbage, not literature."[11]

From the first page of *The Scarlet Gang of Asakusa*, the reader is confronted with perhaps unfamiliar names and places, and this can have the unintended effect of making the story seem exotic or elitist. Notably, the American movies, ice cream, and pork cutlets mentioned in the novel would have seemed just as exotic, if not more so, to Japanese readers in 1930 than the *yukata*, Sensō Temple votives, and other things Japanese do to today's readers of this translation. An extensive glossary of terms and phrases is found at the back of the book. I have chosen to put explanations there, rather than in footnotes, in order to retain the look of the original and avoid diverting readers' attention from the story.

As Donald Richie explains, *The Scarlet Gang of Asakusa* is an amalgam of past and present, high and popular cultures, and this affects the content and form of the novel. From the very first page, Kawabata engages with Edo (1603–1868) history, culture, and literature, and the first chapter establishes the themes of simultaneous lament for a fading way of life and celebration of the new sites and entertainments that have replaced lost landmarks and pastimes. Kawabata also incorporates Heian (794–1185) literary classics, and the narrator alludes to the tenth-century *Tales of Ise (Ise monogatari)* and *The Tale of Genji (Genji monogatari)*, written around 1000. The protagonists of these works, Lord Narihira and Shining Prince Genji, perform a jazz dance in an Asakusa revue. In addition, the narrator refers to kabuki plays and actors, and he even equates himself to Edo poet and "debauched man of letters" Ōta Nanpo. Legends about Asakusa sites are told to the reader in the voice of a wise storyteller.

The new Asakusa entertainments described in *The Scarlet Gang of Asakusa*, especially cinema and dance revues, also shape the narration, an effect I have tried to convey in the translation. Short sentences are interspersed among very long ones, often giving the narrative a jazz or rondo syncopation. Kawabata depicts Asakusa iconographically through selected places, behaviors, and objects presented in various cinematic languages. Urban images are captured in the prose equivalent of differing camera techniques: close-ups, panoramas, tracking shots, montage, crosscutting, framing, among other filmic styles. The narrator describes the city as seen from atop the Subway Restaurant Tower and from bridges spanning the Ōkawa, and he shows the reader in detail the myriad things sold on Asakusa streets. In addition, Kawabata incorporates stock lines from the movies, especially *yakuza* or Japanese gangster films popular at the time. (These lines would have been read by a *benshi* or film narrator, since talkies were not popular in Japan until after 1935.)

Dance revue programs, movie billboards, popular songs, and advertisements are quoted throughout. In this translation, different typography makes these various voices more visible on the page, a technique not used by Kawabata but borrowed from Western modernist works, such as John dos Passos's early 1930s trilogy *USA*. In the same spirit, dashes instead of quotation marks are used to set off dialogue, as done by James Joyce and André Gide, among other Western modernists. Kawabata's use of quotation marks for emphasis and irony has been retained.

Kawabata stated that although he had no models for Yumiko and her Scarlet Gang and had himself created the name for this gang and the others in the novel, he had thoroughly researched the situation of Asakusa juvenile delinquents and the poor. Kawabata, often accompanied by Folies dancers, wandered Asakusa almost daily, but, in the end, only incorporated a hundredth of his notes in the story.[12] He consulted books by popular writers Ishizumi Harunosuke, Satō Hachirō, and Soeda Azenbō, who lived in or frequented Asakusa, and the names of the latter two appear in the novel.[13] At times, the narrator quotes directly from these guidebooks and from newspapers, roundtable discussions in literary magazines, fictional stories, and other texts about Asakusa, but he does not always reveal his sources. For example, at the beginning of chapter 10, he quotes the first two lines of Soeda Azenbō's 1930 book *Record of the Asakusa Underworld (Asakusa teiryūki)*. Chapter 14 includes a few lines from Tanizaki Jun'ichirō's 1920 *The Mermaid (Kōjin)*, and, in this instance, the narrator states the name of the author but not the title of the work. The narrator also tells the reader stories Kawabata has written, without giving their titles.

Kawabata incorporates Asakusa slang in two ways, both of which have been retained in this translation: in some instances, the characters define the terms in conversation with the narrator; in others, the slang is given in katakana, the Japanese character system often used to indicate foreign words, followed by the definition in parentheses. The latter is the case for such terms as *zuke, gure,* and *daigara,* buzzwords for the different strata of vagrants who made their homes in Asakusa Park and were listed in Ishizumi Harunosuke's 1927 literary guidebook *Little-Known Asakusa Stories (Asakusa ritan),* which Kawabata might have read.[14] The character Haruko uses a form of inversion common among *yakusa* in which the second character is said before the first; for example, she says *enko* instead of *koen* for "park." Other such inversions exist in Tokyo slang, including the term *doya,* used instead of *yado* in the poor neighborhood of San'ya located near Asakusa to specify a cheap hotel in which beds in shared rooms are rented by the night.[15] All English slang in the translation was in common use in 1930. Kawabata also makes many puns, which I found to be the most difficult aspect of the translation. For example, he playfully uses both meanings of the word *fūten,* "vagabond" and "lunatic," when he writes, "Almost all of the hobos in Asakusa are crazy. Asakusa is one big insane asylum."

In addition, I have tried to replicate the fragmented narration, confused syntax, and wordplay of Kawabata's style in this novel. A lively and nuanced mode of expression is apparent from his very first sentence. Throughout, the narrator directly addresses the reader in a friendly tone as he guides him through Asakusa, and the main narrative is written almost entirely in the present tense, as if the actions were occurring right before the reader's eyes. However, as Richie discusses, the story is not told consistently from one point of view, and at times the narrator describes events that he would not have been able to see. For example, he gives detailed accounts of what transpires when Yumiko is alone with Akagi on the boat and what Left-Handed Hiko tells the young girl in the house of assignation. There are abrupt breaks and rapid jumps from one topic to the next. Much in the story remains vague or unsaid, and at times it is up to the reader to decide what has really happened or who is speaking. It is common in Japanese to omit the subjects of sentences, but Kawabata does this almost excessively in *The Scarlet Gang of Asakusa*.[16] I have been very careful not to add any explanation or smooth over any gaps.

I have not altered Kawabata's use of run-on and fragmented sentences, and I have tried to remain faithful to his unorthodox use of language. A short, disjointed sentence represents a brief sex scene, but I will leave this for the reader to discover.[17] Inanimate objects perform human tasks, and body parts, especially eyes, become the subjects of sentences. Adverbs are sometimes used as adjectives to provide more immediate sensory impressions, as when the collars of the Casino Folies dancers are open "whitely" (see chapter 11). Kanji, or Chinese characters incorporated into Japanese writing, are used to convey visual images. For example, the character 井, usually read "i" and meaning "a well," is used to depict a pattern stamped on a kimono.

In the interest of clarity, I have adjusted the erratic punctuation of the original, which includes excessive use of dashes and open-ended parenthetical phrases, and its strange paragraphing.

Because *The Scarlet Gang of Asakusa* was written for newspaper serialization, the narrator occasionally repeats his own or the characters' remarks and recaps events in order to refresh the memories of previous readers and orient new ones. For instance, he opens chapter 6 by telling readers that he talked about the attractiveness of the Scarlet Gang members in the preceding section, and then he continues this discussion by giving an example from a conversation he had with Yumiko at some unstated time in the past. Several slightly conflicting accounts of what happened to Yumiko on the boat are given in the second half of the novel.

One final note: While most fictional characters are identified by their first names, Kawabata gives the full names of the historical figures who appear in the novel. These names are given in Japanese order, last name first.

MUCH WRITING and revision were necessary in attempting to capture in English the beauty of the often elusive formal aspects of the Japanese original and the visions of Asakusa, its characters and history, that Kawabata strove to show. I have many people to thank for their help and support during the translation process. I would like to thank Richmod Bollinger, who translated *The Scarlet Gang of Asakusa* into German, for introducing me to this project and for her advice, especially on the first twenty chapters.

I would also like to express my sincere gratitude to and admiration for Donald Richie. During the last stage of this project, he helped me greatly in my effort to construct a convincing, consistent narrative voice (one of the most difficult tasks I faced) and to make the novel more readable in English. I have learned much from his stylistic suggestions and from our discussions about Japanese literature and Tokyo past and present. His years spent capturing the intricacies and emotions of Japanese urban life will always inspire me.

I would like to thank Laura Cerruti, Rachel Berchten, and Stephanie Rubin, my helpful and encouraging editors at the University of California Press. I am grateful to copy editor Jan Spauschus, the press's two anonymous reviewers, and Liza Dalby for close readings and valuable comments. Nicole Hayward did a wonderful job of designing the book. Junko Kawakami acted as go-between, helping obtain rights to use the illustrations included in this text. Fumiko Kitamura carefully checked the accuracy of the English translation. Anthony Yori created the map, and Emily Box and Meredith Dunn helped proofread the manuscript. William Sibley introduced me to *The Scarlet Gang of Asakusa* in his Japanese literature class at the University of Chicago and gave me my first copy of the novel. Norma Field, Brett de Bary, and other colleagues at the University of Chicago, Cornell University, and the University of Illinois at Urbana-Champaign were always available to answer questions about translation and Japanese modernity and to give advice. Thank you to friends who did not run away when I asked their help in finding just the right English word. Thank you to my family for their continuing support.

Generous financial assistance from the University of Chicago and the Japanese Ministry of Education, Culture, Sports, Science, and Technology and a Mellon postdoctoral fellowship at Cornell University provided me with the means to do the extensive research and numerous revisions needed to accurately translate the novel. The Museum of Modern Art, Kamakura, kindly gave permission to use Koga Harue's 1930 oil painting *Makeup Out of Doors* for the book cover, and the estate of Ōta Saburō allowed the inclusion of the original drawings. The Shitamachi Museum in Tokyo provided the historical photographs. For this translation, I have used Kōdansha's

1996 edition of *Asakusa kurenaidan,* which is the same as that included in volume 4 of the *Collected Works of Kawabata Yasunari
(Kawabata Yasunari zenshū)* (Shinchōsha, 1982). The only difference
is that newer forms of kanji characters are used in the Kōdansha
version, and, subsequently, some of the *rubi* glosses that indicate
how the kanji are pronounced have been omitted there.

NOTES

1. *The Scarlet Gang of Asakusa* appeared in *Tokyo Asahi* twelve times in
   December (December 12–15, 17, 19–22, 25, 26, and 29), thirteen times
   in January (January 5, 8, 10, 11, 14, 16, 17, 19, 24, 25, 28, 29, and 31),
   and twelve times in February (February 1, 2, 4, 6–9, 11, and 13–16).
   For more on the serialization of the novel, see, for example, Kawabata
   Yasunari, *Asakusa kurenaidan ni tsuite* (About *The Scarlet Gang of Asakusa*), in *Isso ikka—Gendai Nihon no essai* (Collected Essays on Modern
   Japan) (Kōdansha, 1991), 272–273.
2. This was the first time that "Whitening Powder and Gasoline," "The
   Fettered Husband," and parts of "Asakusa Diary" were published. "The
   Aquarium Dancer" was included in the April 1930 issue of *New Youth
   (Shinseinen),* a popular journal that contained detective fiction, erotic
   tales, and other stories of the seductive and dangerous aspects of
   modern urban life.
3. Six of Kawabata's fictional works were made into movies in the 1930s,
   and Casino Folies star Umezono Ryūko, mentioned in *The Scarlet
   Gang of Asakusa,* appeared in the 1935 film version of "Asakusa Sisters"
   ("Asakusa no shimai"). See Van C. Gessel, *Three Modern Novelists: Sōseki,
   Tanizaki, Kawabata* (Tokyo: Kodansha International, 1993), 205, notes
   59 and 64.
4. Members of the New Art School were, in addition to Kawabata, Abe
   Tomoji, Asahara Rokurō, Fukada Kyūya, Funahashi Seiichi, Furusawa
   Yasujirō, Hori Tatsuo, Ibuse Masuji, Iima Tadashi, Jinzai Kiyoshi,
   Kamura Isota, Kasahara Kenjirō, Kimura Shōzaburō, Kobayashi Hideo,
   Kon Hidemi, Kuno Toyohiko, Kurahara Shinjirō, Nagai Tatsuo, Naka-
   mura Masatsune, Narasaki Tsutomu, Nishimura Shinichi, Ōno Matsuji,
   Ryūtanji Yū, Sasaki Toshirō, Sō Akira, Takahashi Takeo, Tsubota Katsu,

Tsunekawa Hiroshi, Yagi Tosaku, Yasutaka Tokuzō, Yoshimura Tetsu-
tarō, and Yoshiyuki Eisuke. For more on the New Art School, see G. T.
Shea, *Leftwing Literature in Japan: A Brief History of the Proletarian
Literary Movement* (Tokyo: Hosei University Press, 1964), 195–197; and
Alisa Freedman, "Tracking Japanese Modernity: Commuter Trains,
Streetcars, and Passengers in Tokyo Literature, 1905–1935" (PhD diss.,
University of Chicago, 2002).

5. In general, New Art School writings were more journalistic than
New Perceptionist works, which conveyed sensations from multiple
viewpoints and often reduced material culture and urban places to
abstraction.

6. *Modern Tokyo Rondo* was the first volume of Vanguard Jazz Literature of
the World's Biggest Cities (Sekai daitokai sentan jazu bungaku shiriizu),
a series that included translations of Ben Hecht's 1921–1922 *One Thousand and One Afternoons in Chicago*, a collection of urban sketches published for the *Chicago Daily News;* Philip Dunning's *Jazz: Broadway;*
stories set in Shanghai, Paris, and Moscow; and an anthology of *Greater
Tokyo May Day Songs by Ten Proletarian Authors (Meidei uta—dai Tokyo:
Puroretaria sakka jūnin)*. Selections in the first volume included Ryūtanji Yū's "Pavement Snapshot: From Night to Morning" ("Pēbumento
sunapu—yonaka kara asa made"); Kuno Toyohiko's "That Flower! This
Flower! Oh! The Grime of Modernism!" ("Ano hana! Kono hana! Aa!
Modanizumu no aka yo!"); Asahara Rorkurō's depiction of Tokyo's Maru-
nouchi business district, based on a verse from the 1929 popular song
"Tokyo March" ("Tokyo koshinkyoku"); Yoshiyuki Eisuke's story about a
department store; and works by Abe Tomoji, Hori Tatsuo, Kurahara
Shijirō, Sasaki Fusa, Nakamura Murao, Ibuse Masuji, and Nakagawa
Yōichi. Kuno Toyohiko, ed., *Modan TOKIO Rondo: Shinkōgeijutsuha
jūninin* (Modern Tokyo Rondo: Works by Twelve New Art School
Authors), Sekai daitokai sentan jazu bungaku shiriizu (Vanguard Jazz
Literature of the World's Biggest Cities) (Shun'yōdō, 1930). Most of these
works are reprinted in Yoshiyuki Eisuke, *Yoshiyuki Eisuke to sono jidai—
Modan toshi no hikari to kage* (Yoshiyuki Eisuke and His Times: The
Light and Shadows of the Modern City), ed. Yoshiyuki Kazuko and
Saito Shunji (Tokyo shiki shuppan, 1997).

7. Printmaker and book illustrator Ōta Saburō was known for depicting

what he saw as modern Tokyo, especially café waitresses, revue dancers, and other women associated with the erotic aspects of the city. Born in Aichi Prefecture, Ōta came to Tokyo in 1901 to study art, and in 1910 his works were first accepted by the Ministry of Education Exhibitions, or Bunten, as this national salon was commonly known. From 1920 to 1922, Ōta studied Western art in Europe and was influenced by fauvism and cubism. See Unno Hiroshi, *Modan Toshi Tokyo: Nihon no 1920 nendai* (Modern City Tokyo: The 1920s in Japan) (Chūō kōronsha, 1988), 50; Jackie Menzies, *Modern Boy, Modern Girl: Modernity in Japanese Art, 1910–1935* (Sydney: Art Gallery of New South Wales, 1998), 155.

8. The phrase "ethnographer of Japanese modernity" is from Miriam Silverberg, "Constructing the Japanese Ethnography of Modernity," *Journal of Japanese Studies* 51, no. 1 (February 1992): 30–54.

9. Koga Harue left his home in Fukuoka Prefecture in 1912 to study at the Institute of Watercolor Painting (Nihon Suisaiga Kenkyūkai) in Tokyo, and he exhibited his first work in 1913. Koga was greatly influenced by Western modern art, especially surrealism and montage techniques, and he cited Paul Klee as an inspiration. Like Ōta, Koga illustrated books, and in 1932 he designed covers for the humor magazine *Tokyo Puck* and the literary journal *Era of New Art (Shinbungei jidai)*. Koga also wrote poetry and criticism. Menzies, *Modern Boy, Modern Girl*, 153. See also *Koga Harue sōsaku no genten: Sakuhin to shiryō de saguru* (Koga Harue: Exploring the Origins of His Art through His Works and Materials), Special Exhibition Catalogue (Bridgestone Museum of Art, Ishibashi Foundation Tokyo and Kurume, and Ishibashi Museum of Art, 2001).

10. Kawabata Yasunari, preface, *Asakusa matsuri* (Asakusa Festival) (Kōdansha, 1996), 203.

11. Jay Rubin, *Haruki Murakami and the Music of Words* (London: Harvill Press, 2002), 286.

12. Kawabata, *Asakusa kurenaidan ni tsuite*, 280.

13. Ibid, 279. Kawabata Yasunari, *Asakusa kurenaidan no koto* (On *The Scarlet Gang of Asakusa*), in *Kawabata Yasunari zenshū* (Collected Works of Kawabata Yasunari), vol. 33 (Shinchōsha, 1982), 168. Although they are not mentioned in the novel, Kawabata was also interested in the late 1920s and early 1930s surveys, classifications, and sketches of modern practices and behaviors conducted by Kon Wajirō and his associates,

and he wrote an essay about their 1930 collected volume *Modernologio*. A memorial stone for Soeda Azenbō on the grounds of the Sensō Temple shows how influential this writer was in Asakusa.

14. Ishizumi Harunosuke, *Asakusa ritan* (Little-Known Asakusa Stories) (Bungeishijō, 1927), 69–70. For the sake of clarity, I have not maintained the great deal of slang defined parenthetically in the conversation between members of a factory-girl kidnapping gang in chapter 47.

15. See, for example, Edward Fowler, *San'ya Blues: Laboring Life in Contemporary Tokyo* (Ithaca, NY: Cornell University Press, 1996).

16. See Edward Seidensticker, "Edward Seidensticker on Nagai Kafū and Kawabata Yasunari," in Donald Richie, ed., *Words, Ideas, and Ambiguities: Four Perspectives on Translating from the Japanese* (Chicago: Imprint Publications, 2000), 25.

17. I am indebted to Richmod Bollinger for this insight.

the scarlet gang of asakusa

AUTHOR'S NOTE: It is hard to know what kind of trouble the following novel might cause members of the Scarlet Gang or any of the others who make their dens inside and outside of Asakusa Park. I hope, however, that it will be forgiven, because, in the end, this is just a novel.

the piano girl

1

EVEN NOW, right now in modern Tokyo, just like in the old Edo picture books, he's still here, it's said—the bird catcher: the copper-colored fittings on his tanned suede pouch, the pipe hanging from the agate fastener on the pouch  strings, and the old-fashioned tobacco case filled with that sweet-smelling Kokubu stuff, mixed in with a few green stems to keep it from drying out—all dangling from his waist, and his white drawers, his black leggings, the white fingerless mittens, and a plain blue cotton kimono hiked up around his hips. The man who told me this is an inspector at the Metropolitan Police Office, not a person given to idle reminiscence.

But I am. I want to talk like they did back then in the old Edo days. Take this road. Yes, we ought to determine, my dear reader, if this road on which I am about to lead you to the hangout of the Scarlet Gang is the same road on which it has been said, in the old days of Emperors Manji and Kanbun, men with swords in white scab-

3

bards tucked into their white leather *hakama,* all white right down to their steeds, traveled to and from the Yoshiwara while making their horsemen sing bawdy *Komuro bushi* songs.

Let's now suppose it's past three in the morning and even the bums are sound asleep, and I am here walking through the grounds of the Sensō Temple with Yumiko. Dead ginkgo leaves flutter down, and we listen to the crowing of the cocks.

—That's funny. It's chickens they keep at the Holy Kannon Temple. Having said this, I freeze in my tracks. Four dressed-up young girls with very white faces are standing right in front of us.

Yumiko laughs: You'll always be a tourist. They're the Hanayashiki dolls.

Then with the first gray of dawn, it's said that the bird catcher hunts out the little birds with his long pole. But this is something a late riser like me isn't likely to see.

And lately isn't prominently displaying the girls' pictures forbidden even in the Yoshiwara, and so they put little photos in glass cases and you have to peer at them as though they were butterfly specimens?

And (another example) that musical instrument that blends the typewriter and the piano—we all know it as the "Taisho koto," but now some enterprising shopkeepers are calling it the "Showa koto." That's how it is these days. Just no nostalgia for old Edo. Here, let me unfold it before you, dear reader, the newly revised "Showa Map" drawn following the reorganization of the city after the shake-up of the 1923 Great Kanto Earthquake.

Look, right here the Asakusa motor bus runs along the asphalt road between Uguisudani in Ueno and the Kototoi Bridge. Walking north from the bus stop in back of the Sensō, the Asakusa Kannon Temple, you see Umamichi-machi is on the right and Senzoku-machi is on the left. Go on a bit, passing the Kisakata Police Station on the left, and the Fuji Elementary School on the right. Then, after the Sengen Shrine, you come to a crossroads. Walk along the stone wall of the shrine, and you pass the public market, then the Kamiarai Bridge, spanning the banks of the Yoshiwara canal. But before reaching the bridge, there is a certain alley . . . Well, to say "a certain alley" sounds like I'm beginning a real old-fashioned novel. The members of the Scarlet Gang haven't done anything that criminal. They're much less likely to prey on you than the local rickshaw pullers, and I could just as well write out the address.

—Mister! Hey, Mister! A rickshaw puller calls out to you in Asakusa Park, in the Yoshiwara, thereabouts: You look like a guy who knows how to have good time. How about something different for a change?

An agreement is reached. The rickshaw man at once takes off his rubber-soled cloth boots, puts on his wooden sandals, tosses his rickshaw-man cap into the rickshaw, flags down a one-yen taxi, haggles the fare down to fifty sen, and off he goes with his customer. Each man has his own territory, secret (he never tells the others), where he keeps his woman, who, when things get tough, he sells off to passersby. It doesn't matter if she has a nine-year-old, a four-year-old, or is six months pregnant with the next.

But now, dear reader, if you happen to be interested in pilgrims' votive stickers, then you've seen those stuck here and there on shrines advertising the Scarlet Troupe. The Scarlet Gang likes to call itself the Scarlet Troupe because it wants to think of itself as a theatrical group and harbors hopes of staging something spectacular— or what it would consider spectacular—in this small booth set up on a vacant lot. One young member has already started up on the Nakamise. She sells rubber balls while doing the Charleston.

2

THE SCARLET GANG uses votive stickers, but they do it in a way all their own. It's not that they are curious enough to want to learn that the practice of using votive stickers was begun by Emperor Kazan, who stuck them on all the places of wor-  ship he visited, and that stickers were even designed by ukiyoe artists like Utagawa Toyokuni. Also, they don't believe in their efficacy enough to go around slapping them on shrines and temples just for that reason. I'll give you an example. One day that little tyke Boat Tokikō (his father is a boatman on the Ōkawa, so he is called Boat Tokikō) said to me: You know the Five Story Pagoda?

—The one at the Sensō Temple?

—Yep. On the third story counting from the top or the bottom, on the corner near the Nio Gate, there's this ridge-end tile sticking out. It's got a monkey's face on it, and its eyeballs are all gold. Well, I want to stick my sticker flat on the monkey's face.

So just like that, under the cover of night, they stick their Scarlet Troupe votive stickers at truly inappropriate locations. For example, the middle of the three big paper lanterns at the Nio Gate entrance to the Sensō Temple, or on the black-lacquered bottom of that lantern from Irifune-chō, or the horns of the cow statue in the grounds of the Ushijima Shrine over in Mukōjima.

And it's not that members are truly aspiring artistes. It's that they want to scandalize everyone at least once with such displays of outlandish and unexpected originality. Like (I am just reminded) when they asked me to write a play for them and one of them made this endearing request: Let's not just *handle* (that's Asakusa lingo for shaking hands) Akikō. Can't we please take turns doing something more interesting with him?

And thinking about that . . . Right—it was when I was walking through the Rokku with this same Akikō. A crowd has gathered around Gourd Pond, people laughing their heads off. The late summer sun is warming their backs, and I peep through and am I surprised!

Just at the neck of the gourd-shaped pond there is this little island, wisteria-trellised bridges extending from either bank. There, next to the fatsia bush under the weeping willow in front of the Tachibana fish stew shop, a large man is standing, eating the wheat crackers that have been thrown to the carp in the pond. Ankle-deep, he rakes them in with this bamboo pole some two meters long. Then he stands up straight and noisily munches his crackers.

—What a nut. He ought to pay the carp a commission.

And everyone on my side of the pond laughs. Then after he's greedily gobbled up some fourteen or fifteen of the carp's crackers, the man calmly makes his way out of the pond, very dignified, just as though there were nothing at all strange about his behavior.

But Akikō runs after him: Ken! Ken! The man stops behind the Bug House, and Akikō gives him a ten-sen coin. Then turning to me, he says: Until a couple of days ago he was a *zubu* here.

—A *zubu*?

—That's a kind of beggar. Wanders around. No place of his own. I heard the other day that he'd pulled himself together, dragged himself out of the gutter, and did pretty well as a worker. But now he's back. Times are tough.

—What? He's not crazy then?

—Can't someone eat carp crackers in the pond without pretending to be crazy? But I don't know. Maybe he really is crazy. Sane people nowadays eat things out of garbage cans in broad daylight. Anyway, he's back here again. But he's got the reputation of being so full of himself that even the *zuke* (his beggar buddies) won't help him. He's hungry.

Ah, since the members of the Scarlet Gang are like this . . . Well, my dear reader, why don't you just let me take you to their hideout. You remember that "certain alley"? I didn't just wander there on a whim. I had my own agenda. But as for finding that beautiful young short-haired girl playing the piano at the end of that blind alley— that was pure luck.

3

AND AS FOR that "certain alley"—before you reach the intersection near the Kamiarai Bridge on the banks of the Yoshiwara, you turn left onto a small side street almost in front of you, and there you'll see a vacant lot.

There's a felt-and-cork-sandal-maker's shop on the right and a water moxa treatment shop on the left. Noticing a "For Rent" sign at the back of the lot, I step over rows of ceramic pipe and piles of dead weeds and go into that dead-end street. Naturally, a tenement district. The ground floors of the houses on either side of the entrance are crammed with stacked sacks of charcoal, and the inhabitants all seem to live upstairs. Men's shirts and ladies' undies are slung across the alley on a bamboo pole. If I lived back behind this gate, think I, then I wouldn't have to worry about anyone recognizing me.

As I duck to pass through the laundry gate, I look to the left. I can just about see the top of the lookout tower of the Nihon Dam Fire Department. Must be somewhere near, I mumble to myself, and then past the third house from the entrance, I stop short—as if a bunch of bright red flowers has been suddenly thrust at me.

A young woman in a red dress is pounding the piano in the entryway. The bright red stands out against the black of the piano, and the white of her legs, bare from knees down to feet, is young, fresh. The entryway isn't much wider than a wooden sandal is long, and from where I stand, just outside, it seems as though I can reach in and give that black ribbon around her waist a tug. This ribbon is the only decoration, but because the dress is sleeveless with a low neckline, it's something like an evening gown. No, even here at home she's wearing something for the stage—a dance costume? Traces of white powder cling to the nape of her neck, and above it her hair is cropped close as a boy's.

Just as she turns toward me in surprise, a twelve- or thirteen-year-old girl comes running in. She too stares at me suspiciously. So I begin to walk on.

On the house hangs a round wooden sign, the words "Piano Lessons" carved and painted green.

The younger girl turns to the elder: I hear the Casino Folies is showing again at the Aquarium.

—Really? And they're on the stage with no stockings. Maybe I can get myself a job with a revue like that. Oh, how about the bikes?

—I could borrow them.

And with that the two of them seem to have gone upstairs.

The house for rent is two doors down, but before I even get there, it hits me: That's it, that's it. I clearly remember those two girls. I remember where I saw them before.

The Hōsendō, the shop of the fan maker Bunami. Once I bought a dancer's fan for my younger sister in the country. Then leaving the store and heading toward the big crowds on the Nakamise, I noticed a shop at the corner selling musical instruments. There were harmonicas, mandolins, violins, Western flutes, Chinese flutes, Japanese flutes, wooden kotos, portable kotos—the young woman sitting in the shop skillfully playing away on the newly renamed "Showa koto" those songs you all now know so well thanks to the movies, my young lady in the alley looked just like her.

What's more—already, the end of autumn, they're hawking New Year's calendars on the streets of Asakusa, and this year there are lots of women selling rubber balls. The balls are all the same and so is the way of selling them. All sewed up in red and green cloth, as though entwined in colored thread, the ball is a little too big to fit into the palm of the hand. So the seller suspends it from a string tied to her middle finger and makes a great show of bouncing it off her hand and paddling it up into the air—bounce, bounce, bounce—in order to make a sale. Most of them are either middle-aged women or young girls, and the balls sell because the sellers look so pitiful.

But there is one young girl selling her balls better because of her beauty. A red ribbon droops from her bobbed head, and beneath her short open skirt, her legs (stockings rolled) dance the Charleston—cha cha, cha cha—while through her dark encarmined lips she whistles jazzily along. She keeps time, bouncing that ball like a tambourine or like castanets.

Well, the little girl in the alley looked just like her.

I decided to rent that vacant house in the alley. After that, as I'm walking along the road in front of the Miyato Theater on my way to the Asakusa motor bus stop (the one always announced as "Miyato-Theater-behind-Asakusa-Park"), two old bicycles approach from behind and pass me. One of the young riders could have been the twin brother of the piano player in the house in the alley.

I jump into a one-yen taxi I have hailed and yell out: Follow those bikes!

sumida park

4

WHILE SHE did her Spanish number (and I did not make this up—this is a true story), I clearly saw that the dancer on stage carried on her biceps needle marks from a recent injection, though a small piece of adhesive tape had been stuck on top. In the grounds of the Sensō Temple at around two in the morning, sixteen or seventeen wild dogs let out a terrific howl as they all rush after a single cat. That's what Asakusa is all about. You come to sniff out the scent of a crime. But that's not why I followed those two old bikes.

Seems there are more police detectives than ordinary people wandering around Asakusa after one-thirty in the morning, but since I am neither a private eye nor a public investigator, if that piano player had not been so pretty, I probably would have just gone home.

But before my taxi has passed the headquarters of the Asakusa Military Police Detachment, it's rolling side by side with the two old bikes. Soon we'll reach the Kototoi Bridge.

A group of women construction workers, towels wrapped around their heads, walk like men across from Honjo. Stalls selling Chinese noodles and soft round rice cakes full of sweet bean jam are being set up on the bridge. On the opposite shore, the flimsy tin roof and thin wooden scaffolding over the Ushijima Shrine, now about to undergo repairs, look as though they could be blown away by the racket of the river steamboats. At the holy cow statue where you'd turn to go to Shinkoune-chō, the driver quickly stops the cab: Want me to wait?

The two have stopped to buy a couple of sticks of *chitose* candy.

Well, think I, seems like they know they are being followed. Fooling around, maybe even offering me some candy. Preparing a wry smile, I let the taxi go and head for the shop where the candy stall is.

The boy, whom I can think of only as the piano girl's twin brother, looks to be about sixteen, a couple years younger than she. He is wearing his flat cloth hunting cap backward, has on filthy corduroy trousers, and his face is truly dirty. Only his ears are clean, as lovely as carved mother-of-pearl. Those ears and those surprised eyes turned toward me, and these must have made me blush. He leaves the candy stall in a hurry.

Then at the Makura Bridge—looking to their left at the big billboard for the Sapporo Beer Company's Makura Bridge Beer Hall, they go into the park.

The Five Story Pagoda of the Sensō Temple stands just opposite the large crane that has been erected in the middle of the Ōkawa to build a railway bridge where the Makura ferry station used to be. Floating above the lead-gray water, the pagoda with its green-colored roof seems less a building and instead fondly reminds me of some kind of big plant.

The new Sumida Park runs from here all the way to the Chōmei Temple. Or, to put our new landmarks to use, it covers an area defined by the asphalt path that accompanies the riverbank from the business college boathouse to the end of the boat racecourse. Here is the Showa Mukōjima Dam.

—Ready, set . . . calls a cheerful young wife as she lines up alongside her husband. And it seems now everyone wants to run straight down this asphalt path.

—Go! Lunging forward, her felt sandals striking hard, she starts running beside her husband. And each holds a little boy. Twins, looking absolutely identical from their navy blue trousers with the blue ribbons to their twin haircuts.

And just behind this picture of domestic bliss—my two youths.

—Oh, yeah? I'll give you a flat tire, taunts the boy with the beautiful ears as he lines up his bicycle with that of his friend and takes from his pocket a jazz whistle—a small gold-colored affair, pipes lined in a row, the kind sold at night stalls and very popular with the kids this year. He blows it hard and off they set on their bike race.

A dog lets out a howl. The Sumida-maru No. 9 barge comes upriver, towing the Azuma-maru No. 7. The school's rowing skiff comes ashore to rest its oars. Two hairdresser's assistants, hands wrapped in their aprons, go running to it.

I take the passage under the Kototoi Bridge so I won't lose the youngsters. It's chilly. Even so, bums apparently sleep here, judging from the large chalk-lettered signs on the concrete piers that say things like "No Sleeping Here," "No Lying Down."

Then I spot the two again just as the red and green lights on the Subway Restaurant Tower begin to blink on and off. They are standing on the Kototoi Bridge looking down at the dinners being served on the boats below.

It was then, on that bridge, that for the very first time, I spoke to a member of the Scarlet Gang.

5

THE KOTOTOI BRIDGE (opened in February 1928, constructed by the Earthquake Reconstruction Bureau) is bright and flat, spacious and white, like the deck of a modern liner. Still more, it looks as though a clean, healthy line has been  drawn above the sluggish waters of the Ōkawa, littered with the city's garbage.

But when I cross the bridge again, the glow from the advertisements and from the street lamps falls on the dark water below, and the melancholy of the city seems to flow by me. In the twilight of the Asakusa riverbank now under construction, I can see in the distance the cut stones gleaming white and the workers building a bonfire, their packhorses beside them.

Looking down from the railing of the bridge, I can faintly hear the sound the high tide makes. It is suppertime on the three cargo boats moored to the concrete pier.

Steam rises from the rice cooking on the portable clay stove in the stern of one of the boats. A young woman with a towel wrapped around her head carries a wooden rice tub across to the gunwale. Red laundry has been hung to dry on a sculling oar laid across the prow. In the next barge, mackerel is grilling under an oil lamp. A miso paste strainer, firewood, buckets, and such are scattered about the roof.

A few people on their way home from work stop to look down at the small barges, but the families there take no notice. A river steamboat passes, and a child rinsing scallions in the river staggers in the wake. Behind me, someone asks: Isn't that Toki's boat there?

—Toki-i!

Turning around, I see it is the two bikers I had earlier lost sight of. The kid washing scallions looks up.

—Tokikō, right? I'm gonna toss you some candy.

—Hey, my dad said you could borrow the boat, says the voice from the river.

—We can? You sure?

—Uh-huh, it's okay so long as you don't do anything bad with it. And in return, you got to take all four of us to go hear *Yasuki bushi.*

—Okay, I get it, but don't yell so. Here's the candy.

The candy clatters on the barge roof. At that faces appear on the three barges, all looking up. I am surprised. They are all children, all seven of them.

As the boy throws the candy, as it patters down on the roof of the barge, a crowd gathers on the bridge.

The boy, a dead ringer for the piano girl, says nothing but stares noncommittally ahead for a while and then quietly slips behind the crowd. I go right up to him and directly ask: Why do you want to borrow the boat?

He turns abruptly away. Then, foot cocked on bike pedal, he looks at me with an air of innocence and says: Well, we could even use it to sell a woman.

—Seeing twins like those two boys over there in Sumida Park must get at you.

I'd aimed at a possible opening, but he just whistled.

—I assume that the girl playing the piano in that house is your twin sister and so . . .

—Oh, I get it. You're following me around because you like her.

—Not at all. I'm merely thinking of renting the house next door.

—Huh? You want to live in that haunted house?

—Sure, why not?

—You're too much. I mean it's a gambling joint. Hang around there, and you'll get beat up good.

With this he gave a whistle to his friend, and they jump on their bikes and ride off.

Thus, my first encounter with the Scarlet Gang ended, as you see, in failure. But I will only bore you, dear reader, if I continue to tell the story in a proper order. So let us leave these youths and quickly turn to other things.

For instance, I later learned that this Boat Tokikō goes by boat to the Asakusa Elementary School on the grounds of the Sensō Asakusa Kannon Temple. Every morning his father brings him as far as the Kototoi Bridge. But because the barge works on the Ōkawa, he can't always be on time when school lets out. So Toki has to hang around in Asakusa until he is picked up that night, or even the next morning. In such a manner did Toki become one of the children of the park.

But in telling you all this, perhaps I have an ulterior motive, dear reader. I want to make you feel fondly toward the members of the Scarlet Gang. So maybe I've carried on a bit much about how attractive they are.

cropped-head o-so-and-so

6

MAYBE I'VE CARRIED on a bit much about how attractive they are—that's what I said.

But as Yumiko told me one time: Yes, it's like that—there's no denying that I'm attractive. Because I'm attractive, Asakusa puts food on the table. It's like that at the musical instrument shop and the merry-go-round, too. In Asakusa there are just too many beggars trying to cash in on the wretched ugliness of people.

Then Yumiko added, half pulling my leg: But of course you couldn't possibly understand the depths of the real ugliness of Asakusa.

The attractiveness Yumiko is talking about is quite physical, but the attractiveness of the Scarlet Gang I may have been speaking too much about, dear reader, is something a little different.

Okay, let me give you another example.

It was in the middle of November. I was talking about something I'd seen in the newspaper that day.

—Wasn't there something in the evening paper about the arrest of a woman called Cropped-Head O-So-and-So?

—O-So-and-So? I don't know any O-So-and-So. Look at me. This here is cropped hair. I hate calling it "bobbed." Cropped-Head Oyumi—absolutely not.

Coyly smiling, one cheek dimpling, she takes a few steps ahead.

—Well, you hang out a sign that says "Piano Lessons" so you must be a "cropped head."

—But there are many kinds of cropped heads in Asakusa.

—Sure. Anything goes. They even shave girls' heads like monks so they can't run away from the reformatory.

—Oh, like Oshin, right?

—She's been arrested, taken to the Kisakata Police Station over ten times, escaped from reform school seven times, been hanging out in the park for seven years since she was ten, and . . .

—Yes, that's Oshin the *gokaiya*.

—What's a *gokaiya*?

—Someone like her, Oshin—someone who does it with guys like day laborers, cart pullers, garbage pickers, and the homeless. Most of them are kids under fourteen or fifteen or women past forty. Few of the women you'd marry end up sleeping out in the open. If they use their heads they can get by, though, like being someone's mistress, even if it's only something like six times a month.

—Oshin. I wonder how much younger she is than the famous Tangerine Oshin?

—My, my, where did you hear about her?

—She's the heroine of every bad girl worth the name. I don't know much, but when she was about thirteen or fourteen, she organized a gang of girls called the Falcons. She was the leader, made a den at the Hachiman Shrine in Fukagawa for her twenty or thirty followers, and by the time she was sixteen, she'd done a hundred and fifty men. That's about it. Pass the history test?

—I knew it. Just a dreamer at heart. There are all kinds of Oshins—want me to introduce you to the Cropped-Head Oshin?

—Nope. Already got my hands full with this Cropped-Head Oyumi.

—There you go again . . . But anyway, I'll point her out to you sometime. Morning is good. Why don't you go look for her with Akikō? Go when the bums get up and emerge from their palaces. Even if you don't see Oshin, you're sure to come across a *gokaiya* or two.

Apparently she didn't forget. Soon after, Akikō invited me out in the morning mist of the park.

The street lamps stay lit all night. Their light is the first to welcome the morning mist.

Hisago Street, usually called Yonekyū Street, lined with decorative gaslights shaped like lilies of the valley—there on that street is the only eatery open all night in the park, the main shop of the Azuma chain, where we eat steaming bowls of *gyudon* while listening to the radio blaring out commands for the early morning gymnastic exercises.

This seems to be around the time when the bums get to enjoy the posters outside the movie theaters. No one bothers to drive them away, no one calls them dirty. Bathed in the early morning sunlight, they happily stare.

In this Asakusa that usually gets up late, the barber shops—for some reason always the first to open—are still closed, and in front of one: standing there in front of a mirror stuck on a pole, an eye-catching girl is putting on her makeup.

7

AKIKŌ'S FACE this morning—he's the boy
I lost sight of on the Kototoi Bridge—
now that the dirt has been washed off,
it's as white as that of a painted child
on the Asakusa opera stage. He walks
quickly, the fingers of both hands locked
around the back of his neck, as if trying to hide its smoothness, his
cheeks buried in both elbows.

From one elbow dangles what looked like a primary school student's shoe bag.

—Your lunch box in there?

—No, my makeup kit.

The sunlight casts soft shadows carrying yet the scent of morning dew. Not a single shop has opened.

Walking alongside the Nihon Theater, we take a shortcut through
a back street, behind the kitchen of the Sudachō Restaurant, and
end up on Kitanaka Street, known around here as Raccoon Dog Alley. In the afternoon, the red flags of the bargain sales are hung every
which way, but in the early morning the asphalt streets look clean
as those of a toy town.

On the street is just one person, the "lovely lunatic," standing
there before the mirror stuck on the pole. The shock at seeing her
so beautiful is like being doused with cold water.

Akikō runs up to her.

—Hey, you better run on home, Sis.

She turns around, and I see that her hair is done in a strange
style like an autumn version of the *shimada*. Her face is covered with
white powder, heavy like the sugar on candy. And the red collar of
her kimono, with its embroidered white plum blossoms, looks
somehow sad. Akikō stares at her half-open kimono skirt, then

closes it, straightens the hem and asks: Did you really leave home when it got light? You opened that kimono all by yourself? You came out here while it was still dark, didn't you?

But she—as though to prove she's really crazy—walks off without a word.

We turn onto the Nakamise. The tin shutters of all the shops are still down. In front, the street vendors are rolling out their one-mat shops. A country person, wearing a padded kimono from the inn he is staying at, is buying pencils, a dozen for ten sen.

Geisha making morning visits to temples. Children going off to school. Beggars. Nannies. Day laborers. Men going home after a night on the town. Bums. The mix isn't surprising, but these crowds at the Sensō Temple street stalls at seven or eight in the morning all look as though they know nothing of the fleeting world of pleasure. This is one of the wonders of Asakusa.

But at the stall left of the Nio Gate:

CONTRIBUTIONS TOWARD MAJOR REPAIRS
OF THE MAIN HALL OF THE TEMPLE ACCEPTED HERE.

CONTRIBUTIONS TOWARD NEW TILES FOR
THE ROOF OF THE MAIN HALL OF THE TEMPLE ACCEPTED HERE.

Since I can clearly make out these messages on the wooden signboards, there is still some time before Asakusa gets really crowded. Sound asleep, a beggar wrapped in a red blanket lies slumped against the signboard stall.

To the right, behind the Kume no Heinai Shrine, some twenty bums are squatting down for their breakfast. Steam rises from a pot of leftover rice and vegetable scraps warming under a tree near the clay wall. The man ladling out the porridge to the basking bums says: Some for you. And some for you.

And he gives them each a ladleful.

Beside the Kannon Hall, the stilt-maker energetically cuts his green bamboo. The pigeon ladies who sell beans to feed the pigeons are eating some themselves for breakfast. Six of them, heads covered with towels, are sitting in rows along a small metal-sheeted table. Hordes of pigeons—the grounds, the roofs, completely covered.

Four or five chickens are perched on the stone lantern behind the monument commemorating the victory of Japan's troops in Manchuria during the Sino-Japanese War.

Wading through the pigeons, we go into an open place with a cluster of trees. Here and there bums have their morning meetings among the benches.

Newspaper boys walk by them. The bosses have come to buy their day laborers. Lots of people, but most just sitting stonily, silent like lonely lunatics deeply despairing.

Just we are about to leave through the back of the park, Akikō pulls my sleeve: Look!

Two of the men who water the grounds are resting on a bench. The man who got a cigarette butt from the other—no, not a man, it's a woman. This person runs duck-like, wiggling her behind. Despite the two-layered padded kimono, the rubber-soled cloth boots tucked in the men's waistband, it's a woman—hideous.

—See? She's one kind of Cropped-Head O-So-and-So. Most of them are like this. The dregs of Asakusa. But as long as she can still run, she's still a woman. Because most of the bums are no longer human enough to run. Well, if you've had enough cropped heads, go on home. I've got to drop my sister off, change my clothes at the costume shop, and I've a little bit of business to take care of.

The Cropped-Head O-So-and So leans, sagging yellow cheeks, toward the man on the bench and offers the discarded cigarette butt.

The man has a worn-out shoe on one foot, a straw sandal on the other.

the bug house

8

THE HANAYASHIKI TIGERS are asleep. He rests one heavy paw on her stomach. Domestic bliss. But, of course, the Hanayashiki and the Bug House (two small spots known as fun for the entire family), of which even you, dear reader,  are aware, are not famous for the way tigers sleep but for the wooden horses of the merry-go-round.

—Look, young miss, more fireworks!

And the young woman from the Bug House helps the young miss down from her wooden steed and dashes outside.

—Look! Look! The pigeons are so surprised that they're flying away.

And with this, the young woman careens into a gent in a Western-style suit.

—Stupid.

—Oh! I beg your pardon, Mister.

She glances up at him, blushing, then dabs at his overcoat with her handkerchief as though her white powder had gotten on it. Turning to the young miss, she says: See how the pigeons have flocked there on the roof the Healing Buddha's Temple. Their head feathers look a lot more modern than my hairdo does.

—Hey! Just stop fooling with me.

She turns, glares straight in his eyes, then turns and slips into the ticket booth. The band begins, the horses revolve.

The man stands where he is and reads the billboard:

THE ONE AND ONLY MAN WITH A MOUTH IN HIS STOMACH.

THE MOUTH ON HIS FACE IS JUST FOR TALKING.

HE EARNS HIS KEEP EATING THROUGH HIS STOMACH.

He glances furtively at the merry-go-round—mirrors on all eight sides of the wooden octagonal center axle, the band sitting on a lotus-shaped mirrored platform at the top of the mirrored shaft, around it the wooden horses and wooden autos turn, carrying the little misses, the little masters. Above the band, autumn leaves made of colored paper hang from branches. Green paper banana leaves wave against the whitewashed ceiling.

Nursemaids, women shopkeepers, housewives, workers, fathers— there they sit on benches, lean against the walls, watch the horses go round and round, nice folks with silly grins. But that's not all. Up behind the ticket booth ten or so construction laborers, gentlemen, soldiers, shop clerks, and even students are standing around.

Here the man thinks: Not bad—full house. She's doing a good job of pulling them in. And he too pushes his way inside.

The girl who is doing all the attracting, wearing a dark green work smock over a cheap black silk kimono stamped with a red pattern, like 井, a large leather bag hanging from her leather belt, comes into view as the merry-go-round turns, speaking to the young miss astride a white horse: Looks like I've got him.

Combing the bangs back from her forehead, she looks up and stares hard at the man, puckering her lips as though blowing a whistle, tapping the toes of her felt sandals to the tune of the "Navy March." The man winks.

—What do you think I am? Stupid?

As she walks around toward the front of the merry-go-round, the mirrors reflect the nape of her neck, her short hair.

This ticket girl is, of course, Yumiko, whom you already know. She is the piano girl from the back alley.

This merry-go-round with its little misses and little masters is a fine showcase for her beauty. As the wooden horses revolve, men can gawk at her figure from all angles, as though she were a mannequin girl on display.

And on the second floor, the six-year-old girl genius Miyoshiya Fukuyakko has just finished her comic *manzai* routine.

—Ladies and gentlemen, as a living example of modern medical science, we present before your very eyes the man who eats through a mouth in his stomach, announces the master of ceremonies, who has taken over the stage.

It is said that the Man with a Mouth in His Stomach was born in Asahigawa on Hokkaido, and because of the sake, and, indeed, pure grain alcohol that he drank to endure those snowy winters, he suffered a stricture of the esophagus. For this reason, he had a new mouth made at the Hokkaido Medical University. His hair is cut in a bowl style, his upper neck shaved, Harold Lloyd glasses, a white flannel robe like those worn by judo athletes—he pulls it open wide to give the audience a look at his stomach.

Downstairs, the man forcefully beckons Yumiko with his thumb, the rest of his hand somewhere down near the pocket of his pants. The young miss who watched the pigeons now jumps down from her wooden steed and goes over to stand in front of him.

It is the little girl from that back alley.

The man reads the characters written on the red paper flag she is holding up: Tonight on the third floor of the building next door—

The building next door is the Aquarium, and on the second floor is the Casino Folies revue.

9

THE ONE-OF-A-KIND mystery man, the one with his mouth in his stomach, yanks at his robe, pulling it wide open. But I ask you, dear reader, could any theater be as pathetic as this? Only three rows of benches for spectators in front of the  stage. Behind them, an empty room with a bare floor.

Behind him, treetops (seen through the glass window filled with the afternoon light of a late autumn sun), a landscape of a small hut in the remote countryside.

Even more forlorn are the dusty glass specimen cases of cicadas, beetles, butterflies, and bees lined up at the window, which gave the place its old name, the Bug House. They remind me of old Asakusa of the Meiji and Taisho years.

—Unfortunately, the mouth the doctors made in his stomach has no teeth. In other words, it's like the beak of a bird.

Just like the master of ceremonies has told us, when the man unties the cotton cord around the beak, something like a tobacco pipe stuck in the stomach is revealed. He sticks a glass funnel in the mouth of this pipe and pours in milk mixed with pieces of mashed bread.

—In spite of being in this sorry state, the gentleman here still can't forget the taste of sake. He drinks about one-fifth of a liter at a time. He tastes it with his real mouth, but he drinks it through the mouth in his stomach. Sometimes when he drinks he gets carried away, and he's had his sprees in the Yoshiwara. Look, now he's embarrassed. But anyway, this mouth in his stomach lets him live, fit as a fiddle. Isn't the progress of medical science truly something amazing?

> Longing for your love, the lights grow dim,
> I loosen my deep scarlet sash
> But I am lonely . . .

And as the band below stops playing, the merry-go-round filled with the little misses and little masters comes to a halt.

After reading the message on the red flag that has been thrust at his chest, the man in the Western-style suit, surprised, looks at Yumiko.

She has turned her back on him and is fixing her makeup. But she is intently watching him in the mirrored column.

As the children climb off and new ones climb on, the band starts to play. Yumiko walks from steed to steed selling tickets. She says to a waitress in a white apron: Today it's bye-bye to these wooden horses.

—You're just threatening to leave.

—I have finally found the enemy I have long sought. Well anyway, something like that would be nice.

The horses start to rock back and forth as the merry-go-round again begins its circle.

The "young lady" with the red flag has disappeared.

That night, however (following the flag), the man has already been waiting for two hours on the third floor of the Aquarium.

For some time, a girl with braids has been standing near him, giggling, looking at the ground. Still giggling, she now leans against him and pokes him with one hand.

—You're a little dopey, aren't you?

—What? Responds he in an involuntarily sharp tone: Whaa . . . what the hell? Why did you come with your hair in those braids? If this is a joke, it's not a very good one.

—Short hair just stands out too much. Like it better?

—That's a wig, right?

—I'll take it off any time you like. Just calm down. There are *deka* (Asakusa jargon for police detectives) down in the pit.

—All right. Never mind. Let's go around to Mukōjima. I want to hear about how Asakusa's changed all these years.

—But . . .

—You know a better place?

—No, but here I'm always being followed. On land I'm surrounded by danger on all sides.

—On land? You sure do talk big.

—Couldn't we meet on a boat?

—So that's what you have in mind.

—But I'm a little scared.

—You've been screwing around with me since this afternoon, and now you say you're scared.

—I'm not scared of you. Me, I live half my life as a man. Men are nothing at all. But my older sister went crazy because she fell heavy for one. So, as her younger sister . . .

the aquarium

10

Asakusa is Tokyo's heart . . .
Asakusa is a human market . . .

The words of that popular writer Soeda
Azenbō: Asakusa is Asakusa for everyone. In Asakusa, everything is flung out
in the raw. Desires dance naked. All
races, all classes, all jumbled together
forming a bottomless, endless current, flowing day and night, no
beginning, no end. Asakusa is alive . . . The masses converge on it,
constantly. Their Asakusa is a foundry in which all the old models
are regularly melted down to be cast into new ones.

As a part of this "foundry," even the Aquarium is in the process
of being recast in the latest model.

The Bug House and the Aquarium, left behind in the fourth district of Asakusa Park, seem memorials to the Asakusa of days gone
by, and the dancers of the Casino Folies have to pass the fish swimming in the tanks of the Aquarium and go by way of the model of

the Palace of the Dragon King to get to their dressing rooms. Just back from Paris, the master painter Foujita Tsuguharu has come to see the show, accompanied by his Parisienne wife Yukiko.

If the so-called Japanese-Western Jazz Ensemble Revue, an incongruous muddle of different musical numbers, is a part of Asakusa, Model 1929, then maybe the Casino Folies, Tokyo's one and only purveyor of the imported modern revue, is, along with the Subway Restaurant Tower, a part of Model 1930.

Eroticism and nonsense and speed and comic-strip humor of current events and jazz songs and ladies' legs . . .

But the seats on the third floor are not crowded enough for the conversation between the man and Yumiko to be overheard.

—So you're saying that just because this old-fashioned big sister went crazy over a man, then the little sister wised up and turned into a new-fangled *zube* (Asakusaese for "bad girl"). Right?

—Is that how I seem to you?

—Stop putting on airs. It's annoying. Park girls used to have a lot more guts.

—Absolutely. I'd like to be like that, too. They way I see it, when you fall in love with a man, and if it comes so you can really love him, then life would be wonderful. You'd understand if you took a good hard look at me. I'm not a woman. Looking at my sister, I vowed as a child that I'd never become a woman. Besides, men don't have any guts, do they? Not one of them has ever made me a woman.

Isn't it, isn't it so? The Doton Ditch!
Town of rainbow lanterns, sleepless sparrows . . .

Drowning out the jazz band in its box, "Naniwa kouta" blasts from the Casino Folies basement restaurant gramophone. On stage they are doing "A Platform in Shinjuku Station," scene four of "The Boy Companion."

—Look, most of the girls up there don't wear stockings. Can't they afford them? And if they could, would that mean they are doing something bad?

—You jump to conclusions. You were a young punk when you were a kid, right? But these dancers are just fourteen- or fifteen-year-old children. The oldest must be around twenty. You should see them when they leave after the show. If they were doing something bad on the side, would they walk into some grimy shop and have sweet red bean soup, wearing their kimonos, all cheap silk or muslin, worn to threads? So they don't wear stockings, "going stockingless" it's called, and show off their bare legs on purpose, you know. They don't use white makeup on their arms and legs either. When it's hot, you can see the red bumps—mosquito bites.

Yumiko then scrunches her shoulders as if she were cold. She takes a white satin scarf from her lap and buries her white cheeks in it, saying in hushed tones: When I'm with a man, I'm always sizing myself up—weighing the part of me that wants to become a woman against the part of me that is afraid to. Then I feel miserable and even more lonely.

—Come on. To make it with somebody these days you have to play innocent, say a lot of fool things, do everything in a roundabout way. It's like what they just said on the stage: "I'm going off to a world where there's food and fun," and "Why not love me in a more materialistic way," and . . .

11

1. Jazz Dance: "Titina"
2. Acrobatic Tango
3. Nonsense Sketch: "That Girl, That Girl!"
4. Dance: "La Paloma"
5. Comic Song . . .

And

There are eleven scenes in this variety show. And right, the dancers are in such a hurry to change their costumes in the darkness at the end of the stage that you can see their bare breasts.

And then—

6. Jazz Song: "Ginza"

On this street, wide as a kimono sash,
Sailor pants and penciled eyebrows,
An Eton crop, now ain't that chic?
Swinging a snake-wood walking stick . . .

Silk hat tipped to one side, black velvet vest, red ribbon bow tie, collars open whitely, thin walking stick tucked under the arm—of course, she's a girl dressed as a man, and her legs are bare. Then she links arms with two girls in skirts that just about cover their bottoms to form a line while singing the "Modern Ginza Song" in chorus as they dance, moving about as though really strolling the avenue.

Blackout—the next scene begins: "The Fukagawa Revelers' Dance." Braids swing out as two dapper youths in light blue *happi* coats caper.

—Yep, even an old-timer like me can understand this one.

For the first time, the man takes an interest in the stage.

—That little one dances pretty good, doesn't she?

—She should. Her grandmother or someone like that was a famous dance teacher.

—Ryū!

—Hanajima-a!

The audience shouts out the names of their favorites.

—They're really popular. Which one do you think is Ryū?

—The little one. She's named Umezono Ryūko. Hate to disappoint you, but I hear she's only fifteen. Saying this, Yumiko drops her face into her white scarf and hangs her head.

—Dances like this one—I can't stand them. For someone like me who grew up downtown, they bring back all sorts of memories from when I was little. It's not fair to make them dance like that with their hair all done up in braids. The men stare and get excited, and the women watch and feel strangely sad.

—So that's why you came here in those braids.

—A braided wig is the best way for no one to know who I am. When I meet a man who is better behaved (not at all like you), then I become like a girl in braids. But okay, I'll do what you want. But doesn't this revue remind you of old theaters like the Nihon and Kinryū? Kawai Sumiko throwing her name cards from the stage, middle-school students linked together like rosary beads and dragged away by the authorities, and . . . That was when the opera was really something.

—What? You think I'm one of those opera nuts? says the man, clearly surprised.

—How would I know? I'd just started grade school back then. That was more than ten years ago—five or six years after my big sister went crazy. Her lover was an Asakusa man. I hang out in the park because I want to meet him.

—And? So, when you meet him you'll avenge your sister?

—Just the opposite. My poor sister. I'm sure to fall for that man, too. I want to fall crazy in love with the man who made my big sister crazy. Of course, I was upset about what happened to my sister. I was determined never, ever to be a woman. But come to think of it, even as a child I was probably jealous of her, too. I used to try to be like her, practicing being in love. So I want to meet him no matter what might happen.

—So whatever happened to the boat? Remember the boat? All these strange stories about your sister. They have nothing to do with me.

—Oh, but they do. I'll tell you even stranger ones on the boat. Okay. It's four or five days away, but let's make it next Tuesday.

Saying this, Yumiko gives the man a scrap of paper.

—The boat'll be at the place marked on the map on the back of this paper. Come at three o'clock. Okay?

Then, suddenly, without his even noticing, she has disappeared from the Aquarium.

12

NUMBER NINETY-EIGHT. Bad luck. Hmph.

Be wary of new love.
Just let it be. Sorry
Will be entangled he or she.
This love makes others worry.

—It's a fortune card from the Sensō Temple. Hey, that's pretty clever.

On the back of the card is a pencil-drawn map. On the stage is the finale:

(Something something) modern boy.
(Something something) modern girl.

Singing the refrain of "The Modern Song," the girls dance off the stage. End of the show.

But Yumiko is nowhere to be seen. The man stays seated until the others leave. As the audience thins out, the walls, seats, floor of the theater begin to reek. The stench of beggars wafts in.

Dear reader, I mean this literally. Since the revue first hung out its flags, beggars and vagrants have become patrons of the Aquarium. Beggars and bums watching the modern-style dancing of the powdered naked bodies. This bizarre scene of local color is also Asakusa. Students, the "Ginza people," and others like them have also little by little come into the picture.

Still, even now, every night without fail, you'll probably spot some odd man, his face masked with beard, grime, and dust, dressed in rags, leaning against the pillar to the left of the pit, absorbed in the jazz dances. Outside, three men, five men, stand in the cold to stare at the dancers as they leave.

Holding the fortune card in his right hand, the man clicks his tongue and glances behind him. At the theater entrance with its rows of red banners is a bas-relief of a mermaid, plaster fish swimming above her.

—Looks like I don't pull much weight here in Asakusa. Even that little girl didn't take me seriously. Kindly giving me that map. And I took it.

It's true. You don't need a map to get to the riverbank. It would be simple to put Yumiko's map into words, and it would go something like this: From the Niten Gate, the east entrance of Sensō Temple, you go straight on Niten Gate Street until you run into the riverbank at the end. That's the place.

Cross the streetcar tracks and bordering the river is Yamanoshuku-machi and, at the riverbank, the park is under construction. The Kototoi Bridge is on the left, and directly to the right, the iron bridge of the Tōbu Line is being built. At the dock are twenty to thirty small boats, one of which is the Kurenai-maru—the name "Kurenai-maru" is carved and painted on the stern in red. There is no need to go on and on with the directions. The riverbank is quite visible from the Niten Gate.

The fortune on the other side of the map reads:

The one for whom you wait will never come.

And so, the man intentionally comes to the riverbank later than the Tuesday three o'clock date and . . . Startled, he withdraws into the shadows of the trees. There are indeed twenty or thirty boats, but only one has a pair of black silk ladies' stockings hung long on a pole to dry. What a contrast they are to the laundry on other boats— a brazen signal.

With the quick instinct of someone who has often just escaped danger, the man reads this as a warning sign.

—Okay. So she's inviting me out onto the water. Well, that's just fine by me.

And, deadpan, he walks toward the reclaimed land where the park is being made and steps across the cut stone. A young boy in a floppy bell-shaped hat approaches him.

—Mister, you get here with the fortune card from the temple of the Holy Kannon?

—Who the hell are you?

—She's waiting for you on the Kurenai-maru.

—You're no boatman.

And the man hands him a five-yen note. He can tell a person's motive by the way they accept money.

—It's not much of a tip.

—Thanks, but I've been paid already. This way, please.

He lays a narrow plank from the concrete wharf to the Kurenai-maru. The man walks across.

Then—what the man sees—in the cramped cabin of the ship, sprawled on top of the bedding, Yumiko peacefully asleep.

Her short hair disheveled, her forehead like a child's; her eyelashes, her lips stand out from her face, each like a living thing in itself. Her deep red skirt has slipped above her knees. She is not wearing stockings. Those bare feet are perfectly parallel, soles like pink shell work, her face turned toward the ceiling. The charcoal fire in the clay stove softly illuminates her feet, her sleeping figure.

silver cat umekō

13

WAS IT AROUND the time that the Kurenai-
maru left the riverbanks of Yamano-
shuku?

—Here is our Annual Charity Collection Pot. Please contribute something
toward our New Year's rice cakes for the
poor.

I turn around at the cry of a lady officer of the Salvation Army and
then stop short. It is beside the small Kaminari Gate Police Box. It is
at the entrance to the Nakamise. The ginkgo tree just in front of the
police box, the telephone booth and the mailbox and the charity pot
behind it, and then the "Mirror of Virtue" to one side. There is a bulletin board next to the mirror. I read the one and only announcement:

GATHERING AT THE HANAKAWADŌ

THE SCARLET TROUPE

My smiling face is reflected in the Mirror of Virtue. "Kisakata
Police Station," "Notice Board for Public Use," "Subdivision of

Asakusa Veterans," and more words like these are embossed in red around the edges of the board.

The clamor of children hawking calendars surrounds me.

Right next to a police box, right in the midst of the bustle of the Nakamise—doing the unexpected, posting a notice out in the open like this keeps people from being the least bit suspicious. Yep, still bamboozling. Clever kids, I mutter as I decide to go along to the Hanakawadō.

Hanakawadō, a name renowned for its association with the famous Sukeroku of old Edo times. Dear reader, I'm not a member of the Scarlet Gang, but I do know that Hanakawadō is their secret way of saying the Subway Restaurant. This is because it was called the Hanakawadō Building when it was being put up in the autumn of 1929.

The old Twelve Story Tower snapped in half in the 1923 earthquake. The Subway Restaurant is only half as tall, some forty meters, but it has Asakusa's only observation tower, complete with an elevator.

From the observation tower, let's look out for Yumiko and the man on the Kurenai-maru. But because boats don't have stoplights, I doubt we can make out the expression of the boatman. So let me put it another way. As the Kurenai-maru goes upriver toward the Kototoi Bridge, the face of the boatman standing in the stern seems quite pale. Is it that the man has found a way to make Yumiko do what he wants? Then perhaps it is a look of jealousy.

—You're no boatman.

So said the man before he went aboard. Indeed not. He is a typical young punk who has already been put in the Kawagoe Reformatory a few times.

So this Umekichi had not just fallen into the hands of the Scarlet Gang. Rather he was picked up by them and shaken awake from a nightmare that had lasted many years.

Since he is a prime example of those delinquent youths who make their homes in Asakusa, let me tell you a bit about Umekichi's confessions of love:

First, age six. Umekichi was made a plaything by a woman over forty.

Second, age thirteen. While playing outside the stationery store in front of his school, he became friendly with a girl one year older than he was. She was the daughter of a company employee. He was invited to her house. Nobody was at home. That didn't bother the two of them. After that he went to her house to play three or four more times. Rumors spread, and the entire family moved far away.

Third, age fourteen. On a bench in front of a candy store, he met the daughter of a haberdasher. The two of them went to Ueno Park, to street fairs and cheap rooms for rent over twenty times.

Fourth, age fifteen. At a movie theater in Asakusa Park, two young girls sat next to him. He had met one of them at a different theater. They left together and took him to a house with two sliding-door entrances, both with real glass panes.

Fifth, the same age. Umekichi went to a much larger house. While he pretended to sleep, he saw a white hand take a fifty-sen piece from his coin purse and put it into a bud vase hanging on the alcove post. When she was not around, Umekichi looked in the bud vase, and he found eight yen and fifty sen in fifty-sen coins. He left with the money.

Sixth, the same age. A seventeen- or eighteen-year-old and her twelve- or thirteen-year-old sister were watching a play in Asakusa. When the younger one saw what the nearby Umekichi was doing to her big sister, she dragged her out. He followed them. They were the daughters of a book-lender. He began visiting the shop to rent story books. He invited the elder daughter out six or seven times. Her mother put an end to this.

Seventh, the same age. He spent four months playing around with a waitress in a Chinese restaurant. In order to pay for this, he became the "punk boy" of a skirt-chasing older youth.

Eighth, the same age. He got about one hundred and fifty yen out of one of the girls from the house with two entrances. She came to him because she liked it. Her father was a master at the horse races, and Umekichi knew that he sometimes came into big money.

14

UMEKICHI'S CONFESSIONS of love take on a more criminal tone after fifteen. If I disclosed them all here, dear reader, I would shatter the dreams you enjoy in your warm beds.

Dear reader, you in your warm bed, were I to introduce you to the Grasshopper Kid, you would imagine one of the smartest among the *gure* (homeless strays of Asakusa). But I hear that he doesn't even know how to pile up cushions or to fold and put away the bedding. If you told him to make the bed, he would probably roll up everything, pallet and quilt, round and round into a ball. He'd never before used such things.

But our little grasshopper is not as foolish as the famous Oshichi, the greengrocer's daughter. He is well versed in the way of juvenile law. (Author's note: Not the present laws but those before them.) He had been dragged to the police station some twenty times and even sent to that prison on Iojima, but he spoke firmly before the public prosecutor each time: I won't go straight until I'm fifteen.

Well, he kept that promise. At fifteen, after he was sent to Iojima, he began to work hard for the first time. He is said to have sent a pouch full of little shells that looked like beautiful grains of rice to a probation officer who had once been kind to him in Asakusa.

Just try getting hold of an Asakusa *gure* and asking: What about your parents?

The answer might surprise you: I don't have any parents yet.

—Yet?

—Yeah. The other day Shinkō, my pal, he got a dad, but I'm small still so I don't have one yet.

You, dear reader, must understand that even if children have parents and a bed to sleep on, it is an extravagance these days to educate and supervise them.

I'm sure that you, dear reader, know that the bums in Asakusa live on leftovers from the eateries. But did you know that the destitute and the day laborers come to the bums to buy food scraps—in other words, leftovers of leftovers—for two or three sen a bowl? In such a world as this, it is no wonder that forty or fifty thousand juvenile delinquents fall under the jurisdiction of the Metropolitan Police Headquarters.

And do you know how many of these are former apprentices, errand boys, shop boys, trainees, waiters, and child laborers at the local steelworks? For example, just listen in for half an hour or so on the conversations of the nannies who come to pass the time in Asakusa Park.

—But if it's like that, then just what's going on with today's Japan? What's going on with today's Tokyo? Isn't all of Japanese society today, all of Tokyo today, just a bunch of old crooks? In the midst of these elderly delinquents, Asakusa is a young punk. And bad or not, youth has charm, energy, and a progressive spirit.

So says Mr. Tanizaki Jun'ichirō. And according to an article in the *Asahi* newspaper, from 11:50 P.M. on the last night of 1929, JOAK will install two microphones in the compound of the Asakusa Sensō Temple in order to bring to you, dear reader, the clatter of the visitors, the ringing of the bells, the noise of coins being tossed into the offertories, the hands clapped in worship, the gongs tolling one hundred and eight times, the crowing of the cocks, and other aural aspects of the atmosphere of New Year's Eve.

I'm thinking of having members of the Scarlet Gang stand in front of the mikes and shout: Hurray for 1930! Anyway, this broadcast will come off because Asakusa, as "Tokyo's Heart," represents the mood of a pretty lean year in the depths of the recession.

I also hear that in Asakusa there is a beggars-only bar. They put a naked girl on the table and get drunk while spinning her round and round. Also, near a house close to the Komagata Bridge, there is supposedly a place that gives "singing lessons in the Kiyomoto style." But the people there are most suspicious. A sixteen- or seventeen-year-old girl comes to greet you, but it all ends up with lots of liquor and not a note of music.

On rainy nights, carrying large oiled-paper umbrellas, the streetwalkers come out of the flophouses in Honjo to solicit bums who stand under the eaves of the theaters and along the earthen walls of temples. Unobserved, young hoods follow geisha on their way to houses of assignation.

But the terror of Asakusa lies not in any of these things or what happens in places like Okuyama in the dead of night. Rather, as autumn turns to winter, it lies in the turbulent vortex of people at the November Yoshiwara fairs, the cockerel market at the Sensō Temple, New Year's Eve here in Asakusa. How did it come that Umekichi got sucked into this whirlpool and spit out as Silver Cat Umekō?

15

UMEKICHI NEVER talks about his mother
and father. Maybe he's an orphan or a
bastard. And even if not, probably they
were the kind of parents he is better off
without.

When he was thirteen years old, he
became an apprentice at a Western-style umbrella shop in Shitaya
Ryūsenji-machi. This is the area where Miss Higuchi Ichiyō wrote
Comparing Heights. The mistress of the shop was bedridden, some
prolonged illness. He hated even looking at her—all pale and
gaunt. On top of that, her seven kids worked him hard. Umekichi
ran away after three days.

He became an apprentice to a liquor store in Kanda. (As I told
you before, when Umekichi was fourteen, the daughter of a haberdasher became his second sweetheart.) He stole money to show
his girlfriend a good time and got kicked out of there.

While he was loitering around Asakusa Park, the newspaper boys
got to know him and let him into their gang. In less than three
months, he got into a bloody fight with one of the older boys and
was driven out.

After being picked up by a beggar in Asakusa Park and spend-
ing three nights in the big garbage dump on the Komagata riverbank (he and his buddies called it the "Azuma Hotel"), he began to
wander around, starting from Honjo and Fukagawa, eventually getting as far away as Chiba.

Umekichi always said: Never again in my life will I have as much
fun and get into as little trouble as the half year I was a hobo.

Then he went back to Asakusa once again. He became a shill for
an Indian selling rings on the sidewalk. (His job was to pretend to
be a customer.) The Indian loved him as if he were a girl, but Ume-

kichi broke off with him just in time, saying: You can go to hell, idiot. If you want to make out with a Japanese, you better go bleach your skin.

When Umekichi was sitting idly in Asakusa Station, a kindly-seeming old man took him home. He was actually a well-known cat-catcher. Before long it was the old man who was caught by the cops. Then Umekichi was taken in by one of the old man's cat-catching cronies and began prowling the streets as a junior cat-catcher trainee.

When the cat-catcher spots a cat, he lets loose a sparrow tied on a string. Sparrow flaps its wings. Cat pounces. Cat-catcher slowly pulls the string. Cat is lured closer. And the trick is to grab the cat quick enough.

Nabbed tabby is beaten to death at once. In the dark of the park or the shade of the shore, it is stripped of its hide. Cat-catcher hides the pelt under his clothes, wraps it round his waist. It brings in a lot at the samisen store.

Homeless, Umekichi stayed at flophouses here and there with the senior cat-catcher. It was about this time that he became part of an Asakusa gang of young punks. He was fifteen then. Before long Umekichi and his cat-catching colleague were hauled off to the Nihon Dam Police Station in the Yoshiwara, but Umekichi, being just a kid, was let off light.

He reappeared in Asakusa, but for a while he had the feeling that the police knew who he was, so he fell in with a group of peddlers who were pretending to be from an orphanage. While passing himself off as an orphan and pressing people to buy paper and pencils, he met a student selling medicine. This seemed more profitable, so Umekichi quickly changed into a struggling young student peddling pills. Money came easily, and he had no idea that a middle-school uniform and cap could be such bait for girls.

Then before he knew it, even his nickname had moved up a rank—from "Cat-Catcher Umekō," he became "Silver Cat Umekō."

Now as a member of Yumiko's Scarlet Gang, Umekichi is about the right age to fake being a college student, but, actually, he is close to making an honest living working as a barber's live-in apprentice. This is the shop where we saw the "lovely lunatic," said to be Akikō's elder sister, doing her makeup. Yumiko had helped him get this job.

Besides—

Squeeze. Touch. Talk her up. Make a big production. Oh, you dropped something. Keep pushing your case. Baby. My, what have you done? A setback. Follow her. Make a request. Give it your best shot. Lift her skirt. Thanks. Throw the towel away. And so on. Let's suppose Umekichi tries using these age-old techniques for seducing women on a girl.

Yasuki bushi at the Tamaki Theater. The girl is not impressed.

The finale, the "Ginza Song" backed by the Japanese-Western Jazz Ensemble. Eight dancers with long-sleeved kimonos:

Ginza, Ginza, dear old Ginza . . .

They begin to sing, and the girl bites her lip and looks at her lap. He glances at her. Her lashes are wet with tears: Wow! What luck. What innocence!

Umekichi gently tries to put an arm around her shoulders, but . . .

16

THE YOUNG WOMAN has abruptly stood up and left the theater without looking back.

But Umekichi, confident of his talents, figures her as good as had. Thanks to his school cap with its dubious badge

and his *hakama,* he has transformed himself into a college student.

When a woman wants a lover . . . The young women of Tahiti are said to tuck white flowers behind their right ears. In Asakusa (yes, that's right, even if it is not such a remote South Sea island) an artificial rose stuck in a young woman's hair can show she is tender-hearted. By the same token, a single red rose can be even a sign she is a bad girl.

Of course, even in Asakusa Park, the age of the tough, extorting "brotherhoods" has passed, but, dear reader, if your own son were to strut around with his cap at a jaunty angle . . .

—Hey, just a minute. A voice would halt him in his tracks.

—Whose boy are you?

The voice could very well be intimidating or even worse—"Boy" as in "gang boy" means you belong to someone.

Anyway, this young woman in a worn muslin kimono and a soiled sash, with only the artificial silk bow at the back looking new, tied high and red under her breasts, her heavy makeup making her look strangely sad. Well, she's of several minds about herself. Umekichi would do well to take advantage of this.

So taking a woman's handkerchief from his pocket, he runs after her and says in a far too friendly tone: Didn't you drop this?

—Oh, thanks.

—Why, you're the very person who was next to me at the Tamaki Theater just now.

The young woman stuffs the hankie up her sleeve and swiftly walks on. Umekichi seems a little surprised by this, but: Look, at the theater your eyes were full of tears. I saw it. Has something made you unhappy? When you went out to wipe those tears, you dropped this handkerchief. It is still damp.

—Then you're kind enough to offer to listen while I tell you what's making me sad?

—Huh.

—Of course, you know I'm way ahead of you on this one.

—Hey . . .

—You probably want me to give you back the hankie, right? But you don't mind if I keep it, do you? I'm sure you've got three or four in your pocket just in case, right? You must have less obvious ways to get a girl. Let's see your latest.

—Oh, what a dumb move. I didn't recognize you. Very interesting disguise. Keep the hankie. May come in handy for the tears.

—Yes, you're right, the young woman replies as she makes a show of dabbing at her eyes: That "Ginza Song," whenever I hear it, I get all weepy.

—So you got the Ginza bug.

—You know, at the Tamaki, whether it's *Yasuki bushi, Ohara bushi,* or *manzai,* they're all standing up and cheering like they'd called in some geisha. It's like a real get-together for factory workers and ditch diggers. Then what is it? As soon as they start on "Ginza, Ginza, dear old Ginza," as soon as they hear that jazzy tune, they all quiet down, like peasants kneeling in front of a lord. Just what is it about the Ginza? What can the Ginza mean to that bunch at the Tamaki? I bet a lot of them have never even seen the Ginza. Like lots of Ginza young ladies don't know anything about Asakusa. Now look, I've gotten all worked up . . .

—A bit of Marxist thought there?

—And you're Mr. Silver Cat, aren't you?

—You got it. I must be getting senile or something. I almost didn't recognize you. That thing on your head. It's a wig, isn't it? The kimono get-up's all borrowed, too, right? I went fishing and ended up on the hook.

—Actually, I'm on my way back to return everything I borrowed.

Want to come with me? Even though you know who I am, you still want to make me?

—Only if I'm sure that you're a woman first.

—That's for you to find out.

17

THE YOUNG WOMAN at the Tamaki Theater— another of Yumiko's disguises.

Generally speaking, could you say that the Japanese have no interest in dressing up like this? I remember that at a dance held in the Kaihin Hotel in Kamakura, not one Japanese came in disguise, even though it was a costume ball.

Yet in the new Ginza there is a shop that rents disguises, in other words, a costumier. Once, for a joke, I even wrote about it. But come to think of it, in the Ginza, makeup alone is enough. It's not a part of town where disguises are really necessary.

They are really more of an Asakusa thing. Never need to look very hard here. You can always find people in disguise.

Right under your nose, you can find lady bums dressed as men. You just laugh them off. But a man dressed as a woman, face thick with white powder, elaborate Japanese-style wig, all decked out in red, slipping off with another man into the dark alleys behind the temple—this sends chills up your spine like you've just seen a peculiar lizard or something.

And even when it isn't dark. Smack in the middle of the busiest part of Asakusa there is this splendid costumier cum disguise shop—it even has an advertisement tower with a red neon sign rising unabashed from the roof. What makes this store different from others is that because it caters to both stage actors and vaudeville entertainers, it stocks everything from wigs to pistols.

As Yumiko remarked: I'm something like a mannequin girl for this shop. I give them a security deposit and pay the rental fee, so they couldn't find a better advertisement than me. In return, if the members of the Scarlet Gang were to storm Lord Kira's mansion, they would lend us the clothes. Unfortunately, like Amanoya Rihee, their clothes lender, our Showa counterpart is just as greedy. That's the problem.

Someday I'll show you this shop. I'll even introduce you to the people who go there.

But at any rate, when Umekichi, taken in by Yumiko's disguise, decided at her suggestion to take up a more respectable occupation, the allure of disguise seemed to play a big role in his choice. At first he said: I wouldn't mind being a surgeon.

—Oh, so you want to do operations, do you? Just like you, Mr. Silver Cat! Can't get over what it feels like to skin a cat, and now you want to start on people, right?

—One quick, straight cut across the stomach, and you peel off the skin while the blood is still warm. It's quite a feeling. But even if I can't get a chance to cut open someone's stomach, maybe I could work in a restaurant kitchen or be a barber's assistant.

So that's how Umekichi became an apprentice in a barbershop.

Surgeon, cook, barber—all three have something in common. First of all, metal instruments gleaming bright, particularly the sharper blades.

You could even say that this taste for the blade is what has kept Umekichi from sinking (even while having his ups and downs along life's rocky bottom) to the level of the homeless, the beggared—what has kept him from falling asleep forever in this world-of-nothingness garbage can of Asakusa. This taste pulses through his life, a thread of vitality.

And then there is the white coat. The local barbers and cooks come to Asakusa Park in their white work clothes. Not only do these costumes stand out among the throng, they also, just like sharp blades, attract the local girls. Umekichi knew this.

So he became a barber's apprentice, and as he shaved Yumiko's neck, he fell in love with this woman who is so much like a razor herself. Something about her told him that she shares his taste for the blade.

This is why he has taken Yumiko and her man, a playboy of some sort, aboard the Kurenai-maru and is rowing upriver, just as Yumiko has asked him to.

But sharp blades easily nick. And while on the Ōkawa, drenched in wintry mist, Umekichi, concerned about Yumiko, becomes pale, and . . .

the dirigible and the twelve stories

18

THE SOLES of her feet, like peach-colored carved shells, bathe in the glow of the brazier when . . . Okay, the man comes in, and there is Yumiko, fallen asleep while drying her feet by the stove.

He had read those black stockings hanging out to dry as a danger signal and is now relieved yet disappointed—she's even alone.

Nothing seems to be hidden in this narrow cabin.

Just a simple whore after all, he thinks, smiles, but those legs are so slender, beautiful. Boyishly pure legs.

He is wearing a tasteful beige Japanese-style cape-coat with a hunting cap of the same material. His head bumps against the ceiling as he stands, arms folded, staring at Yumiko's legs.

The cabin seems to grow lighter as his eyes get accustomed to the darkness.

Yumiko's bare legs lie one against the other as though trying to keep warm, calves nestled, toes turned under, the hollows of her knees perfectly aligned.

The impression she gives lying there with her legs pulled up is so cute that he thinks: Just a kid. But where the red skirt has slid and her garter shows, he sees a coarse, adult carnality.

Abruptly, the boatman Umekichi lets drop the gangplank. There is a thud, and the boat sways sharply. The man stumbles to the belly of the boat, and Yumiko looks up: Oh, sorry. I was really asleep, wasn't I?

She presses her legs tightly together and pulls down her skirt a couple of times as though to show that it barely covers her knees.

She turns away from him and lowers her head: I've been waiting, anxious, and when it gets dark, there are so few boats on the river. We ought to hurry. Oh and could you close that window? Our boatman tends to be the jealous type.

The man pulls shut the cabin skylight, also the door to the cabin, and it is suddenly a dark and secret room. He throws himself at her to wrap her in his arms, but he falls into the bedding. She is no longer there.

—I'm looking for a lamp. You know, I promised to wait for you here on the boat, but I didn't promise to stay awake. Sorry, but I was really that tired. Yesterday everything went wrong, and I got no sleep at all. Lost my makeup things, slipped getting into the boat, got my stockings all wet . . .

An oil lamp on the dirty little table comes on, and Yumiko kneels there in a pure white coat, her hands properly arranged, a well-brought-up young lady.

—There's no sake.

—Just where are we going?

—Upriver.

—Well, it doesn't matter, but I'm not the kind of guy who likes guessing games. So just come out with it. Tell me what you're up to. If you want to have a good time, I'll play along. If you want help, just ask. But make yourself clear.

—Haven't I made it clear? I want to try and see if I can fall in love with you.

—Come off it.

—Why? You're already in love with me. Why wouldn't I want to be in love with you, too? Come on. Make it happen.

—Look, if you've got a grudge or something against me, just come out with it like a man.

—If I were a man, I would do just that. I do have a grudge against you, a big one. But because I'm a woman, you really scare me. Got it?

And Yumiko opens her big eyes wide and looks him straight in the face. Then, hearing the sound of an approaching motorboat, she quickly shuts them, and her shoulders tremble.

—I've known you for a long time.

19

YUMIKO CLOSES her eyes. But putting it that way will give you no indication of what it is really like. Those eyelids of hers flutter so fast that you can almost hear them, and you can still see every movement of her eyelashes. Her eyes are that big. Her  lashes that thick. And the whites of her eyes have a bluish tinge. The ups and downs of those eyelashes are enough to enflame a man with a fan of emotion.

—I've known you for a long time, she repeats.

The man stands up, walks right over, and takes her in his arms. Sitting on his knees, she stretches her bare legs toward the little stove. Then, smoothing the hem of her white coat just as a child would . . .

—Yes, just like that. The way you take a woman in your arms hasn't changed. I want to remind you of something. It was night, after that new dirigible had floated over Tokyo twenty-four hours straight. Red and green, those two dirigible lights—from below they looked as little as tiny lamps. The sky was black, full of rain clouds. When it crossed the river, the green light went out—just like a shooting star. Then while we were staring with surprise, the red light was suddenly hidden by the clouds. Since you're from Tokyo, you'll remember those lights. There, that night, on the roof of some big concrete building, right there on the observation platform, you took a woman in your arms in just this way, didn't you?

—Amazing, what a good little actress you are. So what's next? The princess's speech out of some fairy tale?

—Fairy tale? That's true. I was only in the fifth grade then. Hiding under the platform. Trembling all over as I watched you two. And now you're holding me just like you held the other woman back then. Hasn't my wish come true just like the fairy princess? Happy ending, dream come true.

—You're that jealous. Well, do me a favor and try to remember just what I did to that woman.

—Yes, you want me to tell you so you can do the same thing with me. Well, you put your left hand on her chin and made her look up.

And abruptly, Yumiko turns around, her face close to the man's as she glares at him.

—Look, let's just stop this. There's no sense in my going crazy, too. But you do remember that concrete building, don't you?

Above their heads they can hear the sound of Umekichi's foot-

steps. On most boats, the boatman's place is at the bow, but on the Kurenai-maru it is at the stern. So Umekichi, not used to sculling from the stern, moves back and forth on the planking over the ceiling of the cabin where Yumiko and the man sit in the flickering light of the sooty oil lamp.

—Just opposite the Kisakata Police Station. Remember? The Fuji Elementary School.

—Ah! And he seems to have swallowed the bait.

—There. So we're not into fairy tales anymore. Still that school does now seem somehow fairy-tale-like. Three stories, all concrete, and on the morning of September first, the kids were let in for the very first time. Then came the earthquake. Then came the fire. And since it was the only building that didn't burn down in the back part of Asakusa, we . . . All our houses had burned up, and so we went there. And speaking of fairy tales, didn't you feel happy as a kid the day we stood on that roof and watched what was left of the Twelve Story Tower being blown up. Remember? The bugle of the demolition team. How cheerful it sounded.

—So you're claiming to be Ochiyo's kid sister?

—Suppose I am. How long were you going to play dumb?

20

THAT SYMBOL of old Asakusa, the Twelve Story Tower, was beheaded in the 1923 earthquake.

Until then, I'd been a student living in a boarding house in Hongō. I'd always liked Asakusa, and so less than two hours after that 11:58 A.M. earthquake, I was on my way there with a friend, going to determine the damage.

All sorts of rumors were floating around the hills of Ueno.

—Can you believe it? Enoshima Island keeps sinking and then coming up again.

—Look! The Twelve Stories just snapped off at the top. There were lots of sightseers up there. How awful! They all got tossed off! Just went to look, and they got dead people floating right in Gourd Pond.

There were some egg boxes stacked by the roadside. We ate six or seven, raw. Couldn't say we stole them, couldn't say we were given them, couldn't say we bought them.

The grounds of the Sensō Temple were full of evacuees— Yoshiwara whores, Asakusa geisha among them, colorful like a field of flowers in utter disarray.

Come to think of it, Yumiko—then in the fifth grade—was likely to have been in that crowd.

—Well, well, so you're writing a novel about how I got to be what I am. That's a funny twist of fate. And she half shut her eyes and seemed to be looking fondly back at the good old days.

—But where has she gone, and how, that girl I used to be when the Twelve Stories was still standing? When I think about it . . . Any-way, you can write as much as you want. I don't mind. Go on, even if they run me out because of something I've done, someday I would like to read it to someone.

The Twelve Story Tower (getting back to our subject) was surrounded by buildings still on fire when my friend and I got there, but the fire hadn't yet gone as far as the stalls and theaters of the Rokku.

Like dragonflies, and just as unconcerned, we perched on the rocks by Gourd Pond and let our feet dangle in the water while we munched on biscuits and watched the big fire some ten meters away.

After things had calmed down a bit, the demolition team came out to blow up the corpses of the bigger buildings left. The stump of the Twelve Stories was among these. As Yumiko is telling the story in the belly of the boat:

—That trumpet, so cheerful sounding—it could be heard as far as the school. Wherever we looked, nothing but scorched earth and every now and then a little tin-roofed barrack. From the roof of the school, you could see out over the whole park. The rooftop platform of the school was packed, and we waited for about an hour for the demolition to begin, didn't we? And then there was the bang of the first detonation, and we saw a waterfall of bricks. I thought that one side of the tower would stay standing, sticking up like a sword, but it fell down with the second explosion. And we all cheered—hurray, hurray—and then burst out laughing. Remember? After the last sword of a wall fell, all those people down there raced up until the brick mountain was black with them. We were so surprised. It was like soldiers seizing a brick mountain. From far away, all of us watched, and we could have shed tears of happiness. Why? Shouting hurray when a tower collapses and scurrying up the bricks even before the smoke has settled?

—That's kid stuff to keep a guy waiting while you unreel fairy stories.

—That's not what I'm doing. When you abandon a woman just like that, isn't her loving you more because of it just the same thing?

—What do you mean?

—It was like that, wasn't it? Didn't you often wake my sister up in the middle of the night by tapping her on the head with a rice paddle? When I woke up and found myself lying on cold concrete, I longed for nothing more than to be sold into a house with real tatami on the floor. In my open box of singed sheet iron with a straw mat for a roof . . .

the great kanto earthquake

21

ISN'T THE KURENAI-MARU now approaching the Kototoi Bridge? Wheels, automobile horns heard above their heads—footsteps like rain.

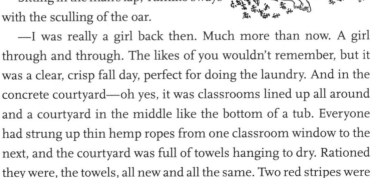

Sitting in the man's lap, Yumiko sways with the sculling of the oar.

—I was really a girl back then. Much more than now. A girl through and through. The likes of you wouldn't remember, but it was a clear, crisp fall day, perfect for doing the laundry. And in the concrete courtyard—oh yes, it was classrooms lined up all around and a courtyard in the middle like the bottom of a tub. Everyone had strung up thin hemp ropes from one classroom window to the next, and the courtyard was full of towels hanging to dry. Rationed they were, the towels, all new and all the same. Two red stripes were sewn in each one. Just that brought tears to my eyes. Bright red lines fluttering all around the courtyard. That red, it touched my girlish heart. But you know, there were burnt walls, all collapsed, fallen tiles, singed electrical wires, charred rusty tin plates, and clouds of dust and ashes all over the place. It was a time you thought it was perfectly normal to see people beaten to death with iron bars and twins born in the middle of the street and dead horses and humans, too, floating together down the Ōkawa, and you thought it was normal not to have anything to eat for a couple of days. And love, that was no ordinary love.

But now, in the spring of 1930, there are big festivals celebrating the reconstruction of Tokyo. A new Tokyo has risen from the earthquake, and, of course, out of all the ruins, an Asakusa reborn. But as Vice-Bishop Gon states right in the preface to *A History of the Sensō Temple:*

> In the thirty-sixth year of the reign of Empress Suiko, the Goddess Kannon of Konryūsan-Sensōji emerged from this very site on the Sumida River. Since that day, our temple has enjoyed a more than 1,300-year history as the most important place of worship in all the Empire for our country's people and receives daily proof of supreme divine grace. At present, our temple welcomes an average of fifty to sixty thousand visitors each day.
>
> As the fires of the earthquake in the twelfth year of the reign of Emperor Taisho, those that reduced most of the imperial capital to ashes, were encroaching upon our temple complex and the more than one hundred thousand evacuees who sought shelter here, and as there seemed to be no escaping imprisonment in an agonizing inferno, the revered image of the Buddha used its magnificent powers to put an end to the raging flames of hell and save temple and people alike. Among those who witnessed this miracle, there was not one who did not heed and mend his ways to become a devout believer honestly and from the bottom of his heart. Henceforth, from near and far, the faithful compete to find traces of this miracle, and it is hardly surprising that the large number of people who seek to learn more about the history of our temple of their own volition has and will continue to increase.

That is why the famous offertory chest in front of the Kannon Hall . . . For example, according to temple records, in just one month, October 1929, 16,002 yen was tossed into this offertory chest, which is 4.954 meters long, 3.169 meters wide, 69.7 centimeters high, with nineteen crossbars, and a hole underneath to collect all the donations. The revenue from the sale of incense, candles, prayers, fortune cards, and all sorts of votives amounted to another 5,000 or 6,000 yen. And the restoration of the main temple hall, under way since the summer of 1928, will take three or four years and cost an estimated 600,000 yen—consisting, of course, of the contributions of these pious folk.

—More than 100,000 people were saved during the quake, including me, and, if you figure out the cost per person, Yumiko once told me: It cost six yen to save a life. But we didn't figure out any such idiotic calculations back then. The three-gun salute, an emergency signal, sounded from near the Imperial Palace, and the Twelve Stories and the Hanayashiki were on fire, and a real sea of flames had reached the Yoshiwara and then spread east. And around two in the afternoon, the little halls of the Sensō Temple were really burning. The fire came from the south, too, moving along the river from near Kuramae. And later, come to think of it, I met the abbot. We'd escaped to the garden of the Denpōin, and the old abbot was sitting on a wicker chair on the lawn, and when the Kannon Hall got all covered up in the smoke, he stood right up and recited the sutras as hard as he could. Then suddenly the wind stopped, and the smoke around the Kannon Hall cleared away.

According to Yumiko, the old abbot, in poor health since returning from his spring trip to India, passed out in the early morning that day, September 1, on his way to the toilet.

22

MORNING—THAT IS, one o'clock in the morning at the Denpōin. The old abbot had a light stroke and passed out in the hall that led to the toilet. He came to around five. But his acolytes knew nothing about it until after dawn.

The big shake-up came at noon. The abbot was carried on the back of a monk out of harm's way to the lawn near the pond.

Soon the whole place—from the room next to the old abbot's infirmary to the space under the floor of the main hall's study—was so crammed with evacuees there was no room to budge. Though twenty-four lesser parts of the Sensō temple complex were on fire, 15,000 people packed themselves in.

The clothes of the some sixty monks, their black robes, formal vestments, and even their undergarments were reduced to ashes. Only six or seven of their scarves were left. Wearing dirty Western clothes or *yukata,* they took care of the evacuees.

The Sensō Temple Hospital, the Sensō Temple Women's Hall, the Sensō Temple Kindergarten, the Sensō Temple Children's Library— among the Sensō Temple's six "public welfare facilities," these four buildings are now part of the temple complex, and the desire to help people from the time of the earthquake continues today in this form. The Asakusa Elementary School behind the Kannon Hall, where Tokikō of the Kurenai-maru goes to school, is left over from the earthquake.

On the morning of September 4, the military began to hand out food to the evacuees in the temple complex. Then at the Fuji Elementary School, all the burned-down walls, broken windows, blackboards, desks, and so on were cleared away and things were put in order as best they could be. And from September 8, the homeless and those just living in shacks were welcomed in. Nearly a thousand people crowded into the classrooms from the first to the third floors. It was a school that had been built for two thousand kids.

—The red of those towels touched my heart, but my big sister was the kind of old-fashioned downtown girl who slept with two bells under her pillow. Yumiko tells the man her memories.

—I am a daughter of the earthquake. In the middle of the earthquake, I was reborn. It's like I told you at the Aquarium. I'm going to become a man. I'm never going to be a woman. When hundreds of people sleep, lying together on concrete, legs touching, without anything to cover up their bodies—then a girl starts to hate becoming a woman. There was no running water or electricity. In the middle of the night, when the candles went out one by one, it was pitch black, and sometimes you'd find yourself sleeping right next to a beggar. Really. Did you know there were beggars mixed in with the crowd? But there was a couple that was the best behaved of all. They would go up to the roof garden in the middle of the night when they wanted to be alone with each other, but they were still beggars, this couple, after all? And then there was my big sister you used to hit with a rice paddle to wake up, and . . .

—The crazy sister you keep talking about, you say that she's Ochiyo?

—Look, if you think you can get off that easy, you're making a big mistake. Anyway, I was really impressed with those beggars. Then the first thousand people slowly went away, and I felt so lonely to be left behind.

Just as Yumiko says—the evacuees were chased out, starting with those in the first-floor classrooms. This was because there was no more space for rations in the ruins of the Asakusa Ward Office courtyard. When the rice sacks were brought into one classroom, the people there moved to another. This happened in the second classroom and then in the third until the whole first floor turned into a warehouse for rations.

And because school was to begin again on October 1, exactly one month after the earthquake, the third floor had to be cleared out for the kids. Of course, this meant the evacuees had to go live with acquaintances for a while, or go back to their hometowns, or move into the municipal barracks, or scrape together enough to build shacks of their own. So forty days after the earthquake, only fifty or sixty households totaling roughly two hundred people were left on the second floor.

—It was just this second floor, but the fall wind really blew across the wide concrete ground—yes, it was like that. There, in the middle of the classrooms, we made our own little nests; collected rusty pieces of tin from the rubble, found straw mats and tattered scraps of cloth, and each family hid, tucked away in its little beggar home. This made it even more lonely. I wonder why everyone wanted so much to live hidden away like that. Only the beggar couple and their kid slept out on a single straw mat like before. If we hadn't put up those tin walls around us, would you've stuck a rice paddle in through the space at the bottom of the wall and woken up my sister?

23

THE SENJU AZUMA Steamboat Company— the name sounds impressive enough, but since the old Mukōjima embankment has become part of the new Sumida Park, the ferries look like old-fashioned toy boats. And when they  get near the Kototoi Bridge, the picture-book sellers on board get

out at the pier and act as if they were part of the crew, calling out: This stop is Kototoi—Kototoi. Make sure you have all of your personal belongings with you as you exit the boat. Good-bye and thank you for riding with us today.

And their way of greeting the passengers as they come aboard is just as serene. Because things are so dignified, dear reader, people still call these putt-putt barges "one-sen steamboats," even though the fare has gone up to five sen. And when one of these old steamboats passes by, it makes all sorts of waves and acts like it owns the Ōkawa.

The Kurenai-maru itself is nothing but a broken-down tub. It's such a small boat that it's a joke even to give it a name, but because Boat Tokikō had asked him, Umekichi, who is fond of blades, carved the letters "Kurenai-maru" on the tail and filled them in with red paint.

When Umekichi came to borrow the tub, Tokikō's father told him to watch out for boat burglars, but it was not the kind of vessel on which even the clever Umekichi (who had himself a quick look-see) would have found anything to steal.

And so, each time the Kurenai-maru rolls on the waves, Yumiko gets to feel the man's knees, and she tightly knits her brows.

—Ugh. I can't stand it when my legs get so warm. Just like I hate holding a dog or a cat. Getting all warm from some animal's body heat gives me goose bumps, Yumiko remarks and quickly springs up and goes over to remove the glass globe of the lamp.

—Let's get some more light in here.

—If you hate animal heat so much, you didn't have to sleep next to Ochiyo back then.

—I guess not.

And she grasps the glass globe with her handkerchief and breathes into it a few times, clouding it with her white breath.

—But I don't remember ever having slept in my mother's arms. Anyhow, at that time, each family got only one mattress. But I was really surprised! That rice paddle came in from beneath that tin-sheeted wall and poked my sister on the shoulders or on the neck. But I wasn't sleeping. I clearly remember it. My sister touched her head lightly with one hand. Then she turned over, squared her shoulders, and pushed herself up with both hands, and, then scrunching up her shoulders, she slipped right out. She took those hemp-soled straw sandals she kept behind her pillow. It was just like that. The thwack of those straw sandals when she dropped them on the concrete floor ten or so meters away. It was completely dark. No electric lights on in the whole neighborhood. Then my sister came back. And what do you think? She was trembling all over. She was looking for something. Then she felt for the ends of my braids with her hands. She jammed those braids into her mouth and quietly sobbed.

—Who do the hell do you think you're talking about? Your very own sister! Aren't you ashamed?

—Absolutely. So, look, I chopped off all of that dirty hair. I just hated my sister.

—You tell me that because you were just a kid, you hid under the roof tower, quivering with fear? That was . . .

—Right. The night the dirigible came. But isn't it interesting? Now that little kid has got you on the boat, and she's telling you these memories of love for her big sister who's gone crazy.

—Could you shake all over one more time just for me?

—Really . . . And Yumiko polishes the glass globe, her head lowered, cheeks flushed, lost in thought.

—So many things happened. The doctor from the Metropolitan Police Department medical consultation group got drunk every day. And those funny craftsman brothers—they'd go and steal rationed pickled plums in the middle of the night, and, if someone's child died, right, they went around collecting presents from everyone, even if it was just one sen or even a sheet of writing paper, and they held shows where evacuees could show off their hidden talents, and they got people together for a pilgrimage to the ashes of the Yoshiwara. But then weren't they caught gambling and got dragged off with three or four other men to the nearby police station?

24

FOLDING HIS ARMS across his chest, the man leans back on the plank wall of the boat cabin.

—Now that you know I'm the little sister of your ex-lover, have you suddenly lost interest in me, just like you did her?
Yumiko asks, smiling but seeming like she is going to leap right at him. She looks at the figure of the man flickering in the light of the lamp bright inside its now clean globe. On her toes and bending over slightly, she warms her hands over the small cooking stove.

—It's pretty plain the only thing you care about is what I think of you.

—So? Kind of like me, don't you? Little sisters are not the same as big sisters in all ways—right down to how they kiss.

—I don't go in for kissing. Too much trouble.

—Same here. But I wonder—the police dragged off some guys for just gambling to kill time, but why didn't they go out and arrest you, Mr. Akagi?

—Good kid. Even remember my name.

—I'll be a real good kid and help you remember. Because you're a bit of a dimwit. You know, if you are going to do bad things, it's important to have a good memory.

And she scoots over to him: I wonder why you were so easily taken in back there at the merry-go-round, a fun spot for good boys and girls, and even got yourself coaxed into coming out here to the middle of the Ōkawa.

—Oh, that . . . and he smiles as if humoring a child: Just kidding around. I get a kick out of it. Besides, I've kept away from Asakusa for two years.

—But why did the winds of fortune . . . Ah, right. The winds. You came like something the storm blew in. You came to my sister. That evening, the automobiles from city hall and the Metropolitan Police Department crossed the temporary bridge over the Ōkawa. On the east bank of the river, the water came up to people's waists, and there wasn't a single building left. Not only in the east, but the shacks all over the park were blown away. You couldn't walk in winds like that, and girls were crawling over the ground on their hands and knees, crying, rain beating down on their hair, braids caked in mud. Since our school didn't have glass in the windows, we wandered around trying to escape the darkness that couldn't even be cut with the light of a match, clutching our rationed mattresses, our few belongings, and the next morning you were there with us. Then with pieces of tin, old boards, tattered cloth, we tried to cover up the windows.

—Spare me the sob stories, will you?

—The sound of hammers striking nails—I can hear it even now. I'll never forget that sound as long as I live. Not just fixing the windows. Fixing our school. Education was the first issue the new government tackled after the Meiji Restoration. And education was top priority for the new Russia, too. I clearly remember the school principal's speech. About four hundred out of two thousand students came on October 1, the first day of class. We walked right over the scorched ground. All our homes had been destroyed in the fires—not one was left. We were so happy to see each other again that we cried. This was the school we made. We ripped apart wooden beer crates, nailed the boards together, and these became our desks and the teacher's platform. We hung straw mats to separate the classrooms. The students in the higher grades worked on the school like crazy every day. The teacher wrote out math problems on walls still stinking of smoke. But we couldn't make blackboards. Classes of twenty or thirty students sat on five or six straw mats laid out in front of the walls. It was a great school. We were as happy as could be, but, if the world were to fall apart again, I wonder if we'd pour our hearts into putting it back together like we did then. But my sister got lonelier once school started. When she heard the voices reading from textbooks, the singing of songs, and the chants during gym class exercises, she would look up from the second-floor window, tears running down her cheeks.

—If you want to blame me for what happened to your sister, just stop beating around the bush and come right out with it.

the arsenic kiss

25

TWO WARDROBES MADE entirely from paulow-
nia wood, a mandolin, a sixty-centimeter-
high mirror, a tea chest veneered with thin
strips of strong-grained ebony and other
woods pasted on in patterns, an oblong hibachi made of zelkova wood, and even a
variety of things sold at the Otori shrine, ranging from a *kumade*
bamboo rake to a *hagoita* paddle with the picture of a zodiac animal, placed next to a miniature unpainted wood Shinto shrine—
all the fixings of downtown homes. I hear there are even thatched
cabins of cargo boats that are just like the living rooms of well-to-
do homes. But on the Kurenai-maru, Yumiko puts the glowing coals
from the little cooking stove into a bucket coated with straw ash.

—Oh, you're frightening me. But am I blaming you? From our
insurance, we only got back ten percent of what we'd lost in the earthquake. But my sister's love was not insured.

—Well then, you ought've insured Ochiyo just in case she had
to be carted off to the insane asylum. But you can't do that anywhere

in the world, so how I can be expected to shoulder the blame for someone who went nuts. What if all jilted women went nuts? That doesn't matter to me, and anyway, Ochiyo didn't seem at all that nuts when I left.

—And where did you say your good-byes? At the front door of the police station, right?

—That's good manners in my circle. Ochiyo didn't squeal to the police. Though I didn't want to take advantage of her kindness, I didn't want to commit any love suicide with her either.

—Good to know that. Yumiko takes a small medicine bottle from the pocket of her white overcoat and drops some arsenic pills, small as millet grains, one by one into the palm of her hand. And then, with her eyes half-closed as if in a trance: One little pill contains five milligrams of arsenic. One little bottle contains five hundred pills, enough to kill many people. This little bottle—it is my pleasure.

—You don't say.

—Look, at times like this when you sneer at me, you seem as old-fashioned as a doll from a folk customs exhibition. Do you think I am trying to scare you with these? Silly man. This is a toy. No, that's not it. This is something I need. I always take these little pills to make my skin clear and white, to get a silky sheen down to the soles of my feet—that's why I take them. This whole time I've been looking at you, thinking I could kill you with them at any time, and that pleases me. Even a heart truly darkened with hatred brightens at a thought like this. But you often end up liking the person you wanted to kill. But no, I didn't bring them with me because I was meeting you. I usually eat in the park, you know.

—That's a load of crap. Before, you bragged that you're always being shadowed on land.

—Ah-ha, but on land you could've run away any time you wanted.

And it would've been a real inconvenience if your old buddies tailed us. On water I have the upper hand. And because I take them with meals, I always have these little pills on me. In the park these days in Asakusa, you can eat a square meal on ten or twenty sen, and it's not worth going to the trouble of cooking at home.

—Lemme look at 'em. Akagi, arms until now folded, stretches out his hand.

The poison makes him view Yumiko in a different light.

This is not lost on her.

—If I fall in love with you like my sister did, I'll kill myself with these little pills. I wanted to see you so badly that I didn't care if it killed me. That is, if you make a real woman of me.

She gently takes his arm and, dropping six arsenic pills into the palm of his hand: Even if I've been bluffing about dying . . . It's easy to say you'll die, but if you have the poison in your pocket and say you'll die, doesn't the passion of love grow even stronger? Here, swallow them.

Akagi smiles wryly, and it seems as if he's going to toss them away.

—Don't! Don't waste them! And Yumiko presses her mouth to the palm of his hand. Crushing the little pills with her beautiful front teeth, she stares right into his face, a pale smile filling her eyes. Then suddenly, she lunges at Akagi. Forcing her lips into his mouth, she kisses him. The poison burns his tongue.

26

LIKE A PANTHER leaping back after a single deadly blow, Yumiko ducks down and stares at Akagi. The soft shadows cast by her thick eyelashes contrast strangely with the hard expression on her face.

When Akagi came aboard the Kurenai-maru, Yumiko told him she had lost her makeup kit in some commotion the night before, and maybe this is why she has not powdered her face, and her beautiful skin shimmers with a lack of sleep luster.

And one of Yumiko's bare shoulders shows where her unbuttoned overcoat has slid from the momentum of Akagi's push.

Akagi spits again and again. The arsenic burns his tongue. Panicked, he grabs the teakettle and gargles, over and over, but there is no place to spit out the water.

Seeing his cheeks filled with water, Yumiko bursts out in wild laughter.

The pills have stained Yumiko's even, grain-like teeth a dark brown, and a few drops have trickled down and moisten her dry lips. Akagi can't help looking at those lips. Desire.

Then he shudders. Poison.

—Hey! As he opens his mouth, water spews out over his lap, and, grabbing Yumiko by the shoulders: You idiot! Gargle! Gargle, you hear! You're nuts. Just like your sister!

Freeing herself from the coat he's grabbed, Yumiko takes a few steps and then slips down to the floor, laughing. Her belly twitches so much that the muscles of her thighs can be seen, one by one.

She firmly shakes out her disheveled locks, and as she lifts her face, her lively eyes are now glistening with tears.

—You! You might know what you call good manners, but you don't know how lovers ought to behave. I kiss for the first time, and you just spit and gargle.

Yumiko starts laughing again. Her quivering body gives a strong sense of her nakedness.

—How awful. I guess it's best not to become a woman after all. Oh, how strange. How strange.

—Hey! Akagi grabs her neck and, pressing her face to his chest, pounds his fist against her cheek and forces her mouth open. Then with his other hand, he pulls down the long sleeve of his undershirt and wipes her tongue and teeth.

Yumiko laughs under her tears, tears of nausea. Wiping those tears against Akagi's chest: B-b-but, but I'm okay. That, that was just playacting. I'm sorry. But I just couldn't have managed that kiss in any other way.

Yumiko breathes heavily, lying in his arms, now that he has released his hold. Her moist eyes look up, directly into his face.

—Why do you look at me that way? Now you finally look at me. From when we met at the Aquarium, you've treated me like some kid or some cheap whore. That made me so angry that I made a fuss. Didn't I tell you that the arsenic is my pleasure? Do you understand?

But at that instant, Yumiko blushes up to her ears, and as if it just occurred to her, she fixes her skirt.

—Look, I . . . And Akagi's once clear voice quavers: About Ochiyo . . .

—There is no need to explain anything to me. If I have anything to say, I'll speak for myself and not for my sister. Okay? I watched my sister in love and promised myself I'd never become a woman. That made me miserable. Then I met you, you, the reason for everything, and I thought if I could just become a woman, I'd be so happy.

They search each other with their eyes, and just as they are about to become one, Akagi's arms firmly pull her toward him, and his face lowers to meet hers.

—Idiot!

With the palm of her right hand, Yumiko pushes aside his mouth.

Aren't Akagi's mouth, lips, teeth now all smeared with poison? This whole time Yumiko has held the remaining pills in her hand, and they've melted in her sweat.

—Pull yourself together, stupid!

And suddenly Akagi pales and falls flat on his face.

ubamiya and himemiya

27

BEHIND SANJA SHRINE, the memorial stone  for the Yoshiwara courtesan Zuiun faces the memorial stone for Master Actor Tsuga.

You may well think of women when you think of Asakusa Park, but out of the thirty memorial stones, there is only one for a whore. And this was something the courtesan Zuiun put up in offering to the Hitomaro Shrine.

> *Slowly in the mist of dawn,*
> *The ship disappears.*
> *Full of longing,*
> *I remain behind.*

Even though this engraved inscription of a Hitomaro poem is done with forceful, manly strokes in the style of the *Man'yōshū*, it was taken from her brush. It seems that this "gem among the courtesans" was making some sort of vow at the Hitomaro Shrine.

And so, Himemiya is the only one of the fifty to one hundred Shinto and Buddhist gods of Asakusa Park who was a whore.

Under an order by the city board of advisors issued in June 1891, the twenty-fourth year of the reign of Emperor Meiji, Uba Pond was filled and only the shape remains today. Since it would be regrettable if the memory of the moon over the Asaji Plain, whose shadows have now ceased, were to be lost to posterity, I have decided to erect this stone monument.

Morita Etsusaburō

The "historic site of Uba Pond" indicated by this "stone monument" is right in the middle of the group of houses in the third lot of the sixth block of Umamichi, and Ubamiya and Himemiya now live together with seven or eight other gods in the Senshō Shrine.

Three different versions of the legend of Uba Pond have been passed down, but in all of them Himemiya sleeps on a pillow of stone. That is why this story of Yumiko, who slept on a pillow of concrete (and might now sleep on a pillow of wooden boat boards), reminds me of the following legend.

The reed-studded Asaji Plain of Musashino was a wide expanse where the moon rose over the silver grasses and set on the pampas: While on his way as the day grows dark, a traveler might hear the sad cries of the plover from near the Sumida River. And as he wanders in search of a night's lodging, he might happen upon a forlorn, tumbledown hut with a decayed roof in the middle of this plain of withered grasses. There, in that wretched hut, lived a stone-hearted old woman.

This old hag had a beautiful daughter who looked nothing like her.

—The old woman would dress her daughter in her finest and send her to welcome the weary traveler and invite him to stay the night. She would order her daughter to sleep nestled beside the traveler on a pillow of stone. Then in the darkest of the night, when the old woman thought the traveler would be fast asleep, she would sever the thin rope to which she had earlier hung a large rock. It would fall, crushing the head of the man asleep by her daughter's side. Then the old woman would tear the clothes from the dead and bloody traveler and sink his body in the pond.

In this way, nine hundred and ninety-nine men lost their lives. But the one-thousandth traveler heard the sound of the reed cutter's flute. It sounded like a voice and sang: When night falls, even if you have no place to lay your head, do not stay at the lonely house on the Asakusa reed plain.

Thanks to this warning, the man eyed the pillow of stone with some suspicion. He looked up at the large rock, and right before his eyes, it fell, just as he had expected. Beside himself with fear, he ran from that house and escaped into a large temple. When he awoke from his sleep, unharmed, he found himself in the Kannon Hall. The reed cutter had been an incarnation of the Holy Kannon herself.

—Years later, during the reign of Emperor Yōmei, a young page stayed at the old woman's hut. When the old woman saw how gorgeous and valuable the boy's clothing was, she smiled to herself with delight, but the old woman's daughter, taken with this gentle and beautiful boy, longingly shared her bed with him. Unaware of this, the old woman let the rock drop. But that boy was an incarnation of the Holy Kannon and just disappeared, leaving behind the daughter, crushed and killed.

For some time, the daughter had borne in her heart a dread of her own evil deeds, and she wanted to end her life. The beautiful boy thus served to brighten her death with the joys of love.

—And the evil old woman, worthy of being called a demon, tearfully mourned the death of her child, and she shortly, in utter de-spair, drowned herself in the pond.

The only thing that is different in the second version of the story is that Himemiya is the daughter of a poor samurai family. Also, the incarnation of the Holy Kannon does not appear. Instead, "to atone for her sins," the daughter dresses as a traveler and is killed by the falling rock. When her parents see this, they immediately rec-ognize their "innate Buddha nature" and don the black robes of Bud-dhist priests.

If Yumiko has died from arsenic poisoning on the Kurenai-maru, people might say her feelings were like those of the daughter in these two versions of the legend, but . . .

28

THE THIRD VERSION takes place during the reign of Sushun, the thirty-second em-peror.

Far and wide on the lonely plain, bandits were attacking the travelers who came from the north and the east.

—The Holy Kannon showed mercy on the travelers and ordered Shakara the Dragon King to transform himself into an old woman and to change his third dragon daughter into a dainty and charm-ing young lady, and sent them to live together in a lonely hut in the middle of the plain, where they would receive travelers from near and far. To the hut came many bandits desirous of the beautiful daughter. They boasted of their qualities and offered sake in ask-ing for her hand in marriage. In response, the old woman invited each bandit to sleep alone in a room with her daughter on a pillow of stone. Then she cut the rope and down came the rock, crushing the bandit's head. In this manner, several years went by, and many bandits came to the lonely house desiring the beauty of the daughter and lost their lives to their lust.

And so it came to pass that all the bandits, from Chief Imaru on down, were tempted and thus condemned to death. In time, not one was left, and travelers could then come and go in safety.

—Yet in those days, villagers still used to say: Even if you have no place to stay when night falls, do not stop at the lonely house of the old woman.

Some time later, the Dragon King, still gotten up as an old woman, threw itself into the pond and became the protecting deity Kurikara-Fudō. The dragon daughter was turned into that shining, golden goddess Benzaiten, and the stone pillow and the dragon princess's mirror are kept for posterity as treasures at the Sensō Temple.

Had Yumiko been the dragon daughter of today and poisoned the scoundrels of Asakusa Park one after another, in the end, Akagi, in the role of bandit chief Imaru, would have fallen victim to her charms and been lured to his deathbed.

But—right next to the small police station at Kaminari Gate:

GATHERING AT THE HANAKAWADŌ

THE SCARLET TROUPE

When I read this pronouncement on the bulletin board, I still did not know Yumiko was aboard the Kurenai-maru that very day.

Even in the second of the pilgrim poems dedicated to the thirty-three Edo holy sites one reads:

Prayer: Over Uba Pond, brimming with worldly sins, floats the promise of that lonesome hut.

I have told you the legend of Ubamiya and Himemiya, dear reader, because (as is evident by the fact that it was even made into a pilgrim's poem) it is one page in the chronicle of miracles performed by the Asakusa Kannon. And if we could now return to our story, here I stand at the entrance of the Nakamise, and the noise of the kids hawking calendars surrounds me.

Intentionally avoiding eye contact with the kids, I casually stroll along Asakusa Street in the direction of the Hanakawadō. I come across two "China" girls in front of the Asakusa Post Office. Both are wearing yellow Chinese dresses. As my eyes turn toward them, suddenly: You like that sort of thing?

And an artificial silk *haori* coat with strands of gold woven into it flashes by in its gaudy manner.

—Well . . .

—Then you ought to go see Tsujimoto. Chinese, Korean, whites, he's got them all.

Tsujimoto—I will introduce you to him later, dear reader, because, of all the dubious touts around the park, he is the shrewdest, strangest, and saddest of them all.

—You're going to the Subway Tower, right?

—Oh, you paying?

—Aren't you all meeting in the restaurant?

—Who?

—They're meeting there, the Scarlet Troupe. You're going because you read the message board at Kaminari Gate, right? Did something happen?

—Oh, so that's why you asked if I were going to the Tower. Too bad. It would've been nice of you, really. I was just looking for someone to treat me to dinner. That's a joke—someone's idea of a joke. I hadn't seen the message board. But are you going there? I was just kidding about dinner. You see, I just bought this souvenir on my way home.

And Haruko waves a small paper-wrapped package before my
eyes.

—This here . . .

"This here" is a famous Asakusa specialty. But in this novel, I
want you to guess the name. The riddle is really pretty easy to solve,
though.

—When I buy this, I know the secret. Slide a newspaper across
the counter, and it's absolutely astounding. The shop girl takes it
and quickly hides it in her undies. To thank me, she gives me a big
discount.

the new "light of the fireflies" song

29

FOR EXAMPLE, WHILE walking with the child actor Utasaburō, Yumiko looks much more male than does this boy with his too-beautiful lips. When a pretty girl looks like a man, dear reader, don't you  think that there is in her the melancholy of a sharp blade that easily nicks?

I rented a house in the same row as Yumiko's along that blind alley where you can see the Yoshiwara embankment fire tower, and soon after I caught a glimpse of Yumiko helping Utasaburō put on his *tabi* socks. There in the entryway where the piano stands. While again and again wiping her tears with her sleeve, Yumiko heaves with sobs. Wearing a cloth hunting cap with a wide visor, both hands crammed in the pockets of his man's overcoat, Utasaburō sits in front of her, legs outstretched.

Of course, the boy probably did nothing to make Yumiko cry. But I act like I hadn't seen a thing and slip out of sight.

What does this scene mean to a girl who seems like a man? At any rate, I felt like crying out: So this is the way it is. I will never blame her no matter what she does!

But I must not forget to tell you—Utasaburō is not Yumiko's little brother. And he's just a twelve- or thirteen-year-old kid.

The difference between Yumiko and Haruko: You can compare Haruko with all sorts of other women, and she is more womanly in every way. A real woman has no tragedies—anyone would think that by just looking at Haruko. There is nothing tragic about her, and once you understand that, you understand that a true woman has no tragedies. Well, at least Haruko is that kind of woman.

—Oh, it's really true. Right into their undies, remarks Haruko as she walks with me, looking down at my feet. That's their only hiding place. The shop girls' dresses . . . At that store, they have no pockets. Not even in their aprons. But they really like those newspapers. Oh, I shouldn't have said that.

—Was there something special in today's paper?

—Not just today. Every day. I hear the shop owner keeps eight mistresses. He comes to the shop from one of his mistresses' houses in the early afternoon, counts the money from the day before, has someone take the money to the bank, and then quickly leaves again. And you know what's interesting? His two sons also stay over at his mistresses' houses. They say his wife died, and I just don't see what his mistresses have to do with newspapers, but the shop owner absolutely won't let his shop girls read any. Books aren't allowed either. If someone sends a book to one of the shop girls, the shop owner won't give it to her and sends it right back.

—You don't say? But I guess those things happen.

—I—I didn't make it up. And so, the advertising lights, like electric words. Words so missed by the girls, and these are the only words they can see from the shop. So it's a real thrill when they can get their hands on a newspaper or a book. They hide in the bathroom and read for an hour or more, and, after that they slip it into their undies. Then at night, the manager, he always turns out the lights right away. But interesting enough, it's like the words of the song— "the light of the fireflies and the snow by the window." These shop girls sleep on the second floor, so they open the window, and the light of the streetlamps shines in, and they huddle around that spot . . .

—That's a great story! It is my job to get people to read, you know. Lately, they say that literature—that is, reading words—is losing its charm, but . . .

—No! You can't write about it. Poor shop girls. I hear there are eighteen of them now. If the owner finds something to read lying around, he always looks into where they got it. They won't tell either. But then I hear he makes them all line up. And he hits them one after another, slap, slap. But, in the front of the shop, there he is—the tired, dirty, pale-faced but still friendly-seeming old newspaper seller. When the shop girls close up for the night, he slides the evening papers he didn't sell under the door. But really, please don't write about this. I know. Why don't you write that the customers keep forgetting their newspapers and magazines in the shop?

30

SPRING GRASS, BLOOMING
FLOWER, JEWELED SCREEN, DAISY,
SUGAR-GLAZED BEANS, MINERAL
BLOSSOM, COUNTRY TREAT,
DAWN MOON . . .

I read absently on. These are the names of different kinds of traditional Japanese sweets, appropriate as decorations for a tiered Girl's Day doll stand. Fruit jelly, caramel, chewing gum, chocolate, and so on are lined up inside the glass case here on the first-floor shop of the Subway Restaurant.

To the left is the showcase of prepared ready-to-eat dishes.

—What are you going to eat?

RICE, BREAD, COFFEE, BRITISH TEA—*five sen*

LEMON TEA, SODA WATER—*seven sen*

ICE CREAM, CAKE, PINEAPPLE, FRUIT—*ten sen*

FRIED SHRIMP, CURRY RICE, CHILD'S MEAL—*twenty-five sen*

BEEF STEAK, CUTLETS, CROQUETTES, HAM SALAD, CABBAGE ROLLS, BEEF STEW—*thirty sen*

FULL LUNCH COURSE—*thirty-five sen*

—Oh dear, it is so expensive, the food here. Let's just pass.

The food coupon stalls are lined up to the right of the elevator.

—No one said you can't go up the tower if you don't buy something to eat. Look here. It's written right here—iron tower, forty meters above ground, admission free. To the amusement of the food-stall girls, Haruko waves her wrapped package at me.

—Let's eat this and drink some water. There ought to be some evening papers and other stuff to read lying around the *krap* (lingo for Asakusa Park). Because I added a newspaper I found lying around to my *yarikan* (ten-sen coin), the shop girl gave me this much more of the stuff for free.

The inside of the elevator looks like it is covered in gold-sprinkled lacquer.

—My, my, here it says that the capacity is thirteen people. Two hundred and fifty yen in three years, about how much is that a day? I'll do the math in my head before we reach the top. At the shop where I bought these sweets, the apprentices get two hundred and fifty yen for three years' work, so that's eighty-three yen, thirty-three sen, three rin, and three mō a year, not even seven yen a month. Oh, is this already the sixth floor?

The kitchen is across from the elevator. As we go past it and walk along the black and white checkerboard-patterned brick floor to the rooftop garden,

—Since there are three hundred and sixty-five days a year, that is not even twenty-three sen a day. The shop is open from eight in the morning to eleven-thirty at night, so that's fifteen and a half hours of work for them. They do have free time and don't have to work the whole time, but that is still less than one sen, five rin an hour. What kind of pay is this? Good? Bad? I would not like it.

So says Haruko, and doesn't even look down at the city spread out below.

—First, did you do the math right?

—Let me tell you, I know you can't go by the food coupon stalls without buying something, and I am not doing the math just to show off. Just in the time it took to come up in the elevator, I figured it out right down to the one sen, five rin, I did. Oh look, an Inari shrine! Right over there. Revered god Inari . . . they've even put up flags for him.

The torii gate of the Inari shrine is made of iron.

A tall steel arm swings with a whoosh right in front of us—the Azuma Bridge construction crane.

—This building is like those spiffy socks worn with golf clothes, and on the roof flutter flags of countries around the world. And the uniforms of the subway conductors, they're something special to Tokyo transport. The conductors are just as pretty as the Western hotel bellhops in the movies. Putting an Inari shrine up here is like sticking an artificial flowered ornament in someone's bobbed hair.

The white curtain next to the ladder leading up to the observation tower—four of the restaurant girls are hiding behind that white curtain, playing "Habu Harbor" on the harmonica.

—The musicians must be happy. It's like newspapers in the sweets shop, I guess. One sen, five rin an hour there, and they can only leave the shop twice a year. And then the manager is in charge of them, so it's just like a grade school trip.

concrete

31

THE ROASTED CHESTNUT cart on Asakusa Street—in the roasting bowl, the black sand mixed with chestnuts waves round and round. Watching this, one member of the Scarlet Gang said it well: That's one swell hula-hula dance. More real  than Haruno Yoshiko's, more like some big fat black dancer.

And even though Flute Kame swears constantly on stage at the Yuraku Theater, he would not get nearly as much applause if he didn't then go on and play those jazz songs he is so cussing out.

For example, dear reader, have you listened to *manzai* lately? *Manzai* used to be funny. But in 1929, because the *manzai* people have been pushed by the "modern," by that wild, reckless nonsense straight from America, they have become pathetic clowns in both senses of the word.

For another example, go have a look at the opera at the Teikyō Theater, in which Shining Prince Genji and Lord Narihira do a jazz dance. A different topic, but Your Lordship Narihira, your Mukōjima with its birds of the capital is now all concrete riverbank park. And the shops selling Chōmei Temple rice cakes wrapped in cherry leaves, Kototoi dumplings, and other Mukōjima treats are now also made of concrete.

Nearby is the business college boathouse—by the waterside, it is blue, wooden . . . If you compare the buildings, the one for boats seems much more old-fashioned than the one for rice cakes wrapped in cherry leaves.

But Lord Narihira would hardly understand such things as the charm of concrete.

I hear the Shōchiku Motion Picture Company's Kamata Studio has made a dreadful film of the popular song "Ain't That the Latest!" A musical film called "Ain't That Reinforced Concrete!" will probably be released soon. People who laugh just don't understand the charm of asphalt and concrete.

About this charm—the topic of toilets is distasteful, but there is no better example. In the little park near the Yoshiwara (well, you can't really call it a park. It's more like an open space where the kids of this poor neighborhood play), a few of the kids clean the park toilet, and it's the cleanest toilet I have ever seen.

—You kids clean this place?

The kids give me a questioning look.

—Every day?

—Uh-huh, sometimes.

—Why? Did someone tell you to or make you?

—Nope. The kids exchange telling glances and sneak off.

Then when I asked one of the nannies in the park,

—That? I guess they just like doing it. That toilet building—it's a lot more modern than where they live, and it's the only chance they get to use such a magnificent building, so they probably clean it because it makes them proud.

Not the answer I expected. But when I asked the nanny on the opposite bench, she said the same thing.

No doubt the public bathroom is truly magnificent. Their own homes can't compare. But the fact that the kids love this toilet, doesn't it have something to do with the charm of concrete? Though adults might praise these youngsters in the name of "public duty," don't the kids do it because of the charm of the modern building? Don't the kids love the concrete bathroom more than the teahouse of the Momoyama Castle?

The eight new sights of Asakusa, if I had to choose, I would certainly include the famous garden at the Denpōin designed by Kobori Enshū, where Yumiko and the others took shelter during the earthquake. Yet Yumiko only said: What? That's a famous garden?

Judging by her reaction, there would probably be lots of people who would forget to include this garden, which is rumored to open to the public on April 1, 1930. But nobody could forget the concrete Kototoi Bridge or the concrete Sumida Park. The Subway Restaurant, a reinforced concrete building, would be ranked above the Five Story Pagoda. That temple made of concrete with doors like the iron bars in front of a prison, the Senshō Temple, currently being constructed at the end of Asakusa Street, may (as a truly "modern" Buddhist place of protection) lure visitors away from the Asakusa Kannon.

But, anyway, on the roof of the Subway Restaurant (that "cultural flower in the vanguard of our times" and so advertised on the streetcar posters), waitresses are hiding behind the white curtain, only their cotton socks showing, playing the harmonica—the harmonica, that sad, quaint instrument.

Haruko, who drinks water from the faucet and unwraps the package of sweets she brought with her, is cheerful, but . . .

32

PERHAPS TO prevent suicides, there is
a fence around the roof, and wire netting is strung on top of it. In front
of the Inari shrine, there are eight
chairs and two long-legged ashtrays.
There, I listen to the street noise.

The whistles of the traffic cops, the bells of the newspaper sellers, the sound of the crane's chains, the sound of the engines on
the river steamboats, the sound of wooden sandals on asphalt, the
noise of the streetcars and automobiles, the harmonicas of the girls
up here, the bells of streetcars, the sound of the elevator doors,
the automobile horns, all sorts of sounds from afar—they become
one, and I float along on this wave of sound; it is almost like a
lullaby.

The Ōkawa with its four bridges forming a line downstream is
covered with wintry mist. But, eee, eee—every now and then, a shrill
sound pierces my ears. I could just see it down below. It is the sound
of a toy. Press lightly on the wire lever and a round metal sheet turns
with a screeching sound and gives off red and blue sparks. A beggar boy sells them in front of the post office. A girl around three
years old lies on the asphalt by his feet, crying—boo hoo, boo hoo.
She has been made to cry. Crying is this three-year-old's job, and a
kid who cries much costs a lot. But the boy glares down at her back
with obvious hatred. I have never seen such an icy glare.

For another example, dear reader, when you are in front of the
cinema billboards, just shift your gaze to the other side of the street:

THERE IS NOBODY IN THE WHOLE WORLD AS BAD OFF AS I AM.
MY HUSBAND DIED LAST OCTOBER, AND I HAVE TO TAKE CARE
OF MY SEVENTY-FIVE-YEAR-OLD MOTHER, AND I HAVE BERIBERI,
AND I HAVE TO RAISE THREE KIDS, AND . . .

You'll most likely find things like this written on signs held up by beggar women with bloated legs.

The kids have gone off somewhere. Three of them have each climbed a tree by the edge of the pond. You are not supposed to see them. When they realize they have been spotted, they quickly jump down and start a fistfight right in front of you, dear reader. Then they begin to bawl. Putting on pretend fights is their job, but their eyes are filled with more hatred than if it were a real one.

Now I would like to remind you of Haruko's bright eyes. Her brown pupils slowly ooze toward the white, and the white easily becomes red, but . . .

—Yummy. When the tap water is pumped up here past the restaurant it tastes so good. Absolutely.

Just like a bird, Haruko extends her delicate neck as she drinks and then, smacking her lips, she returns to her chair.

There seems to be something of a country girl about her. That gaudy, gold, cheap crêpe she wears does not seem to suit her.

—You seem so quiet all of a sudden.

—I always get quiet ten minutes or so after I meet a man, I do.

—Part of a plan, right?

—Like for seduction? No. I'm the kind of girl who gets happy easily, and it takes me a short while to make a little small talk.

—Want to go drink really good water?

—Yes, please.

The restaurant runs from the second to the fifth floors, and each of these levels is different, down to the colors of the wallpaper and the decorative lights, and everything is bright, modern, clean. Alcohol is prohibited on the second and third floors. Of course, coffee is served, even on the green-walled fifth floor we now enter. From the west window, we can see the flags of the Ueno Matsuzakaya Department Store.

A cheap-looking girl fills the sake cup of the man now accompanying her. A group of junior high school students sits at the table next to them. Two families with kids are eating cutlets as big as their plates.

At the table near the entrance, two little girls around six years old mount their chairs, and a waitress butters their toast. When they are done eating, they call for the elevator and calmly ride down.

We smile.

—Not bad for such little girls. They are certainly Asakusa kids. Yumiko'd be pleased.

—The others aren't here. Why not? Maybe they're on the roof.

birds of the capital

33

THE COFFEE CUP is already empty. Haruko sucks on the spoon like a child suckling at her mother's breast and gazes idly out the south window.

—The fruit stands are really pretty, aren't they?

—What? She says with a start. Yes, they are. I've been looking at the roofs. The roofs of the streetcars and the buses. They're awfully dusty and dirty. All that stuff that collects on them.

—What are you thinking right now?

—Nothing really. Just relaxing.

—So, that's it. When you're with a man, you get quiet in ten minutes, but after twenty minutes, you've forgotten all about him, right?

—I'm not like Miss Yumiko and hate saying things in dribs and drabs like sewing.

—Sewing?

—Like a needle flashes in the light before it disappears into the fabric again, over and over. To Yumiko, I'm pitiful. To me, Yumiko is pitiful. But anyway, I just can't stand Yumiko, you know.

—Oh.

—That girl, first of all, she's an idiot. Before, you were surprised at my math skills, right? I came to that answer by doing the math. A woman just can't get ahead by acting like Miss Yumiko. Now, Akikō, I like him. He's Yumiko as a man. Though Akikō is younger, he really tries to take care of me. Deep down, I think it's strange. Akikō's sass is considered fashionable, that much I know, but I'm probably careless, and he has sometimes taken care of me without my even knowing it. Women are like that, I guess. So men are always messing around with me . . .

—What do you mean, messing around with you?

—Just like I said. No matter if it is this or that. I can't explain it. But you know, I've thought about it sometimes. I guess I'm just a pitiful girl. No, it's okay. It would be the same to say how good it would be to be a man.

I say nothing but hold out my hand.

—Sorry.

And Haruko picks up the spoon she has been sucking and puts it in my hand—so unconcerned it seems she has not noticed what she's done. Then she continues:

—Before I said I was just relaxing. Completely relaxed. I relax very soon when I'm with a man. It's not necessary to think about anything, do anything. I mean, I don't have to trouble my brain. It's like that for me, anyhow, because, as a girl on her own, I have to look out for myself. But I also need to relax. Men are life's little sleeping pills. The parting, though, that's the waking up in the morning. It hurts. Oh, it hurts so. Sorry for saying something so pretentious. But when a girl is in love, she cries at night, and she cries in the morning when she says good-bye. When she no longer cries in the morning, a girl has really grown into woman. But Miss Yumiko, she fights with men like it's a matter of life or death. You know, you've seen the big billboards in front of the Kannon Theater, right? Sword fight plays—I'll cut down anyone who gets too close. It's just like the ads say. Yumiko hardly sleeps at all. I don't know what she's thinking about that keeps her up. Like some pitiful laboratory animal. How long can people live without sleep?

—But doesn't Yumiko have anyone?

—Really. I don't like that. I really don't. If you wanted to ask me that, you should've just come right out with it in the beginning instead of letting me go on about this and that.

—You are surprisingly good at sewing.

—That's right. I'm just an ordinary girl, so I think I ought to learn how to use a needle. But, oh no, that's no good. Now you act like you really don't care. But in another twenty minutes or so, you'll ask me again if Yumiko has anybody. I just hate that.

34

THE MASSIVE steel arm again drifts towards the glass window, and Haruko looks up at the sound of the chains, her eyes half shut:

—Oh, I'd like to hang myself. To be pulled up there with a yank—it'd be so good. I keep thinking about it. All made up, all dressed up in deep red, and flailing about struggling to get free. So good. And then, after dangling high up there for a while, after I'd gone limp, I'd plop right down into the Ōkawa . . .

—But that's something from the days when the term "poison woman" was in style—something truly flamboyant. Sporting a bathing suit, diving down like a swallow from the top of the crane. You, as a modern woman, should learn how to do the swallow dive.

—Well, really. Now that is the kind of thing you could say to Miss Yumiko. That girl is like a virgin in a box tucked away until her wedding. But what is she so afraid of? She can't be a real bride anyway.

—I wouldn't know about that. Asakusa folk are truly old-fashioned—that's for sure. From hucksters to hobos, right down to panhandlers, they all respect their hierarchical differences, all subscribe to duty, believe in friendship among buddies—just like gamblers back in the Edo days. There are young punks over in Shibuya's Dōgenzaka or over in Shinjuku, but they're a newer breed, maybe because they don't have traditions like Asakusa does. This place is all hustle and bustle on the surface—there's probably no other place in Japan where so much is happening. But essentially Asakusa is like a specimen in the Bug House—that's right, something completely different from today's world, like a remote island or some African village led by a chief, a whole net of time-honored codes over it.

—What's gotten into you? This kind of talk, I don't like it. Students who cut class and go to Asakusa and sometimes get rounded up by the cops—they say things like this. A whole net of time-honored codes. You ever got caught in it? Probably not. So it is none of your business. Just look around Asakusa. Satisfy that curiosity of yours. These codes you laugh at—thanks to them, Asakusa is a real home for people on their own. Just think how it would be without them. Bloody fights, people dying of hunger in the streets. That's the truth. Really. Asakusa would be famous for it. Me, I'd like to hang myself from a crane. And you should go ask the crane what you were just wondering. Mr. Crane, where have the birds of the capital gone? Go ask the birds of the capital if Yumiko has a boyfriend or not.

—I see. The Azuma Bridge is where the ferry to Takemachi used to be. And the Takemachi Ferry was also called the Narihira Ferry.

—And that's where the birds of the capital were?

—Birds of the capital are just plain old seagulls when they're over the Sumida River. Some books say that their beaks and feet are red, but that's nonsense. They were often treated quite coldly in *senryū*.

At the famous sites, even seagulls are birds of the capital.
Crossing the bridge, they turn into birds of the capital.
The ferryman cuts the name of the bird in two.
Too bad, now they are only Komagata seagulls.
And if they are seagulls, Komagata can never be famous.

So this is why they are "birds of the capital" until they reach the Azuma Bridge, site of the old Takemachi Ferry, and then turn into pitiful seagulls as they travel straight downriver to Komagata.

—And this Lord Narihira, he's supposed to be one of history's greatest ladies' men. Yes, he's the type who says oh, you're beautiful to any woman he meets on the street, just to get what he wants. They sing about that even today.

—Aren't they singing about it now at the Teikyō Theater?

But I just remembered, dear reader, that I left Shining Prince Genji and Lord Narihira behind on the stage of the Teikyō Theater.

Well, these high-ranking courtiers wear very aristocratic, high-ranking courtier clothes—except that they carry slender walking sticks and swing their hips:

I'm a pro, in my overalls.
Don't just swing my hammer for show.

Singing "City Symphony," they do a jazz dance—and all of a sudden, up go their sticks, and it turns into sword fighting.

And even Haruko, whom I have called old-fashioned, she shows off as well—cheerfully kissing four or five men in turn.

—The bride of Asakusa tower, that's me. How does it go, that play *The Bride of the Eiffel Tower?*

35

ON STAGE is the Heian capital at its height—and so, as elegant ladies of the court from the time of Shining Prince Genji and Lord Narihira, the girls sing and dance sedately, until, suddenly, from among them, a flapper, a thousand years newer, dances the Charleston until she passes out. Then, using the fashionable term "left girl," they debate love and debate society.

For example: What's the proletariat?

—That's what you call those fellows of the working class who earn an honest living.

And after the quarrel, they punch each other, saying: This is boxing, that's how they fight in the West.

By the way, dear reader, that term "left girl" may sound strange, but it's apparently the latest slang in Asakusa. It is a very rude way of saying "left-hander." If one of the members of the Scarlet Gang says: Yumiko has turned left these days, it's a pun meaning she is left in the lurch and short on cash. And if they say: Haruko is a modern geisha, they are making a pun that she has been influenced by Alexandra Kollontai's book *Red Love*. But the difference between geisha in Russia, the home of the left, and Japan is that the Japanese geisha accepts money.

At any rate, Shining Prince Genji's love letters are being recited as opera songs—that's Asakusa. And on stage, these high-ranking courtiers speak a macaronic mixture of Japanese from all different eras. Then they dance the fox trot, and, hand in hand, all the members of the troupe sing a jazz song, and end up in the big finale—that's "musical theater."

On top of the Subway Tower, it is as easy as pie for Haruko to play the role of *The Bride of the Eiffel Tower*. This is because right now the Casino Folies is using a stage set that looks just like the one for Jean Cocteau's *Les mariés de la Tour Eiffel*. And it is not surprising either that the kids of the Scarlet Gang come riding in from somewhere on a truck—that's Asakusa.

The end-of-the-year sales are already in progress, and like during some cheap exhibition, the streets are all awash in "we've got flags, got banners, red stickers, paper lanterns, music bands, and mannequin girls right here in Asakusa."

In the middle of all this color, the white clothing of a Korean carrying seven or eight (so-called) "polar bear" fur pelts over his shoulder, threading his way through the crowd. From the fifth-floor window, our eyes follow this sight, and, just as this white figure is about to cross the streetcar tracks, a truck stops smack in front of him, and two kids jump out.

—Oh, it's the little runt. But the truck isn't coming from Mukō-jima? From Kototoi? I wonder what's wrong, and Haruko stands up.

That little runt is the younger girl from Yumiko's house.

In her dark red overcoat, with, of course, rouged lips and even penciled eyebrows, she looks like a child actor in the opera. But the little boy runt holding her hand as they enter the restaurant seems a strange match for her—beggar boy that he is.

The little girl comes over by herself. Looking very serious, she comes over to whisper something in Haruko's ear.

—Well, that boy is impossible. On the way up here, he pocketed a screw from the railing.

—But you're impossible, too. Don't you tap your feet to the rhythm of the band every night at the Aquarium?

—So? All the kids do that.

She does not seem at all concerned, but then she pulls Haruko's sleeve like she has got a secret.

—What?

—Big Sister is on the Kurenai-maru, and . . .

—So, we're really meeting at the Tower?

Because the little girl nods, we go up to the tower roof, and the little boy jumps out from behind the white curtain where the waitresses were playing the harmonica.

—Leave that alone. Don't do that.

Without even a grin, the little runt has now slid off somewhere to the side of the Inari shrine. Then he comes back and shows us a scrap of paper he has just found. It is a Scarlet Troupe votive sticker. A sheet of stationery covered with Yumiko's writing slips out from inside.

Waving the paper in front of us: Lookee here! What's this?

the bride of the tower

36

THE BOY IS called Boat Runt when he is
with the girl runt. This is because he was
on a boat when the Scarlet Gang picked
him up. Not a real boat, a stage boat. A
prop thrown away behind the theater
stall. He was a little stray who had been
roosting in that boat.

Boat Runt has been getting by these days as a shill for a huck-
ster, but he is really known for finding strange things hiding in
strange places, like sniffing out the wallets on pickpockets. So now
he has his eye on the potted plants beside the Inari shrine. It's only
a scrap of paper, but it's covered with the precise characters from
Yumiko's pen, looking like writing practice.

The Scarlet Troupe votive sticker that has slipped out—Boat Runt
picks it up and sets it on fire with a match.

I peer at the letter:

When the haze clears, it is light.
When the lightning stops, it is dark.

—What's it say? Asks Boat Runt.

Taking the paper, I read it aloud in a hushed voice as the four of us climb the spiral staircase to the tower belfry:

Mist is light in the morning, heavy in the evening.
Fog is heavy in the morning, light in the evening.
When the haze clears, it is light,
When the lightning stops, it is dark.
Autumn leaves first change colors on the mountain peak.
Spring flowers first bloom at the mountain foot.
The river, quiet in day, is loud at night,
The sea, loud in day, is quiet at night.
Blossoms on the tree open in the morning,
Flowers in the grass open at night.

—What's it mean? Something from a fortune card? Let me see it. And Haruko takes her hands out of the folds of her clothes.

—Ah, I've got it.

—Some kind of code?

—Just scribbles—no, that's not it. Isn't it just like Yumiko, she even has to show off when she scribbles.

—But why did she drop it here of all places?

—I'm not going to chase after a scrap of paper. Well, let's say someone tried to put the make on Yumiko. Tomorrow I'll mail you my answer, she says. And the answer he gets is this riddle. No matter how much he turns it over in his head, he can't for the life of him figure it out. Then finally, after coming up here to the tower, he realizes that she has taken him for a ride. Fed up, he throws the paper away. So it got here because someone coming up to the tower brought it. And if I'm right, even Yumiko can be sweet, you know. But although she writes to him the next day as promised, she gives him no straight answer. That's for sure.

The tower spire—a round concrete tower like a church belfry with windows that look out in all four directions, wire netting on the ledges of the windows, the bottom of the walls green and the tops a light blue, with a glass chandelier hanging from the tower ceiling.

By the east window, four men in a huddle all quickly turn around when we come in, and when they see it is Haruko and the others: Boat Runt, you just come up from Kototoi?

From the east window—directly below is the Kamiya Bar. To the left of it, the construction site for the Tobu Railway Asakusa Station, a fenced-in lot. The Ōkawa. The Azuma Bridge, a temporary bridge with wiring work by the Zenidaka Company. Construction on the Tobu Railway iron bridge. Sumida Park—the Asakusa riverbank under construction. Further on this bank, a group of small boats and stone works, the Kototoi Bridge. On the other bank, the Sapporo Beer Company. Kinshibori Station. The Oshima Gas Tank. Oshiage Station. Sumida Park, the elementary school, the industrial area. Mimeguri Shrine. The Okura Villa. The Arakawa drainage canal. Mount Tsukuba shrouded in wintry mist.

Haruko, hands tucked in the folds of her clothes, wanders aimlessly from one window to the next, and, while glancing out at the rooftops of Tokyo: Just countryside. Tokyo looks like the bottom of a wooden sandal. What's more, a dirty wooden sandal. Like a village turned inside out.

—A village, you say? That's a good one.

And one of the men takes her in his arms and kisses her.

Man number two kisses her without a word.

The last two men quietly wait their turns and then kiss her as well.

The whole time, Haruko stands there, eyes shut, hands in her clothes: The bride of the Asakusa tower. That's me. Got a lipstick on you?

37

GOT A LIPSTICK on you? When Haruko asks this, the girl runt is pressing her nose against the wire netting on the west window. This is because, his hand on her shoulder, Boat Runt is seeking her rouged lips.

From the west window—the Asakusa Post Office, like a garbage bin flipped on its side. The gold letters of the big Kaminari sweets billboard. The Asakusa Ward Office. The Denpōin. Asakusa Street—end-of-the-year shop decorations reminding you of those for the Beetle Festival. Automobiles and streetcars crawling along the main thoroughfare, banners celebrating the new army recruits, the concrete Senshō Temple at the end of the road, its copper roof a dull evening glow. On the right side of Asakusa Street, the roofs of the Nakamise and the movie-house district. On the left side, the telephone exchange office and a large public bathhouse. Ueno Matsuzakaya Department Store. Ueno Station. The gray Ueno Forest and the white steam of the locomotives. The Imperial Museum. The Imperial University's Yatsuda Hall and the university library. Nikolai Cathedral. Yasukuni Shrine. The newly constructed Diet Building. And over this wide sea of houses, on clear mornings and evenings, beautiful Mount Fuji.

Apparently, to them, kissing is just like whistling.

The fourth man, a hatless fellow in a corduroy suit, high wooden sandals made of magnolia, a blue plastic sun visor hiding his face, finishes kissing Haruko and says: Hey, Boat Runt, any word from Ginkō on his bike?

—Uh-huh, he's been keeping watch for the Kurenai-maru. But they closed the cabin window, so he's got no idea what's going on inside. He gave Umekō the sign to come ashore as soon as he can.

—Oh, so that's why the boat went down to the Kototoi Bridge.

And the fellow, turning around with a small telescope still over one eye, looks like a university student, *hakama* peeking out under the hem of his Inverness coat, though he wears a hunting cap like so many of the young merchants do. Another guy is wearing a school cap. And then there is the fellow who looks to be a downtown young dandy type.

—But today, right here, I found a letter from Akikō.

—A letter? And the four of them all look in surprise because it does not seem to be something any of them have thrown away.

Seeing the surprise in their eyes, I turn to face the north window and gaze at the direction they are looking, and, from the north window—the tower roof vent ducts and the flags from around the world. The Nakamise. The gold dolphin-like fish on the roof of the Imahan restaurant. The Niō Gate. Pigeons. The Five Story Pagoda—only the tiles on the highest roof are green. The big ginkgo tree full of dead leaves. The Kannon Hall under renovation. Since the very beginning of December, a tin roof has been put over the scaffolding and a bamboo fence has begun to be put up, and it's like it says on the reception office notice for donations toward the renovation of the main hall: the rooftop fence is 48.6 meters wide, 51.3 meters long, and 36.3 meters high, and 5,000 cedar logs between 9 and 18 meters long, 70 cubic meters of rectangular timber, and also 4,000 wavy sheets of tin are used. The grove of bare wintry trees on the temple grounds. The Yoshiwara. The Senju Gas Tank. The low wintry clouds at the north edge of Tokyo.

—"Mist is light in the morning, heavy in the evening . . ." What the hell does that mean? And the men peer at the scrap of paper Haruko has pulled from her sleeve.

—It's secret code. But, you know, Akikō would have no idea we're all coming up here today.

—Maybe someone'll come later, someone Akikō sends up here.

—Naw. Maybe some odd guy came, and he tossed it out here.

—Boat Runt, orders the fellow in the corduroy suit, looking at the back of the paper: Go downstairs to the restaurant and heat this paper in the stove. If words show up, come right back up here, okay? Be very careful.

—Mister, gimme five sen. For coffee. And Boat Runt holds out his hand to me, and the girl runt says from the side: I've got something.

—It's like this, the guy in the hunting cap says to me: Last night, there was some commotion at Yumiko's, and we found out about it this morning, and she shouldn't have been in Asakusa today because it's too risky. On top of it all, she shouldn't have gone on the boat with that rotten Akagi, and because we're worried about her, we're keeping watch. But secretly, because she tries to act like she's so tough.

—Hey look! The fellow with the telescope yells from the window.

—There, Akikō's being dragged off the boat—his chest is showing. The sleeve of his white coat, it's dark red! Blood!

—Isn't that the water police?

A white motorboat approaches, kicking up on the water the shadow of the Kototoi Bridge.

the *hōzuki* plant market
and the foreign girls

38

A WHITE MOTORBOAT approaches, kicking up on the water the shadow of the Kototoi Bridge.

That is how far I got in my writing. Right—then from February to July, about five months, I let *The Tale of the Scarlet Gang* rest.

—The sleeve of the white coat, it's dark red! Blood! The fellow watching with the telescope from the Subway Restaurant Tower yells this out, while the white-coated Yumiko is being dragged into the boat cabin. So I must continue from here.

But the Ōkawa then was covered in the winter misty dusk. Though winter, that was still 1929. In the streets, the end-of-the-year sales had begun. Now it is already 1930, and the midyear sales have started. And firefly and bug sellers—in the nighttime Asakusa Park, these signs of summer already lag behind the change of season. They're even later than the flowers of the flower girls.

Those flowers—the bunches sold by the roadside flower girls are, for the most part, late this season, but, dear reader, have you ever bought flowers in Asakusa? There are no other flowers that lose their petals so quickly.

—Maybe I should sell flower bouquets, too, but in the Ginza style, says Haruko.

—There already are Ginza-style flower girls, you know. Behind the Tokiwa Theater and the Park Theater.

—Oh, you bought flowers from them?

—Don't be silly.

—They don't sell just flowers, you know. I hear they tuck their name cards in their bouquets. They write on them let's meet at such-and-such time and such-and-such place.

—And so they sell flowers that lose their petals fast. I wonder where they meet.

—Oh, get a hold of yourself. Those flowers—you thrust a toothpick all the way from the head of the pistil down through the flower stem. You get interested in them at first sight, smile when you look at them again, and the third time you see them, your heart throbs. Probably the same ploy used at the counterfeit shops. Asakusa is a training ground for phonies. The phony masterpieces they sell are still okay. But the photographs are worse. They've got movie starlets in swimsuits, and . . . But they're really just ordinary pretty girls with their clothes off. And the photographs of innocent girls in grave danger and such that they say are original, they're really stills from a samurai movie. And the photograph of Kan'ichi kicking Omiya on the beach of Atami is all tinted in bright colors. The group of mermaids not wearing a stitch but their socks? It's just a photograph of group gymnastics at some girls' school sports meet. And their books are even worse. There are so many of them, those little booklets you so often find stuck in women's magazines. Those. White paper is pasted over the covers. But the titles beneath show right through, and you can clearly see: *Guide to Knitting and Handicrafts* and *Western and Chinese Cooking Made Easy* and . . . These phonies are palmed off all nicely packaged. Just like novels, don't you think?

—Just like the Asakusa revues.

—All the same. But if you prick a live girl's nude body, out comes real red blood. And Haruko blows the little lantern-shaped *hōzuki* flower she holds in her mouth, making a croaking sound like a frog.

July 9 and 10 are the Asakusa Kannon's days of grace. If you happen to be a believer in the Kannon, dear reader, here are her days of grace:

January 1	(equivalent to 100 days)
February 28	(equivalent to 100 days)
March 4	(equivalent to 90 days)
April 18	(equivalent to 50 days)
May 18	(equivalent to 100 days)
June 18	(equivalent to 50 days)
July 9 and 10	(each equivalent to 46,000 days)
August 24	(equivalent to 4,000 days)
September 20	(equivalent to 6,000 days)
October 19	(equivalent to 1,000 days)
November 7	(equivalent to 6,060 days)
December 19	(equivalent to 4,600 days)

So for example, if you visit the temple on July 9 like Haruko and me, in just that one visit, you are supposed to receive as much grace as in 46,000 ordinary visits. And if you come on the days of grace for three years and three months without missing a single time, you are guaranteed divine blessings of "all prayers answered, recovery from illness, a prospering family lineage, and entry of the whole family into Nirvana."

No mere mortal will ever know how they come up with these convenient figures, but people who don't know better and go to the temple on other days are truly cheated. So that's why on the 46,000 give-away days, the Kannon Hall, which closes its doors in the evening even on New Year's Eve, is all decorated and welcomes visitors until late at night.

There is also the *hōzuki* plant market.

Full of green *hōzuki* plants hanging upside down. Isn't it just like summer after rainy season has ended? And from the charms to protect against thunder sold on this day, you can hear the thunder itself.

39

A PROCESSION of Polynesians scares the Sensō Temple morning pigeons. This is a tour group.

A Korean woman, a kid tied to the waist of her white Korean skirt with a black sash in the Korean style, walks barefoot along the asphalt. Her canvas shoes dangle from her hand. In one night, any number of such women passes by. In front of the Shōchiku Theater on Matsukiyō Street.

Four Chinese kids play tag under the eaves of the Shōchiku Theater, which has already turned out its lights. All four have pigtails. Calling out like monkeys, they run around the brass bars of the gate in front of the ticket booth just like monkeys, trying to escape each other. It is already after the booth has closed. These are the kids who go to the cafés from the back part of Asakusa up to the area around the Yoshiwara, selling fortunes slips and beans and dried squid. Soon it will be time to start selling. Japanese, Koreans, Chinese—in one night, some forty or fifty of these kids come to the cafés, and, at a glance, you know they are Chinese from their pigtails.

Suddenly, Haruko waves and calls out to white girls who have come up from behind and are now walking past us: Varia!

From here on, I will let Haruko do the guiding, dear reader. To put it differently, in the recent movie version of *The Scarlet Gang of*

Asakusa, Yumiko has died. But on the Kurenai-maru, she only held six five-milligram arsenic pills in her mouth.

—Varia! And the girls Haruko called to rush down the street, clippety-clop, like wild fillies, as if blown by some erotic, violent wind.

The two girls, arm in arm, whistling, stockingless, in dark red thin dresses that look like some kind of dancing costume, nothing on underneath, hatless—just as though they mean to say that it is the same to them whether or not people whose skin is colored look at their white flesh, that they scorn the lust of the Japanese.

—Hey, these foreign bitches act like they own the place.

—Don't know about that, but, lately, in the park, there are so many more of these foreigners. I heard someone say that sooner or later this place might turn into some international gangland. But, oh no, don't believe what I say. And Haruko waves her hand again as if saying good-bye on a pier: Mira! Varia!

I am surprised. The taller of the two turns right around, and, lifting her short skirt a little, she curtseys and blows us a kiss.

—That's why I hate them, those foreign girls. And Haruko turns away in a huff: Just sixteen, that girl. But those long legs are so feminine. But the little-girl waists of the Japanese dancers, there's nothing juicy about them, just dryness. I hear the older one, Mira, is eighteen. They take the streetcar right home from Kaminari Gate, so forget about it. You ought to go ask Tsujimoto for different girls. I hear he has a few cute fifteen- or sixteen-year-old white ones. I hear he has them strut around the Nakamise. Of course, they pretend to be revue dancers. These two, they have a younger sister who is fourteen and an older one who is twenty-one, and all four dance together at the Mansei Theater and call themselves the Danilewsky sisters.

The Russian dancers' bare legs are glossy in their transparent whiteness, covered with scented oil, and, when they strike their high heels on the night asphalt, those legs are as fresh and firm as the green *hōzuki* plants. They are just the sense of summer itself, much more than the bare feet of the Japanese girls peeking out under the hems of their *yukata*. And on stage, the Russian dancers freely drip with sweat. The audience can see it running under their white powder.

Already in early June, a month ago, Haruno Yoshiko, dancing at the Denkikan, was bothered by her own sweat. She told me that the more she tries not to sweat, the more she sweats.

By the way, when Yumiko lured Akagi aboard the Kurenai-maru, the legs of the dancing girls at the Aquarium were like deep red glass due to the cold. Roughly seven months since then—dear reader, I must admit to you that trying to describe those seven months in Asakusa is even more impossible than trying to capture last year's sunshine.

Now, beside the Matsukiyō Police Station, Haruko pulls one of those Scarlet Troupe votive stickers out of her kimono sash, as if it were grease paper to dab her white powder.

—Okay, I'm going to say my good-byes now. Left-Handed Hiko from over in Juku asked me to take care of some tricky business. Not at all sure I can handle it, but I've got to try my best because the codes of our Asakusa, they say so. Bye.

Juku means Shinjuku.

the red sash society

40

THIS POLICE STATION is located where Asakusa and Matsukiyō streets meet. If you go out the back gate of Asakusa Honganji, it's on the left, west of the Tawaramachi streetcar stop. You can say that, in the east, Kaminari Gate is the main entrance to Asakusa, and in the west, it's Matsukiyō Street.

The human wave that floods Asakusa amounts to roughly a hundred million people a year, and the money sunk annually into shows, eateries, and geisha houses amounts to roughly 12.6 million yen (at least according to the statistics), and it's said that the tobacco shop at the west entrance once took in two hundred yen in a day.

Then business at that tobacco shop suddenly plummeted. That tobacco shop is now shut out of the park by the new road. The city reconstruction office has turned their booming business into a thing of the past. The road is too wide to cross just to buy tobacco. But the other side of the street has gotten so crowded that, even though Russian girls swagger about, they escape people's notice.

—I guess you will need the red ones tonight. And I glance at the votive sticker in Haruko's hand. We're on the sidewalk of the lonely side of the street.

—Oh shoot. That reminds me. I've only got red ones left. I use the green ones way too much, so you can see how much I like to chase after boys.

The votives are the Scarlet Gang's innocent pranks, a downtown kind of joke. But sometimes, they double as their name cards, ID cards, or their warning signals.

On the thick paper like that used for doors, yet so small you can tuck them in the palm of your hand, with the three words—Asakusa Scarlet Troupe—printed in *kantei* style (bold, round white letters), there are both red ones and green ones. The whole system sort of works like streetcar signals.

For example, say Haruko picks up a man and takes him to the shop where they sell Meiji brand candy in front of Kaminari Gate. She drops a green sticker at the store entrance. One of her buddies passing by notices the sticker and shakes the man down for money.

But they never know where, when, how, and what kind of people they will meet. So when they come across someone suspicious, they (when he is not looking) stick a red sticker on the wall of a dirty Chinese restaurant. So the roads that lead to dark, vacant lots are strewn with red stickers. These signal danger and mean to go get help.

If one of the girls disappears, they first ask the beggars (the *zuke* and the *daigara*): You seen a piece of paper like this lying around here? They ask the bums who sweep the front of the eateries late at night or early in the morning in exchange for leftovers.

—Actually, I don't much use the red ones, but I have to pay back a debt to the old Red Sashes. I said I'd let Hiko know when I see those guys from the Horse Votive Club. He won't know them because he just came from Juku. So I go around with Hiko and point them out, one by one, and it's a real pain. Maybe I could just stick red stickers on their backs. Those Horse Votive guys—really! Maybe those Horse Votive animals would sell themselves with red tags stuck to their hides.

—But aren't you taking more of a risk than you bargained for?

—Risk? What's so risky about it? You see, I'm a just a simple girl. I'm not ugly or naïve enough to let any man beat me up.

Haruko laughs so that her shoulders shake: Take a look. Up there on the second floor.

A flowered dress hangs from a clothes hook on the wall. There is also a lady's hat with a large rose.

The old Yamabun Inn. The second floor of this shabby Japanese building stands right up against a Western inn. A white woman sits in a wicker chair in the middle of the tatami with a girl around ten in her lap.

—Signe Rintara and Leene Rintara, singers and dancers from Finland. They perform at the Teikyō Theater.

The tobacco store that no longer does any business is three or four doors down. Only their clothes are gorgeous. Their meager luggage.

41

THE OLD RED SASHES—that's what Haruko said, but it was not really that long ago.

Dear reader, surely you remember that summer when unlined deep-red kimono sashes were all the rage.

Shop girls, telephone operators, downtown girls strolling the night stalls—those kinds of girls loved this kind of sash. This dark red color has a tinge of the bad girl to it.

That time in Asakusa, Haruko wore a red unlined sash. This is because there was a girl gang called the Red Sash Society. At the same time, red sashes were in fashion everywhere. Girls found them irresistible. So, the Red Sash Society was not only in Asakusa, but there were branches in almost all the bustling areas of Tokyo. To tie your kimono with a red sash—to do this alone, many girls became members. Although red sashes were not just the privilege of the Red Sash Society, the name of the group lured in many a girl.

Dear reader, above all else, for the sake of your daughters, watch out for fashion. Intelligent person that you are, dear reader, you might laugh at the girls of the Red Sash Society, but do you know how gullible silly girls are even in Asakusa Park and how easily they can be sold off?

—The craze must have died out by fall. Can't wear an unlined sash all the time, I recently said to Haruko.

—Yes, that was a problem, so we thought about wearing black sashes from the fall—black satin ones! Besides, just at that time in Asakusa, there was a boy gang known as the Black Sash Society. And to top it off, so many of the Red Sash girls' lovers were in that group.

—Loose-Hair Oito was the one who suggested it. This Oito, she is just the smart, big-sister type, and she is now with the Ero-Ero Dance Troupe over at the Nihon Theater, singing "Going to Shimbashi in Azuma sandals with no socks." But back then, she was just eighteen or nineteen. Well, a black satin sash would be perfect for her, but they aren't for just anyone. Some people started to grumble about it. Girl gangs—they never amount to anything. A silly girl like me knows, in the end, she can get by with the least amount of trouble if she just accepts the fact that women are weak. Both Yumiko and Oito could've learned a thing or two by watching me.

—Recently, you were kind enough to introduce me to Oito, but she said, since it would be too risky to walk around with me, to please leave her alone.

—Then you'd better just leave her alone. They're different from the Scarlet Gang, you know. They say, in the old days when Oito walked around the park with her hair down loose, blood fell like rain. Just when I was thinking that I hadn't seen her in a while, I heard she'd become a department store salesgirl. I'm sure she's come back because she's made a lot of money. Absolutely sure. She lures in innocent shop girls like a little-old-lady pimp.

Asakusa and department stores—do you think, dear reader, that Haruko's guess is only nonsense? There is a secret society from Shinkoune in Hongō, just on the other side of the Ōkawa, that has a stronghold in Asakusa. I know the name, but I cannot write it here. I hear many department store salesgirls are among the members. One of the members of the Scarlet Gang even told me which department store, which floor, and which sales counter. I went to that department store just to see them, but when I am near those girls, I feel so sorry for them that I can't look at them as I walk by. That is just an example. But this society has nothing to do with Oito.

I am certain that you, dear reader, are not naïve enough to think that things like this are just nonsense, and in *The Study of the World of Asakusa*, you can find a little more of this nonsense. For example, the Shinshū silk-factory girls and Asakusa—that frightened me, too.

"End of the Shinshū Silk Filatures?" I am sure, dear reader, that you saw this big headline in the paper around July 13 or 14. Shimosuwa, Okaya, Minato, Kawagishi, Konan, Kamisuwa, Miyagawa, Tamagawa, Eimei—more than three hundred silk factories in the Suwa district closed all at once because the price of silk took such a nosedive. Soon this will spread from Suwa to Shizuoka, Yamanashi—throughout the whole country. Already almost one hundred thousand factory girls are unemployed.

Where do they go? Probably some of them go back to their hometowns in the hinterlands or up in the mountains. Others join the fight against the capitalists—but this isn't all of them. The others are welcomed with open arms by the Asakusa regiment of underhanded pimps.

mold and revues

42

GOURD POND IS deep green. This is because green algae multiply in stagnant water like mold in summer. If you go up the bank and through a slightly dark grove of trees, you reach a clearing. It is after two in the morning.

Twenty men are squatting in a circle on the ground in front of the benches. On closer look, there are also little crabs. The men hold crabs attached to strings in both hands and try to get them to fight each other with their claws. The crabs are already white with dust. Claws dangling limply, they do not move. A cop dressed all in white looks on. With a wry smile, he starts walking away.

—Hey! A fellow in an alpaca suit and fake Panama hat, still standing, calls out,

—What's up? You find work?

—Well, Mister, went up as far as Shibaura, but, nope, couldn't get me anything. So picked up these here crabs. Just come have a look in the morning. Kids'll be happy.

—Uh-huh.

The men in the circle all look up, and this seems to make the standing fellow a little proud, as, snapping his fan opened and closed, the plainclothes cop continues on his rounds among the park benches. Nowadays, things being as they are, all the young police detectives have to say a word or two to the old-timers of the park. Though it might seem quite rude, there are just too many newly arrived *okan* (Asakusaese for homeless) for this cop to know all their faces.

—Flies, bedbugs, sick cats, horses with sunstroke, men and women, bars crowded enough to make your head spin, street shows—summer.

—Summer is a circus. Yes, that's it. In summer, everything possible happens. Everyone spends almost all winter indoors. But in summer, there is life in the hustle and bustle of the streets.

So, in summer, the benches and the eaves become beds of heaven. There is no other hotel in all of Japan that has as many beds as the grounds of Asakusa in summer.

It is said that, even with an abacus, you can't count the number of vagabonds in Asakusa.

Anyway, you can't really rely on official statistics. If there is going to be an official survey or something like that, the bums get wind of it before it begins. Then they go hide somewhere. So no one can say for sure if there are five hundred or eight hundred or just how many people stay at this hotel. Still, this summer, there are far too many.

You can't say that they just suddenly multiply like the algae in Gourd Pond—still, this summer, there are far too many. And you don't have to ask the reason why. When even the sword hilt of the statue of Danjurō was stolen, didn't the newspaper reporters blame it on the recession?

"Malnourished children," "family suicide" . . . —strange terms like these are nothing new to you, dear reader. "Recession" and "eroticism"—in 1930, the newspaper reporters only write about these two words. Stories of people during the recession are already boring. And so: "Recession: Killing People and Buddha Alike."

I looked into the donations to the Asakusa Kannon. Ironically, because of the recession, donations have increased. Well, that's only human nature, but that was last year. This year they are said to be so few that they are not worth mentioning.

Under the headline "Buddha Also Suffers Setback," they write about the general standstill of the sales of obligatory presents and votive offerings during Obon.

It is certainly true in Asakusa. Just compare last winter's end-of-the-year sales with the sales of midsummer presents. Anyhow, over in the Nakamise commercial area, they put up a gate advertising the big sales, made dark blue and white checkered canopies for the eaves, and hung morning glories on the canopies. Well, more like day lilies or moonflowers, meager artificial blossoms, but at least trumpet-shaped flowers are blooming. But you don't even hear flutes or drums on the other shopping streets, and they are not decorated at all.

It's not so surprising that the little girl who rode the holy horse in the May Sanja Shrine festival already now in June has to sell her body to support her family.

But my meeting Left-Handed Hiko also had to do with the recession.

—Could you buy me a *yukata?* And I was had, and . . .

43

FRAGRANT WITH FRESH GREEN *MARRONNIER* LEAVES,
A SUGGESTION OF THE ATMOSPHERE OF OPERA AROUND
PARIS CHAMPS-ELYSÉES HANGS IN THE AIR—
DRAMATIC SOPRANO SOLOS BY MISS ODETTE DELTEIL

That is what it says on the billboard of the Shōchiku Theater. A revue in the first week of July. And in the second week:

EROTICISM FLOWING FROM THEIR BEAUTIFUL
PEARL-WHITE NAKED BODIES, THE RUSSIAN DANCER
MISS VARENNA RADOSENKO AND HER TROUPE

At the Mansei Theater, Tamara, Mira, Varia, Luba—the Danilewsky sisters' Metro dancing troupe. Gypsy dance, Cossack dance, Spanish dance, jazz dance, the Mermaid. The Russian girls sing the "Kanda Song" and the "Modern Ginza Song" in Japanese with their sweet Russian accents.

In the Mixed Dance Troupe at the Teikyō Theater, Signe Rintara and Leena Rintara: "Singers and Dancers from Finland," says the billboard. Mother Signe sings the "Okesa Song," while her ten-year-old daughter Leena, wearing a wreath of flowers on her head and a long-sleeved Japanese kimono, does the "Okesa Dance." Then before you know it, Leena is dressed like a man in a black satin suit, silk top hat, and a walking stick in one hand:

Oh, I'm Charlie Chaplin,
The always merry clown.

Singing, she shuffles through a mixture of the Cossack dance and Chaplin's trademark duck walk. And this little girl gets more applause this July than any other performer in all the theaters of Asakusa. In general, the Asakusa masses are kind to foreign performers. They are especially kind to the kids.

After the act, Leena comes down into the audience and sells post-cards with her picture on them. Beautiful. She reminds me of Lin Jinhua, a Chinese girl from ten years back.

Dear reader, please bear with me for a moment as I share with you a sad memory.

—Lin Jinhua is performing in Shinjuku.

That was last January the second. I went to this dump of a tent theater in Shinjuku just to see her. But it was just a phony revue—Lin Jinhua wasn't even there.

A digression, but the bear girl was in the next theater booth. The beautiful bear girl who performed behind Asakusa's Nakamise this spring. There was at the same time a circus tent near the Imahan restaurant. And there, in that circus tent, I saw Lin Jinhua.

Like Leena, she was just ten years old. Her thin, little-girl body performed strange and wonderful "acrobatics"—it was beautiful, like some strange and wonderful insect. A noble but melancholy insect. She, too, came into the audience and sold postcards with her picture on them.

But, recently, just by chance after these ten years, I saw Lin Jinhua again.

—Aw, let's go! She has gotten so ugly—too fat, so short, and those rouged lips on that vulgar face.

Left-Handed Hiko, looking back at me, dumbfounded, shows no intention of following me outside. This is at the Asakusa Egawa-Ōmori Theater.

Still, this July, the legs of Varia Danilewsky remind me of the far and away most beautiful dancer, Anna Lubowsky.

But, dear reader, since you were kind enough to listen to my reminiscences, might I also ask you to read a story I wrote in 1923?

. . .

The star opera actress of the Kinryū Theater walks through the autumn rain in Kagurazaka, sharing an umbrella with her mother, also an opera actress. Her mother holds the umbrella. Although attended by her mother as if by a maid, the daughter walks very respectfully beside her.

Seeing the daughter in her Western clothes and her mother, both exhausted from losing many theaters and homes alike to the fires, people would probably tend to look more favorably on the mother who thinks so highly of her daughter than to think ill of the daughter herself.

The daughter—I don't think she would mind if I wrote down her name. It's Sagara Aiko, who's having a comeback now in the movies.

44

I WROTE the rest of the story seven years ago. Let's skip a bit . . .

To return to the beginning of the story. Only fifteen days after the earthquake, two opera actresses walk through the autumn rains in Kagurazaka, sharing an umbrella.

At that time, I thought of an Asakusa winter drizzle four or five years earlier. Back then the Nihon Theater was enjoying great success with its opera, and even Sawada Ryūkichi played the "Moonlight Sonata" there. A Russian troupe that had fled the revolution performed, too.

One of members was named Gan Starsky. Nina Pawlowa, who should have been at the Kagetsuen in Tsurumi, danced. The three Lubowsky brothers and sisters, Anna Lubowsky, Daniel Lubowsky, and Israel Lubowsky, were also there. The oldest, Anna, was thirteen or fourteen, and Israel was around ten. Anna was an elegant beauty.

A student at the most prestigious high school at the time, I waited with my friend A for Anna to exit from the stage door. The three Lubowskys were accompanied by an old Russian man dressed in rags. Anna's coat, too, was worn to shreds, although it looked great on her.

The four—father and children—walked as far as the roller skating rink to the north of the Mikuni Theater and then stopped. Anna's neck was about level with my shoulder, and I gazed at her skin.

Anna stepped on the foot of a middle school student with her muddy shoe, deeply blushed, and smiled in embarrassment. The student also deeply blushed.

Then the four went to the bank of the lake, and the father bought a few roasted chestnuts.

They entered a seedy flophouse across from the Mikuni Theater.

We stood, looking up at the second floor of that flophouse.

—Tomorrow I'll stay at the room next door and buy Anna for the night. Fifty yen should be enough, said A.

After a while, it started to rain. Just as we sought shelter from the rain under the eaves of the Mikuni Theater, we turned around and looked in surprise. There was someone leaning on that wall, intently gazing up at the second floor where Anna was. It was the middle school student whose foot Anna had stepped on.

I thought about this Anna for a long time.

For a while, I tossed around the idea of writing a long, strange novel set in Asakusa Park in which only lowly women would appear—the factory girls at the cigarette plant in Kuramae, the waitresses at the movie booths, the circus girls and the girls who balanced on big balls—and I considered including this Anna and the little Chinese acrobat Lin Jinhua.

Another one I would add, a truly sad foreigner, was the leader of the water circus troupe that came from America that year. Someone put up a hundred-foot ladder on the burnt-out ruins of the Azuma Theater, and the troupe leader jumped from the top into a small pond. There was a large woman who jumped from fifty feet like a seagull, and she really did look like one, too. Beautiful.

I heard the troupe leader would say good-bye to the other members of the troupe before climbing the ladder. That is, to use a Japanese turn of phrase, he would "drink his last farewell cup of water." At the top, he would say a prayer to the starry sky. From below, we knew that up there in the sky the strong, cold wind blew.

Then he would arch his body backward, plunge headfirst with just a suggestion of looking behind him, leisurely turn a somersault in midair, and then land feet first in the pond.

He was terribly unfriendly during the whole performance. While climbing the ladder, he didn't even give the audience a single smile, and, after he jumped into the water, he swam back to shore with a few overhead strokes and returned to his dressing room without as much as a look around. From start to finish, he looked sad, as if all this did not interest him in the least.

This troupe leader fascinated us. I would have loved to see him jump off the top of the nearby Twelve Stories.

I tossed around the idea of writing a long, strange novel. And, dear reader, in these pages, after ten years, I have finally begun to do just that.

45

BUT, DEAR READER, there is really no reason not to tell you frankly a few of my memories from the heyday of Asakusa opera.

Some opera actresses from ten years back are having a comeback as revue girls, and isn't that just like today's Asakusa?

Okay, let's return to July 1930—the Mixed Dance Troupe of Leena Rintara and the others at the Teikyō Theater, but—

They are mixing too much up together, think I, someone who is not shocked by such things as "jazz *kappore*," but that "mixed dance" "The Reins" as performed by the monk Hōnensai Nyōkai and Matsuyama Namiko is going a bit too far.

Take that "Japanese-Western Jazz Ensemble"—Namiko is a blue-eyed seaman in a sailor suit, and Nyōkai is a Japanese girl in a long-sleeved kimono, and they use a white ribbon as a rein, and with very expressive hand and body gestures, they act like lovers, and while the seaman dances a Western dance, his girl dances a Japanese dance.

Even Sawa Morino, who appeared in June at the Showa Theater with the Tenkatsu Troupe, mixes things together and performs the same dances she did ten years before, like the "Nanny" and "Gypsy Life." When she makes a face, she has wrinkles like a monkey.

On the other hand, Kimura Tokiko of the Otowa Theater—

—She has got to be the boldest, brashest girl in the world.

And she looks so young, unbelievable to those who know her age. Even the bad girls are amazed.

The opening performance of the Nihon Theater's Ero-Ero Dance Troupe:

MAJOR DANCE REVOLT OF THE NAKED IT GIRLS

Yes indeed, dear reader, that's what it really says on the billboard.

Kitamura Takeo and Fujimura Gorō of the Tokyo Theater. Fujita Tsuyako and her Swan Troupe do a piece billed as:

The fat idiot Kawai Sumiko has returned to the Nihon Theater. Sawa Kaoru has moved from the Kannon Theater to the Asakusa Theater. Taya Rikizō and Yanagida Teiichi have also come and gone. Such clearance sales of opera players do not seem so rare anymore.

The fourth and fifth performances of the Paramount Show at the Denkikan—though it was back in June, Haruno Yoshiko's jazz dance and Minami Eiko's Charleston seemed very 1930.

But even the Hatsune Theater, which has kicked out the girl *gidayu* singer with her recitation of "The Setting Moon over the Lonely Castle," has recently repainted its billboard:

ULTRAMODERN VARIETY SHOW TOURNAMENT

"All and everything" is "vaudeville," "variety," "revue."

And "Chinese Okichi" by Kawai Sumiko and her dance troupe and the Casino Folies' "Kiss-Dance"—these numbers have been strictly censured for being quite "erotic."

The day after those two Russian girls passed Haruko and me, I wandered over to have a look at all of these Asakusa revues.

However—

FROM LIFE'S SERIOUS HARDSHIPS

FLOOD OF LUNATICS IN THE CAPITAL

ALL HOSPITALS FULL

PATIENTS WITH MINOR ILLNESSES
GRADUALLY RELEASED TO MAKE ROOM

These are not revue billboards. They are newspaper headlines.

left-handed hiko

46

ALMOST ALL of the hobos in Asakusa are a little crazy. Asakusa is one big insane asylum. But not all the homeless are beggars or hobos. Naturally, the horde of unemployed pours in this summer. Of course, there are more beggars and hobos, too.

But there are fewer leftovers during the recession. Less for the beggars to receive. And there are only a limited number of benches. Yet, from the days of old, there have been strict divisions of territory. If you violate them, you not only lose your place in Asakusa, you can also lose your life. But, at any rate, during this "time of famine," they multiply like the algae in Gourd Pond.

I have heard this: He must've been a day laborer who went from *doya* (flophouse) to *okan* (no house). When this dope earned a little dough, he'd drink like a fish and smoke like a chimney, and the rest he'd blow on fireworks. When he got back to the park, he'd set them fireworks off. Bang-bang. He must've thought it out. He's a newcomer in these here parts, not pulling much weight, and them fireworks would make him a popular guy. But, come morning, he's just a small fish in a big pond again.

The fellows watching the crab fight are probably a bunch of new-comers who couldn't get benches. Wherever I look, the benches are full. When three guys are sitting on a bench, there is no room for more.

I quietly walk into the dark grove of trees. On top of the concrete arch of the bridge:

—That's just a lot of big talk. We gotta make sure the cash is good before we send the men to do the deed.

—A sap like you'll never make it. But, you know, Shinshū is crawling with dames—you can't move without bumping into one. And they're all wandering round the streets in a daze, clueless, so they're real easy to hook.

—Think there'll be many of them good-looking lady-killers around?

—Don't matter. In Western duds, you can make anyone look the part.

—Can you get them Western duds for twenty or thirty?

—Now you're talking like a counterfeiter. So print up ten one hundreds a head.

—Not so loud.

—So go out and make the world a better place.

Since this gives me the creeps, I leave. But, dear reader, they are not hobos. They are three members of a factory-girl kidnapping gang, and you have just been made privy to their secret plans to send some men to Shinshū, where so many girls are unemployed.

I would be happy if they talked about making money as if it were just some dream. But those scoundrels with their same old tricks and close to a hundred thousand factory girls, it seems possible. So you, Shinshū cops, instead of going after social activists, you ought to arrest these guys.

But, of course, this is just wishful thinking on my part. I do not know how useful any cheap tricks of mine would be to the girls. So I ought to keep quiet about this and tell you about a girl I saw right here in the back part of the park.

—That girl, to her, it's just pain. She has no idea what she's doing or what it's all about. And Left-Handed Hiko laughs with a serious look on his face.

—Could you buy me a *yukata*?

Because Hiko asked this out of the blue, I must have made a face.

—*Women's Club yukata*, the "Southern Evening" type. She says she wants silk crêpe.

—You going to give it to someone special?

—Just a minute now. I could beat you up for it. Don't underestimate me. I don't know how you get along with Yumiko and the others, but I'm not dumb enough to hit someone up for money just to give a girl a *yukata*.

—So it is not for a girl's *yukata*?

—You just don't get it, do you? It's for a fourteen-year-old kid. I was fooling around and said I'd give her a *yukata*, but because she's just a kid and took me seriously and because she believes me like a god or something, I can't let her down. Okay, tell you what. I'll sell her to you. She's a girl for sale, you know. Turned into one last week, and so she's available now. But I'm not so cheap as to try to win a little girl's heart with a *yukata*. I'll just throw the *yukata* in the entry—though the place isn't grand enough to have a real entryway—and then get out fast.

—So which is it? The silk crêpe Southern Evening?

—Thanks. It's not that I don't have the three hundred and forty-five yen. But it's dirty money. Your money's better. Just give it to me, and I'll let you meet her. Write just a little bit about her, and you could buy ten or twenty *yukata* in one night.

In other words, it was to revive the Shiroya house that this "Left-

Handed Hiko" came over from Shinjuku. They say a pimp who didn't know better brought him.

It was still June the day I crossed paths with the truck heaped with yellow, white, and red chrysanthemums on the road to Asakusa.

And Hiko came to Asakusa the day of the Sanja Shrine festival.

It is rumored that a few dangerous characters returned to Asakusa mixed in the crowds of this "famous blood offering festival of Asakusa."

47

CLOSED BUT BROKEN shutter doors, a big curtain, like a wrapping cloth or a bedsheet, hanging in front, and the glass panes of the sliding doors to the three-tatami-mat room all pasted over with yellow paper—and in this six-mat room stands a small old dressing table with a mirror. (Why are the mirrors in these kinds of houses usually broken?) And there are four or five cheap cotton women's *yukata* thrown over the clothes rack.

Hiko is lying on his side, head pillowed on his elbow, eyes closed. It is very quiet. He is not bothered by the pimp going restlessly up and down the steps. Now finding himself in a stranger's house calms him; it's like being in a hiding place.

It is after ten-thirty. The girl said she was going to the movies but still has not come home.

—She's probably walking home. It's a bit far to go for a little girl's legs, you know.

—She's probably prowling about somewhere.

—Believe me, she's still just a little kid. She said she went alone, so where would she go?

—Oh, calm down. I didn't say you're lying to me just because she's not here.

—Okay. I live right behind this house. So I know she's not the kind of girl who wanders around at night. And I was told they only gave her twenty sen.

—So then you're near the Fujita café.

—Mister, you from around here? And he gives Hiko a piercing look.

—Nope, but the poster girl is an old friend.

—You don't say.

—What's that talk about Omitsu's losing weight after having a kid?

—I don't know anything about that, but . . .

—You must've had to go all the way around the park on your way here. Probably went by Rokuji of Suiten.

—Where's that?

—What? Don't know him? He's the head of a gang of pickpockets, rivals of the gang at the tailor's shop. He started up a nice radio shop on the side, where I hear he's got a real cutie. I saw the old man with her in the front of the shop. Her kind of wavy hair was up in a *momoware*. That boss Rokuji, he just came out of the slammer, so he lies low. I only know him by sight. I heard it from a kid who was sent down with him. The kid's a tough, roving around the park, and he meets Rokuji four or five days back, on the streetcar, and, when he gets home, he finds he's got four fifty-sen notes in his pants pocket. He was mighty happy because the boss's hand's still fast as ever.

—She'll be back soon. And the pimp sneaks away.

A little old lady comes up to the second floor. She puts a matchbox in front of Hiko. A long, tan face with an old pair of glasses hung from the end of her nose. Hiko still dozes. After five minutes or so, she comes up again. This time with a cheap green glass ashtray and magazines:

—You must be bored. The little one probably stopped off for some sweets. These children's books are probably not what you'd want to read, though.

The *Young Girls' Club*. All six issues, January through June.

As Hiko glances at the photos of the young ladies on the frontispieces, he hears the sound of breathing, as if someone is waking up in the three-mat room next door. He sits up but can't see into the room.

Downstairs, the girl comes home. The pimp comes up to the second floor, looking relieved.

—Hey, there's someone in the next room.

—Oh, that's someone who lives here. A woman. I'll send her downstairs right away.

—You gonna get her up?

—No problem. I'll talk to her.

Then the girl brings in tea like she is expected to, but the girl's looks are so unexpected that even Hiko is taken aback—her shins peeking out from her Genroku *yukata*, baby-blue boy's sash, her braids down to her shoulders like some sassy kid returning from elementary school with a "Hey, I'm home!"

the young girls' club

48

IT SEEMS LIKE this little girl has never worn makeup. When she comes upstairs alone the second time, her face is no longer flushed, and when Hiko asks: Good movie? What'd you see? She runs over, and, still standing, she talks to him as if he were a school pal.

—Uh-huh. Called *Talent*.

—At the Imperial, right?

—No, the Makino.

—Oh, right. *Talent* isn't at the Imperial yet. I waited more than an hour for you, you know.

—Really? I went to Minowa.

—That farther than Asakusa?

—No, closer. Oh, put that on, okay? And she takes a *yukata* with a large court carriage pattern on it and tosses it at Hiko's feet.

—Just a minute.

—Okay. You read the *Young Girls' Club* every month?

—Uh-huh. I got them all starting from two or three years ago.

—They got some real nice *yukata*, don't they?

—They're pretty. And the girl kneels beside Hiko, head still pillowed in his arm, so that her knees almost touch his elbow.

A pattern book for *Women's Club yukata,* an inserted advertisement in the June *Young Girls' Club,* is open wide.

—Want me to buy you one?

—Really?

Her suddenly lit-up face surprises Hiko. The look on her face shows that she really thinks he is going to go out and buy her a *yukata.* She does not think it is a joke, does not think it is a lie, does not think it is strange. It does not even occur to her they are woman and customer.

—Hmmm, which one? And she is a child looking closely at the pattern book. She does not even say "thanks" or "sorry."

—Later, let's take a look at them together.

—Okay. Wait a minute. I'll run over to the noodle shop.

And like an elementary school student who has asked her playmate to wait a bit, she clatters down the stairs.

Hiko's feet hang over the end. It's a child's mattress.

The woman in the three-mat room next door quietly leaves. From downstairs comes the sound of slurping noodles.

—You having some?

—Uh-huh. When there's a customer, the whole house gets to eat noodles.

—Yeah, a real celebration.

The girl gazes up at Hiko with a blank look, as though she's on an operating table.

—When did you finish school?

—This March.

—You really fifteen?

—No, fourteen.

Then opening a white slip of paper with both hands held before her bright open eyes, looking up, she reads aloud in a clear voice: If infected and not treated immediately, various complications will arise that can affect different bodily functions, and more harm will come to the sufferer, for, in the end, the peace of the family will be disrupted, and various detrimental effects will befall the progeny . . .

—Hey!

—It keeps for a long time.

—Huh?

—This medicine doesn't go bad. Says so right here.

—Wow. You can read such big words. I guess it's because you've been reading the *Young Girls' Club* since you were a fourth grader.

—I go to Asakusa's, children's library, even now, often . . .

Her voice falters, and she wrinkles her forehead a little, but her face remains indifferent to what is going on.

They are in front of the pattern book again.

—Which do you like?

—Hmmm . . . I don't know. I'll ask my mom.

Hiko also goes downstairs and peers into the room. There are three women—the old lady from before, a bony woman around thirty, and then there is a young woman wearing only a red woolen undershirt and something wrapped around her waist. Her body, plump, is beautiful.

49

THIS PROBABLY has nothing to do with anything, but I have a cousin in Asakusa's Kuramae. She is fourteen and a first-year student at a girls' school. Two of her classmates from elementary school joined the Purple Gang (one of them is the daughter of a famous comedian).

This Purple Gang isn't a play on the name Scarlet Gang but really exists. My fourteen-year-old cousin doesn't know that I'm writing a novel called *The Scarlet Gang of Asakusa,* nor does she probably know what the Purple Gang is up to. She only knows that those two girls from elementary school have "always swapped letters with boys."

My cousin came to visit me not so long ago, and since I had an appointment that day in Asakusa and couldn't leave her home alone, I brought her along with me and took her picture with six or seven jazz dancers in the Denkikan dressing room.

—Uncle, will the photo appear in a book? She asks me, worried, every time she sees me.

This is because her teacher might find out that she went to Asakusa. At her school, except for visits to the Holy Kannon, going to Asakusa is strictly forbidden.

I also hope she grows up to be a young lady who has never seen the likes of Asakusa Park. In any case, she is the only fourteen-year-old girl I know. And what Hiko said was quite right: Pretty or not, she's still a caterpillar.

Waiting for the girl, Hiko looks carefully at the photos of the "young ladies who do not know the likes of Asakusa" decorating the frontispieces of the six issues of the *Young Girls' Club.*

—They're pretty, but they look kind of flirtatious. She's not at all like that. Usually young girls from Asakusa on up to the Yoshiwara know more than they should for their age, but this little one isn't quite to that stage yet.

No man has ever told her that he would buy her something. So she did not know how to feel. It's not that she is taking a joke seriously. It's just that she does not know when someone is just kidding her.

—I'll ask my mom. And the gentle innocent way she springs to her feet as if she had forgotten what she just did surprises even Left-Handed Hiko.

Let's hope the adults downstairs don't bruise that innocence.

But then the girl comes rushing back upstairs, in her hand the magazine with the inserted advertisement hanging limply out.

—They said "Southern Evening" would be good for me.

—Which one's that? But that's got a cluster amaryllis pattern on it. A little too ladylike, don't you think?

—My big sister picked it out.

—Your big sister's the girl in the red shirt?

—Uh-huh. My big brother's wife.

—Your big brother?

—He went off to work in Hokkaido. And the other one's my real big sister.

—It comes in muslin and silk crêpe. Which one do you want?

—What's muslin?

—It's higher-class cotton.

—I guess silk'd be nice. For the first time, she hesitates. And for the first time, she seems calculating.

—But you have to tell me how to get here again real carefully or I'll never find my way back.

—Okay. I'll draw you a map. Can I use this? And she picks up the paper she'd been reading, and, moistening the point of the pencil on her tongue: Here's the Ryūsenji stop, and this is Asakusa, this is Minowa. Got it?

Then she writes the address and her mother's name as it says on the door nameplate.

Together with her mother, she says good-bye to Hiko, but the little girl only sticks her head out from the sliding door of the room downstairs: When are you coming again? Tomorrow? The day after tomorrow?

She asks this like an adult.

shōkyokusai tenkatsu

50

IT WAS THE DAY AFTER Hiko had extorted from me the funds for "Southern Evening," designed by Yosano Akiko. It must have been the third day of the rainy season. The silk for the *Women's Club yukata* had not come to Asakusa's dry goods stores, they said.

—No choice. Gotta get the muslin one, but that's two yen forty sen a roll instead of three yen forty-five sen, and I don't want to make her think I'm trying to scrimp on just one yen. Could you give me enough for one more?

—How about material for a *Literary Arts Chronicle–The Scarlet Gang of Asakusa yukata?*

—How much?

—Two yen thirty sen.

—One yen ought to be enough.

—You going to bring it to her tonight?

—What do you think I am? For just one or two rolls of cloth— I'll send them off to her tomorrow. Toss them in like the parcel post. I'm not going in there again.

The next morning was midsummer hot.

The front and back doors of the little girl's house are both wide open. That is, the back and front entrances are not much different. There is no entryway. The kitchen is next to the front door. From the kitchen comes the little old lady, wiping her hands. There are two rooms downstairs, one three mats, the other six. The little girl sits alone in the six-mat room, sewing a *yukata*. Sitting straight, her profile is outlined in the southern sun. Morning in a decent family.

—Could you call the kid over, please?

The girl gets up and comes over, serious look on her face.

—Here. And Hiko hands her the paper-wrapped *yukata* material, and he has never seen such a happy look on anyone's face. Her whole face lights up.

—They said the silk isn't in yet, so I bought you an extra roll of the cheaper stuff.

—Okay. And saying only this, she trots off, tells her mother something, puts the wrapped package on top of the old dresser, and then again sits down in front of her sewing in the back room.

—Thank you very much, says her mother who shifts into the room after the girl leaves.

—Please come in from the heat and rest for a moment.

—Well, could I have some water?

Hands him a cup of water.

—Oh, just stop that for a minute.

—But, mom, I just want to finish this half of the sleeve.

—Please stay and cool off a bit longer.

—No thanks. Good-bye.

And the girl lets her needle rest and stares across at him, and, in a loud voice:

—Leaving? See you in a few days.

—Wouldn't you like to stay a bit longer?

—No thanks.

—Okay, as you wish.

—Get over here.

Called by her mother, the girl gets up and comes over. Why, her eyes are full of tears.

Hiko lets slip: Want me to take you to the movies?

—Really? Wait a minute. I'll go change.

Hands already at her sash, she goes into the back room.

—Too easy. Abducting a little girl. So Hiko smilingly says: But not just you. Go ask someone else.

—Really? How about my big sister? And she calls up to the second floor from the bottom of the stairs: Hey, Sis!

51

Entire Ensemble: A Selection of Famous Songs
A Fairy Tale: *The Spirit of the Artist's Brush*
Musical Comic
Big Magic Show
PERFORMED IN PUBLIC FOR THE FIRST TIME
The Ocean Dance

Skits

THE TRAVELING COMPANION

THE SLEEPING CAR

The Cowboy Dance

Skits

THE LIE

FISHING GIRL

The Magical Transformation of the Cannon
A SAD TALE FROM ENGLAND'S WAR OF THE ROSES

New Dance: Scenes of Five Festivals

THE NEW YEAR

GIRL'S DAY

BOY'S DAY

THE STAR FESTIVAL

THE CHRYSANTHEMUM FESTIVAL

Daring Aerial Acrobatics

Egyptian Paradise
NEW MAGIC COMEDY

The Shōkyokusai Tenkatsu Troupe program.

The Showa Theater opened on June 7. At the end of May, the New Tsukiji Revue Troupe performed "What Made Us Come to Asakusa?" and that was after they'd shown such numbers as "What Made Her Do It?" and "The Secret Tales of Tsukuba."

Dear reader . . .

It

IT

It

Written three different ways on the three different banners that flutter in the July breeze in front of the Kannon Theater.

The Nihon Theater came up with the clever name "Ero-Ero Dance Troupe" and even at the Shōchiku Theater, "Dance Ero" is advertised in big black letters. "Ero" is on billboards everywhere you look. This foreign word, left half undone, might still be okay, but if you go and collect all the words from the Asakusa "phony revue" billboards, you will end up with a sex fiend's notebook.

Dear reader, just go take a walk in the evening along the alleys behind the theater booths near the bank of the pond. There, in those back alleys, where you might be relieved of your money some afternoon, are the entrances to the dressing rooms of the "ero queens." They come out in the cool of the evening. There, dear reader, you can see for yourself that when I say the legs of the Danilewsky sisters are beautiful, they are only that way because of the night lights. Their legs are really darker than those of most Japanese.

Now, just as you would expect, the program of the Tenkatsu Troupe is much finer than those "phony revues." The magician's props are dazzling. The way the young dancers look at the audience is cleverly beautiful. But Tenkatsu, old enough to have grandkids of her own, plays the role of a girl student. She is in every act and swaggers about too much. Matsuoka Henry's aerial acrobatics are spectacular. It is also amazing that dancer Sawa Marino has been engaged.

But what surprises Left-Handed Hiko is that so many things are thrown from the stage to the audience. Sawa Marino, playing the artist in "The Spirit of the Artist's Brush," poses as a baseball pitcher and tosses thirty or forty paper bags of sweet bean buns here and there to the audience up in the gallery and down in the pit.

The line "The bread at Fujiya on Asakusa Street is delicious" comes before that. It is an advertisement for the bakery. Then during the magic show, a male helper lets fly from the stage a hundred cards with Tenkatsu's picture on them. Like butterflies, they skillfully fly as far as the back of the pit. Right next to the photo is a printed advertisement for makeup.

They throw Morinaga caramels and pies.

Matsuoka Henry throws apples.

Each time, there is much excitement in the audience.

Very domestic. Many kids are there.

And Hiko's little girl climbs on top of her chair again and again and waves her hands in the air. This way, she is sure something will come her way. Her sister's lap is full of stuff. The little girl is still happy, even on the way home.

But Hiko says good-bye to them and comes to see me.

—Never seen anything like those magic tricks. Absolutely amazing. No idea how they did them. Go see for yourself. Even tomorrow. But the big sister started to cry. The little girl always says stuff like it hurts today or that today it wasn't so bad. She can't stand to hear it. But her mother-in-law won't let her sell herself because she's her son's wife, after all. The husband's probably been sold into a labor camp up in Hokkaido. And the big sister tells me that I should do something for her today. If she could make her mother-in-law believe that she and I have something going on, then from now on, she'd let her start selling her body. I can do without such sentimental playacting. No woman has ever taken me for that dumb. But what about you? You don't get a chance to do a good deed every day? A white, plump babe, can't just toss that one away.

okin of the bank

52

SEVENTY PREVIOUS CONVICTIONS: born in Yokodera-machi in Ushigome, the daughter of a long line—retainer to the shogun—but died a dog's death behind Awashima Shrine in Asakusa Park.

When I say Asakusa's famous Okin of the Bank—well you, dear reader, will probably think of that old drunken bat, the spiteful, swearing harridan who would fall over backward in a crowd.

For example, when Asakusa old-timers are shown any of these recent revues, they smile: Must've been around the time of the war with Russia. There was this show called "The Underwater Dance of the Lady Divers." Compared to that show, today's dances in swimsuits are pretty darn decent.

There was a big tank. Sea grass was planted, and shells gleamed deep at the bottom. A girl diver wearing only goggles and a red underskirt, her hair waving in the water, looking just like one of Utamaro's girl abalone collectors, picked up seashells from the bottom. That was the underwater dance. They said that even a starlet who went by the name "Mermaid Omatsu" would appear.

But you don't even need to go as far back as the stories of the old-timers. By the time Okin of the Bank died at age sixty-two, those ball-balancing girls in the flesh-colored slips had long disappeared from Asakusa.

The Kaminari Gate should have been rebuilt after 1884, but it doesn't seem like it will be any time in the future. Even this main gate burned down because of a woman—Ogin, the daughter of a waste paper collector—but that's Asakusa for you. I can tell you countless stories about Asakusa women.

There were girls serving tea in teahouses starting two hundred years ago. Next came the girls at the toothpick rooms. Arrow girls at the archery stands. It is already Meiji. Proprietresses of sake bars. Then newspaper reading room girls. *Go* parlor girls. *Mugitoro* shop girls. Shooting gallery girls. The girls of the bars under the Twelve Stories. It is already Taisho. The "Taisho geisha." The big earthquake. Along with the Twelve Story Tower, all sorts of girls disappear.

But still, the garden given to the master gardener Morita Roku-saburō by the house of Prince Rin'noji in the Ka'ei era—at least that is what they say, and I don't know if it is because of this or not, but, at this oldest historical spot, now the Hanayashiki, among the show stalls in today's Asakusa, you can find nostalgic things like marionettes, acrobatic birds, and lifelike dolls that vaguely remind you of the days when the chrysanthemum dolls by the famous doll maker Yasumoto Kihachi were at the peak of their popularity.

HANAYASHIKI—ENJOY THE SUMMER BREEZES—
OPEN DAY AND NIGHT—PLAYS—ACROBATIC BIRDS—
MARIONETTES—DANCE REVUES

Dear reader, these words are on the "electric news signboard," and, of course, an elephant and a monkey all drawn in electric lights walk above the entrance, pulling these words along. Though more and more stands are decorated with neon signs in Asakusa in the summer of 1930, the Hanayashiki electric news signboard "takes the cake."

So the most old-fashioned Hanayashiki is like this. And in place of all those different kinds of women who have disappeared, women who are the equivalent of this electric news signboard have no doubt appeared all over Asakusa. Over time, dear reader, I will pick out and show you some of these women.

But in saying this, it would be too bad if you were to think of me as a mediocre copy of the "debauched men of letters" of old like Ōta Nanpo, alias Shokusanjin.

—Inari of the Ginkgo asks Inari of the Kasamori one day: I have heard of your Osen. What distinguishes her from our Ofuji?

This is from Shokusanjin's *Comments on Comparing the Merits of Osen and Ofuji.*

These days, the young people who pass the time in Asakusa's coffee shops and milk halls call a writer who starts rumors to help revue dancers get better known, especially a writer who frequents the Aquarium, by the old-fashioned term "debauched man of letters."

Anyway, the dark brown of kabuki actor Segawa Rokō II's costume when he played this Ofuji, who was competing against Osen of Kasamori at the Ichimura Theater, became popular as the color called Rokō brown. Ofuji was a girl from the Motoyanagi-Niheiji bar. The bar was located under twin ginkgo trees behind the Kannon Hall. Even the peddlers sang about her. Of course, color woodblock prints of her sold well.

Woodblock prints in those days were like today's photographs of movie actresses, and even Ogin, that daughter of a Tawaramachi waste paper collector, was such a beauty that a print was made of her. Some man saw this picture and became so consumed with passion for her that he snatched her away from her betrothed Shinkichi. This man was Kishigami Ryōtarō of Mikasa in Honjo, the second son of a direct retainer with a thousand *koku* of rice. On the night of their wedding, Shinkichi started a fire, and the Kaminari Gate was burned down.

That was 1865, the first year of the Keiō period, when the Meiji era was already drawing near, but to the daughter of a waste paper collector and her parents, a direct-line retainer had an irresistible charm. But Okin of the Bank was also the daughter of a direct-line retainer.

53

WHEN SHE WAS FIFTEEN, Okin was sold off as a bar girl in Kawagoe. This was because the fortunes of retainers to the Shogun declined after the Meiji Restoration, and, at this time, Kawagoe was the starting point of a somewhat precarious trade. Then around 1897, now about thirty-one, Okin came back to Tokyo to work at a brothel on the bank of the Yoshiwara. Her drunken sprees and her eventual criminal record spread wide the name "Okin of the Bank."

When she was nearing fifty, she had no other choice but to tug at the sleeves of men she met on the street and go from one flophouse to the next. By the time she was nearing sixty, she had to make her living under the cover of darkness. She made her home on the ground. She went from *shiki* (Asakusa lingo for home) to *sotoshiki* (homeless). This was because her partners were mostly bums. When she died at age sixty-two, it was a relief. She had worked hard as a woman right up to her dying days. She did not sink to the level of *zubu* or *daigara*. Drunk as she sometimes was, she could still curse with the best of them.

Bums who are lower than bums—that is, those who no more roam about, right, but turn into weathered human figures. From morning to night, they sit on their bench, and, the next day, they are there still sitting again, and so they get weathered, and, dear reader, you probably remember what Akikō said that time in the park:

—See? She's one kind of Cropped-Head O-So-and-So. Most of them are like this. The dregs of Asakusa. But as long as she can still run, she's still a woman. Because most of the bums are no longer human enough to run.

Also, the weathered folk no longer talk. They live amid the hustle and bustle of the commercial district without saying a word.

—Foreigners call them ladybirds, right? Yumiko also asked this that morning in the park.

—Ladybirds?

—Another name for ladybugs. And for "female birds," the Chinese slang for fallen women, for ladies in rouge—also for women who put on their morning makeup right out in the open. There's no further to sink if they've already sunk this low.

Sitting on the chain fence surrounding the shrubbery, two young women do their morning makeup, compacts in hand. The backs of their kimono sashes are all crumpled, and the soil of the night ground clings to them.

An eatery has attached a rubber hose to the public toilet tap to get its water for cooking.

A few field mice nibble on the old rubber-soled cloth boot on the dangling foot of a man sleeping on a bench. These mice are what surprise me the most on this Asakusa morning. I have seen them behind the Bug House.

Makeup finished, the women leave. They are last night's *sotoshiki*.

Roadside teahouses, sake bars, archery stalls, newspaper reading rooms—I am sure, dear reader that you have heard about the current that flows under this one—courtesans, procuresses, harlots, streetwalkers, and today's *gokaiya*. Homeless Okatsu, Lightning Otama, Oyuki the Booby, Squinty-Eyed Ohisa—there are many *gokaiya* like these whose names have been put into print, but Okin of the Bank was not a beggar kid like Bobbed-Hair Oyoshi, nor was she as stupid as the Idiot Okiyo. Instead, she was a prime example of a woman who simply fell to the bottom of the ranks of women.

And I wonder what happened to the little girl from Ryūsenji who was sent off to work two years before Okin.

And, dear reader, you know that Yumiko's older sister Ochiyo is "a ladybird who puts on her morning makeup right out in the open."

the german hunting dog

54

AS IF PAVED with leaden boards, the asphalt gleams, bathed in a rosy hue. How brightly this red colors the sky over the still sleeping city. The freshness of the sound of the streetcars—and it is five in the morning.

In the morning sun that dyes the Kototoi Bridge pink, the striped pattern of traces of last night's urine. And as if it were a blueprint drawn on the ground, Sumida Park is a plain and neat H. The Kototoi Bridge is the middle bar that connects the lines of the Mukōjima embankment and the Asakusa riverside.

Currents in the Sumida River are yellow where the sun hits them, mud-colored where the sun is hidden by clouds. But since the Kototoi Bridge has no steel structures except for its comb-like handrails and its pencil-like light posts, it has all the cheerfulness of a single, strong, simple, straight line of steel. Though the air is rarely clear enough to see as far as Mount Tsukuba, let alone Mount Fuji, standing on the bridge, from out of nowhere, the wideness of the Kanto Plain seems to flow around you.

It is 158.5 meters long. Though it swells in a gentle arc, of the six large new bridges over the Sumida River, the Kiyosu Bridge is the beauty of the curve, and the Kototoi is the beauty of the straight line. The Kiyosu is a woman. The Kototoi is a man.

And so Onatsu presses her cheek against the steel of the railing: Oh, it's so cold.

She is sixteen and always wears heavy makeup. But she has a habit of rubbing her lips together. So her deep red lipstick is often smeared outside the corners of her mouth. Men see this as a sign of her being easy and consequently get lured in.

Of course, her lips this morning are still smeared with last night's lipstick.

—Runt, the fog hangs over the bridge. See, it's still raining way over there.

—Guess so.

—So sleepy . . .

—From tonight, can't you tie Ochiyo to you with a piece of string or something so she has to sleep next to you?

—The fog just hangs on my face.

Her right cheek is all blotchy, as if the white powder has been absorbed.

—You know if it's fog or dew?

The covered truck of some rag picker goes from Honjo to Asakusa, a one-yen taxi carrying a woman in a violet *haori* coat goes from Honjo to Asakusa, a Chinese noodle seller is on his way home to Honjo from Asakusa, a youthful baseball team goes from Honjo to Asakusa, a marathon runner goes from Asakusa to Honjo, another rag picker goes from Honjo to Asakusa, a woman in wooden sandals, no socks, wearing a dress as transparent as white gauze, completely revealing her body, goes from Asakusa to Honjo, and since it has now gotten light, she quickens her pace as if she does not want to be noticed—but why she wears something so thin that she is almost naked beneath is beyond me. Other than this traffic and a few laborers, nobody else passes, not even an empty taxi.

—There was a really thick fog in the middle of the night on New Year's Eve. And thanks to the fog, Yumiko's life was saved, right?

—Yoo-hoo! And Boat Runt is standing on the bridge handrail, a straw sandal in each hand.

He walks on the railing as if on a tightrope. This handrail comes up to an adult's chest, and it is only as wide as the span of a hand.

—You making fun of me? And Onatsu starts running as fast as she can.

They say a boy stole the platinum ball from the top of the lightning rod on the big chimney of the Susaki landfill garbage incinerator. There is also a rumor that a young boy roosts on the top of Asakusa's Five Story Pagoda. Then there is the boy who stole the hilt of Danjurō's sword.

There are many reckless stunts like these, and the public toilet that's been built right on the belly of the artificial hill in front of the Hanayashiki on the east bank of Gourd Pond, its concrete roof garden has already become both a place for enjoying the cool breezes and a sleeping place, its handrail is just as narrow as that of the Kototoi Bridge. And dear reader, have you noticed the man who always sleeps on that railing? His back hangs off both sides, and his legs dangle down, one in each direction.

I've seen a few kids walking on the handrail of the Kototoi Bridge. Always in the morning.

—And now I'm finally awake. And off he goes down the steps to Sumida Park and runs right under the bridge, yelling at the top of his lungs:

—Stu-pid! Stu-pid! Stu-pid!

The echo of steel.

55

Onatsu waits in front of this sign at the entrance to the site of the former Mito Residence.

The bums on the benches under the bridge look up. The echo of steel has disturbed their slumbers.

With a steel roof, concrete walls, and river breezes blowing through, this is a great sleeping place in the summer. Dear reader, you probably read in the newspaper about that strange festival of beggars held just recently in the middle of July. Banging on old buckets and waving old rags like banners, the beggars all got drunk, sang songs, danced. Half in desperation, they offered up prayers for the world in the midst of this recession when they hardly receive handouts anymore.

—People can say what they want, but I know the scene here. The dogs that prowl about Asakusa's Okuyama, I know which spotted mutt is going with which white bitch and which red dog got the brush-off from which black pup near Gourd Pond. Thus boasts Asakusa expert Satō Hachirō. And the first thing he mentions in the "Roundtable Discussion on the Bizarre in Tokyo" is: Even the bad boys now go hungry.

I do not know whether it is because of this or not, but "talent" has gone out of style, and instead it is lately fashionable for a pretty girl be made the leader of a gang.

—Stu-pid! Stu-pid! Stu-pid! yells Boat Runt like a child who really likes the sound of the echo of steel, but acting surprised because he woke up the beggars, he comes running back as fast as he can.

The grounds of the former Mito Residence are vast and green.

Only the oleander has a few flowers. In the middle is a Japanese landscape garden, and the lawn is the deep green of morning in the West.

—See? It's fog.

Something white flows over the green. Freshness, as if you'd just washed your feet. The park opens at eight, but the neighborhood residents are already taking wake-up walks with dogs and kids.

A girl and a German hunting dog sit on a semicircle of lawn dotted with larch trees. This girl, disheveled, seems out of place with the neatly ordered landscape, as if a foreigner were drawing a Japanese picture.

The dog comes bounding toward us and puts his paws on Onatsu's shoulder.

—Tesu, Tesu, that you? If you've been with her, then there's no reason for us to come here. And she strokes his muzzle. His fur is cold, and there is blood on Onatsu's hand.

—Oh! And looking sharply at the girl: Chiyo, something happen to Tesu?

—Yes, he was in a fight. But Ochiyo is smiling.

—With another dog?

—More like beggars.

—People?

—Strange. Beggars are people?

—I'm not kidding, Ochiyo. Crazy ladies are women, too. So you'd better be careful. Onatsu helps Ochiyo to her feet, and, carefully looking her over: Your *yukata* has gotten soaked from the fog. Last night it was heavy. Did you sleep out here?

—Not here.

—Then where?

Without a word, Ochiyo starts to walk away.

—Even though they're beggars, did Tesu bite them?

—Probably Snazzy Sankichi, Boat Runt says between whistles.

—Is Sankichi the fellow who always takes a quick dip in the fountain behind the Kannon Temple?

—You don't know him? He always chases after our Chiyo because she was called a butterfly years ago, and now he walks around Asakusa singing: Ochiyo and Sankichi, Sankichi and Ochiyo.

The white morning fog is growing thinner on the green lawn. The brilliant green stands out against the earth.

In her fish-scale-patterned *yukata* and her fashionable white unlined Hakata sash, Ochiyo looks like a stylish downtown girl, but somehow new dirt is beginning to cling to her. That earthy smell of the bums. Night and day are the same to her. If you take your eye off her, she'll just disappear into the park.

—I was over there. And when we have almost reached the asphalt riverbank, she points to a bench shaded by pine trees.

—There? You mean last night? Did you sleep alone?

—No, there were four of us. Three men, but Tesu took care of them, says Ochiyo, nonchalant.

56

WASHINGTON'S POTOMAC, London's Thames, Paris's Seine, Budapest's Danube, Munich's Isar—Sumida Park, the landscape that the Reconstruction Bureau and the Ministry of Parks Administration boast can hold its own against riverside parks of world cities. With its abundant water, wide panorama, and rows of cherry trees, it covers an area of 187,677.6 square meters, and the Mukōjima embankment is 1,170 meters long.

Onatsu and the others stand right at the south end next to the Tobu Line iron railroad bridge, gazing upriver, and the surface of the Kototoi Bridge becomes hazy in the morning colors, an asphalted, gleaming, still-damp plane.

The river, the bank with its willows, a sidewalk, a row of cherry trees, a sidewalk, a row of cherry trees, a roadway, a row of cherry trees, a sidewalk, a row of cherry trees—this is the ground plan, and the cherry trees form four columns on the narrow rectangle of grass, and the willowed riverbank is likewise covered with grass.

—I thought it smelled like the beach, and now I know why.

—Huh? What do you mean?

Boat Runt cannot read the sign:

DEPARTMENT OF THE INTERIOR,
MUKŌJIMA SALT WATER TESTING STATION

Perhaps because it is Sunday, across the river on the Asakusa side, from the end of the Azuma Bridge to Hashiba, white uniformed figures are putting up a net—amateur baseball.

Boat Runt starts running with the dog. Onatsu calls the dog back. Boat Runt calls to him again. While the dog makes a big arc running back and forth between the two, Ochiyo falls asleep on the bench.

—Newspaper! Get your newspaper! Morning edition with all the want ads! It must be the time when the newspaper sellers make their rounds from bench to bench in Asakusa Park. It must be the time when the cops in white make their rounds inspecting the crowd of homeless.

It might so happen that a young fellow, rubbing his eyes, explains just who the guy with him is.

—He's a soldier.

Though the cop gives him a good shake, the guy next to the young fellow doesn't wake up. When he finally opens his eyes in a daze: Come with me.

Confused, he picks up his soldier cap and jacket from back in the shrubs, and, with his military sack dangling, off he goes to the police station with the young fellow. The regulars at the Open Air Hotel take no notice of scenes like this.

It must be the time when the *tekiya,* trying to make money off the morning visitors to the temple, take advantage of the stores on both sides still being asleep to set up flimsy stalls on the Nakamise.

Maps, inflatable pillows, mice, handwriting manuals, perfume, pipes, socks, brooms, clay masks, the twelve Chinese zodiac signs on belts, kimono collars, live turtles, knickknacks two for fifteen sen, children's clothes, freshly dried gourd shavings, decorative garden stones, sandal straps, citrus fruit, water lilies still with their roots, ribbons, miniature watering carts, stands for flower vases, fans, ornamental hairpins, rubber dolls, sago palm seedlings, handkerchiefs, freshly dried sardines, skirts, rings, charred vipers, thin cord, notebooks with a scale, used books, chirping bugs, warm sleeping clothes for children so that they will not catch colds, mirrors, horoscopes, writing brushes, cut flowers, hats, small boxes made of paulownia wood, seedling trees, suspenders, undershirts, wooden sandals, purses, medical herbs to prevent diarrhea—this is what I saw at the Nakamise street stalls one July morning.

Already on the Kototoi Bridge, stands have also been set up, selling chilled coffee—one cup for two sen and three cups for five sen— and garters and pears and hat cleaners and *go* and chess pieces and watermelon slices.

But only the dog is acting like it is morning because both Onatsu and Boat Runt are sleepy.

This is the dog Komada stole from his uncle's house at Yumiko's request, and she trained this puppy for Ochiyo.

Komada is the fellow who watched the Kurenai-maru with a telescope from the top of the Subway Tower, and he is Oharu's sweetheart. If I don't explain a little of Oharu's past, you won't understand.

While still a maid at an inn in Chiba's Funagata, the fifteen- or sixteen-year-old Oharu's only dream in life was to be a hairdresser in Tokyo's geisha district. One of the summer visitors at the inn promised to arrange this for her. He was not lying to her. Though he cheated her out of the money she entrusted to him for traveling expenses, he set her up as an apprentice to an Asakusa hairdresser. The hairdresser's shop was on the street next to where the Showa Theater is now and near the Aritake Pet Shop.

But before she realized it, without her knowing, she got sold from one man to the next, something a country girl like her is not supposed to understand.

streets echoing with gunshots

57

A REALLY NICE AUNTIE—there are lots of these.

At first she pretends to be a new customer, and she's a really smooth talker. Among the four or five assistants, she is especially nice to Oharu. She asks if she were born in Bōshū. She says she can tell by her accent.

—I spent a summer in Funagata in Bōshū.

—Oh?

—Ah, aren't you from near there, my dear Haru? But of course I'm not so upper-class I can live in such luxury. I was just taking my sister's children to go swimming, as their nanny.

Oharu also meets this nice auntie a few times at the public bath. Auntie scrubs Oharu's black neck with a small rice-bran sack while she sings the praises of her white skin. She treats Oharu to sweet bean soup on the way home. She slips her theater tickets. When Oharu goes to the theater, without her noticing, the nice auntie slides into the seat next to her. There is a young man with her. A university student lodging on the second floor of Auntie's house.

—It would be good if I could give you more tickets, but since I like you so much better than the other girls at the shop, if I only give you tickets, they all will get jealous. So, dear Haru, why don't you come over to my house on your next day off?

—Okay, but . . .

—Oh, it's all right. Ah, I say it's all right, but I forgot that you don't know where I live. I'll show you on the way home today. You have time to come over, don't you?

Her house is in Komagata.

If she lives over in Komagata, why would Auntie go out of her way to a public bath near Asakusa Park? That's what Oharu ought to have asked herself.

Oharu is pulled into the living room. She listens as Auntie tells the university student what a bright future he will have. The university student acts shy, as if she is embarrassing him. But Oharu is just a former maid at a country inn whose only dream in life is to be a hairdresser. So she is not seduced by such talk of bright futures. She hurries home. But on her next day off, she goes to call on Auntie at her house.

And one month passes. Auntie comes to have her hair done after nine at night, her arms full of packages.

—I was just on my way to see relatives in Ueno, and I realized I wouldn't be returning home until very late, and, when you go shopping, there's always so much to carry.

—If you wish, you can leave your packages here.

—Thanks. But if it is all right, I thought that to save on taxi fare it would be nice if my dear Haru could take a small trip down to my place and drop them off.

—As you like.

The next morning, waking up on the second floor of Auntie's house, Oharu finds herself in bed stark naked. Shocked, she runs her hands over her hips, and, yes, she is naked. The man is not there.

She jumps out of bed and turns on the light, and in the dressing table mirror stands her white, naked body. She pulls off the quilt. The sheet from last night is also gone. She opens the wardrobe, and it is empty. There is nothing to cover her naked body, not even a kimono sash cord. Frantic, she slips back into bed. Drawing up her knees, she curls into a ball, trembling, embarrassed, as if afraid to touch her naked body with her own hands. She does not even realize that she is crying.

But she is restless. Not knowing what to do with herself, she gets up again. Sitting in front of the dressing table, she sees her naked body in the mirror, and she begins to calm down. Her own nakedness somehow seems strange to her. So much so that she suddenly stops crying. After trying to catch a glimpse of what is going on downstairs, she turns round and round in front of the mirror, gazing at her naked body. Again, she peeps downstairs and crawls back in front of the mirror, staring at the reflection of her own strange figure. Then falling to the ground, she lies on her side, but, instead of breaking into tears, she bursts out laughing. A new woman is born.

Then, for the next five days, Oharu lies stark naked in this second-floor bed.

58

BUSINESS HOURS ARE FROM SUNRISE TO 12:00 A.M.

PATRONS IN AN OBVIOUSLY INTOXICATED STATE WILL NOT
BE PERMITTED TO PLAY.

LEWD MEANS WILL NOT BE USED TO SOLICIT PASSERSBY.

PUBLIC MORALS WILL NOT BE VIOLATED.

WITH THE EXCEPTION OF THE PROPRIETOR AND STAFF,
ENTRANCE INTO THE INTERIOR GUN ROOM IS STRICTLY
PROHIBITED.

BY THE ORDER OF THE AUTHORITIES, THE STAFF IS
PROHIBITED FROM ACCEPTING FREE TICKETS, GRATUITIES,
AND OTHER GIFTS.

These are the rules posted on the target room wall next to the gun counter. From the front hang long strips of paper pasted with Shikishima cigarettes like the New Year's decorations at shrines. Below, on the second shelf, are Shikishima and Bat cigarettes, and on the shelf below them, dolls and sweets. On the other side of the nearly two-meter-long wooden floor of the shooting gallery is the counter and on top of it are enamel bullets and rifles, and there is a tapestry like a stage curtain, and, on both sides of the gallery, there are mirrors, and, in this stall (same now as in the past and will never change) stands a woman with her hair in the ginkgo-leaf style.

—No matter how old-fashioned this pastime is, we're not about to change all of a sudden into a mahjong parlor. That's only a passing fad. Ours is a business with a long tradition.

—Anyway, for starters, you girls need to get with the times. Cut your *momoware* hairdo into a bob. I would have liked to reply. But anyhow, behind the Park Theater, Denkikan, and the Asakusa Theater, in other words, in the rear of the first and second sections of Asakusa's Rokku, in the best place for shooting galleries, they are lined up one after another. The second most popular spot is the west side of the Rokku, especially behind the Tokyo Cinema and the Asakusa Performance Guild. And another place, though rather shabby, there are still standing, all in all, nearly forty stalls behind the Hanayashiki. From these "streets echoing with gunshots," Oharu appeared wearing Western clothes. Down from the second-floor bed of Auntie's house where she lay stark naked. The shooting galleries were where she shook out a living in Asakusa.

It was the time of local shooting. It was the time of many shooting contests. It was not unusual for a customer to shoot one hundred or one hundred and fifty rounds, and there were many people who could not fall asleep without the sound of gunshots. A one-armed fellow named Ogawa was so taken with the Sakurada stall that he could not bear to leave it, and, even when the stall owner gave him a little money to take a trip (he left with the goal of becoming a great actor in Kyoto or Osaka), the next day he was standing right at the stall next door, firing away. Just a prime example of the charm of the shooting galleries in those days.

Left-Handed Hiko, Loose-Hair Oito, and I, the three of us went with Oharu to a shooting gallery just the other evening.

Since he'd gotten wind that some artist apprentices, members of the Horse Votive Club, frequented the shooting galleries, Hiko wanted to go check it out. Me, I wanted to meet the girl at the Kirakutei stall because she would have lots of material for stories.

The Kirakutei is in front of the Park Theater dressing room. At the dressing room entrance, members of a backstage crew are getting some fresh air. Naked actors look out at us from the dressing room window.

Oharu does not seem to want to hold a rifle, and she only talks about old times with the woman in the ginkgo hairdo.

—As pretty as a French doll. Oharu as a bride. I can still see it now. What's that man up to now? When you used to come to the shooting galleries, people always said the plays couldn't begin because the actors crowded at the window to see you. Western clothes like yours were real unusual back then.

—It's also unusual that you haven't changed a bit these ten years.

—But you didn't even know me ten years ago.

Later, as Oharu explained to me: The girl at the Kirakutei was adopted by a family in the countryside right after she was born. Her real father was a *Naniwa bushi* singer. He had always commuted from his shooting gallery to a *yose* theater in the park. When she was eighteen, the girl went to visit this father of hers, and, while helping out at the shooting gallery, she fell into the business.

That was twelve or thirteen years ago, but, even now, she looks only about twenty-two or twenty-three. These days, she has taken over the shooting gallery and has set her father up with a grocery stand. Then she sent for her adopted parents from the countryside and has also taken care of them.

Oharu's time at the shooting gallery was six or seven years ago. Today it would be hard to even make a tenth of what they took in ten years ago, and, on a good day, they make only about four or five yen.

—The time when our Haru played at being a bride, business was growing. And like the girl said, after those honeymoon days, Oharu picked up her Komada at the shooting gallery.

mirrors and nudity

59

IT GOES WITHOUT SAYING that the fellow who lured Oharu to Tokyo was a ruffian who plundered the summer resorts, and his setting her up at a hairdresser's was really like depositing stolen goods in a safe place for a while.

Oharu still did not suspect a thing, and he sold one of his buddies all the "rights" to her, including the right to sell her off to someone else. The buyer was the fellow from the second floor of Auntie's house. The way Auntie saw it, this Terasaka, a chump, was easy to cheat.

Auntie's house was a "private house of assignation," and Auntie herself was the madam. So Auntie had fetched Terasaka's purchase from storage for him. The way Auntie says it, she uses chumps like Terasaka. For example, if Oharu had managed to escape that night, Auntie would have been with her relatives in Ueno the whole time. She was not worried. Keeping Oharu stark naked so she could not escape was a clever idea. Of course, Terasaka's lodging on the second floor of Auntie's house was a lie.

The miniature stone garden in the alcove of the room, then the dressing table and red kimono rack. Right after Terasaka asked her up to the second floor, Oharu saw through it. When she opened up Auntie's paper-wrapped packages, all she saw were three old cushions.

—I don't know what possessed me to look at my naked body in the mirror like that afterward, Oharu said, but, anyway, in those five naked days, she fell madly in love with Terasaka. She loved him like crazy so she could escape a second danger—though she did not really know this at the time, and at first she was timid, but then in her desperation, she mustered her courage and utterly transformed into such a beauty that she ended up confusing Terasaka.

Instead of selling her, he was made to buy her Western clothes. Then she started to frequent the shooting galleries as Terasaka's bride. When she ran into the girls from the hairdresser's, she just acted aloof and turned away.

To Terasaka and his pals, dropping in at the shooting galleries on their way to and from the park was something like good manners among buddies. The Bat stall across from the Kinshatei was their hangout. It was an unusual stall in that it was not run by a woman but by an old man and his son and the brother of the old man, who sponged off them.

SHOOT DOWN THE STACK OF THREE PACKS OF SHIKISHIMA WITH FOUR BULLETS, GET TWENTY-FIVE SEN.

SHOOT DOWN THE STACK OF THREE PACKS OF SHIKISHIMA WITH THREE BULLETS, GET EIGHTEEN SEN.

SHOOT DOWN SHIKISHIMA ON A PAPER STRIP WITH THREE BULLETS, GET EIGHTEEN SEN.

SHOOT DOWN THE CERAMIC CAT OVER THE SHIKISHIMA WITH THREE BULLETS, GET EIGHTEEN SEN AND A PACK OF SHIKISHIMA.

SHOOT DOWN THE STACK OF THREE PACKS OF BAT WITH THREE BULLETS, GET A PACK OF ASAHI AND SEVEN SEN.

SHOOT DOWN THE STACK OF FOUR PACKS OF BAT WITH FOUR BULLETS, GET EIGHTEEN SEN.

SHOOT DOWN THE FANCY DOLLS WITH THREE BULLETS, GET TWENTY SEN.

SHOOT DOWN THE REGULAR DOLLS WITH FIVE BULLETS, GET TEN SEN.

SHOOT DOWN ACCORDING TO CHARACTER COMBINATION, GET EIGHTEEN SEN.

There are nowadays these nine options, and they would have been just the same back then.

But even though there are these nine options, from the days of yore, Asakusa regulars have always tried for the three packs of Bat. You almost never see anyone try for the three packs Shikishima or the Shikishima on a paper strip.

And sharpshooters like Terasaka have, of course, mastered the three packs of Bat and pay only the bullet cost of two sen per round. The shooting gallery would fold if they had to give up packs of cigarettes each time, so they let them have their fun for just two sen.

So they have contests for sport, and they only count shooting techniques, like the Break Even and Percentage and Twist and Mountain Path.

Anyway, back then, a fifteen- or sixteen-year-old boy would come every day to shoot at that Bat stall. He came at noon and had himself an hour of fun, and then he came back for another hour of fun in the evening. And one day he was there from afternoon and got sushi and sake for the old man's brother, and even in the evening, he still showed no signs of leaving.

60

AT THE END of the counter, all stacked with piles of packs of Bat, there are three packs standing on their sides with two matchboxes between them. You are supposed to take down all three packs of Bat with your three bullets and just leave the matchboxes. In the second round, there are two packs of Bat stacked at a right angle in the back corner of the Shikishima counter. These need to be shot down with a single bullet. In the third round, there are six packs of Bat in a diagonal row. These need to be shot down with just three bullets.

This is the "cigarette contest" that evening—they say the old man who runs the Bat stall puts the cigarettes in positions more difficult than anywhere else in the park, so the regulars gather there to show off their "shooting skills," and it doesn't matter to them if there's a girl there or not. Usually a shooting contest takes place when some fellow makes the rounds of the shooting galleries, gets a bit of pocket money together, and pays for one of the stall owners to sponsor it, for example, reserving a place near the Kappabashi Bridge and getting together once a month with fellows who share his interest. Or a group of blowhards starting up a contest after a stall has closed for the day—just like that night at the Bat.

By the time they'd finished, it was almost one in the morning.

—Look here, sport, you've just been watching all day. We're closing now. Come back tomorrow.

—Okay. And the boy stands in the corner of the stall without budging, looking dejected. Seeing this, Oharu runs right over to him and puts her hand on his shoulder.

—Sport, come with me. Come over to my home, okay?

—Okay. And this mature girl in beautiful Western clothes suddenly speaking to him so kindly has made him blush.

—It's okay. You can stay over if you want.

As they go back to a flophouse in Mukōjima, Oharu gently puts one of her *yukata* sleeves over him like a tender embrace and touches his pants.

—Hey, you got a lot of money on you, sport. Kids shouldn't carry so much money around. You can leave it with us if you want to. You can stay here as long as you want, sport.

—I had more on me this morning, but I gave the old man at the shooting gallery thirty yen. He also said, just like you, that kids shouldn't carry so much money around, but if I'd handed all of it over, he'd've thought there was something fishy going on.

There is two hundred and fifty yen in the purse the boy gave Oharu.

Terasaka, who seemed disgusted until now, looks Oharu full in the face, dumbfounded.

—Look at that! I knew it! exclaims Oharu. It has been just one month since she gazed at her naked body in the mirror.

—Sport, where'd you get that money? You do something bad . . . Terasaka starts, but Oharu cuts him off.

—Don't be stupid. You're not a cop. Don't worry, sport, and just go to sleep. It's late.

There is only one mattress. Terasaka falls asleep right away.

The boy took the money from his uncle's safe. For a while now, he's pocketed two or three yen a day and gone off to Asakusa with it. That's all there is to it. Lured by the mysterious charm of Asakusa. His uncle lives in Ōgawa-machi in Kanda. That's where the boy was used as an apprentice.

Oharu listens as the boy tells her this and gently encircles his neck with her hands, and, while running her fingertips down his chin: That safe, is it a big one?

—The shop's safe is little. But I know where he keeps the key.

—You know, that sports shirt and white pants getup looks pretty bad.

—But this is how I always dress when I run errands.

—All right. But tomorrow we're going to take some of that money and get you some Western or Japanese clothes.

—I want Western clothes.

—And one more thing. From today on, you're our little brother. Wherever we go, you have to call us brother and sister. Okay?

—Okay.

—Oh, and tomorrow when we go buy you Western clothes, I want you to get me something, too.

And Oharu is only one year older than the boy.

61

KOMADA, WHO STOLE the shepherd puppy for Ochiyo, was this boy six or seven years ago.

The first batch of cash had been enough to buy two Western outfits and a gramophone. The three of them enjoyed themselves on the rest of it. But when they went to the shooting gallery to fetch the thirty yen: Oh, I spent it right away. Sport, didn't you say it was for me?

If the money is gone, the boy is nothing but a bother.

—You've got no other choice. Go on back to your uncle.

—It's no fun if there's no money. I'll go get us more.

And seeing the boy so heartbroken and unhappy, Oharu puts an idea in his head. With the money, he could buy her back from Terasaka.

Then the Red Sash Society, the Black Sash Society, the Scarlet Gang. For five or six years, Komada has followed Oharu around, and he has already become part of the Asakusa scene, and, as Oharu herself admits, she would be entirely lost without him.

And Komada is, for some reason or another, still attracted to her charms, smitten like a lovesick puppy. Oharu thinks he should make a fresh start with a nice, capable young woman. She asked Yumiko for help in this.

—Are you saying that I'm that kind of girl? Or that I should go find him a girl like that? Yumiko asked curtly.

By the way, dear reader, as for Yumiko . . .

When I'd reached this point in my story, I met Yumiko in a strange way, and so my novel must also suddenly change course.

I once compared my novel to a boat, and it was actually on a boat—we are riding together on one of those Sumida River Steamboat Company one-sen steamboats.

I get on at the Hama-chō riverbank and am going in the direction of the Azuma Bridge.

A girl selling Oshima hair oil stares at me, her pupils up somewhere near her upper eyelids. A cheap hip-length navy blue coat with white splashes, purple apron, navy blue gaiters, rubber-soled cloth boots, black cloth-wrapped package resting on her knees, and also oiled paper, a round wicker hat with bamboo slats on the sides for support—one stand of hair cuts across her cheek and droops down over her sunburned face. With only a light dusting of makeup, she looks every bit a country blossom but with a touch of the big city in her. She seems to fit in fine with this old-fashioned boat. Muslin waistcloth sticks out from her hem.

Sober-faced, she starts laughing in spite of herself.

—How about a bottle of camellia oil from Oshima? Would make a good present for your wife.

Yumiko!

—I knew I'd seen you somewhere before. Surely . . .

—Or how about some shampoo made with oil from coral roots and kelp roots? Makes your hair shiny and thick.

—As usual, you overplay your role.

—You too. Why are you on this boat?

—After you were taken away on that white motorboat, I wanted to continue writing my story, and I've been going around looking at the Ōkawa River scenery.

—Don't write about the oil seller, okay?

—Disguised as an oil seller. How do you want the story to go on?

—She's looking for someone.

—But you're always looking for someone.

—No, that's not true. She's got to make a living somehow—how does that sound?

—And you can rent an outfit like that at a costume shop?

—Oh no. I borrowed it from a real oil seller.

—And what about this girl?

—Now she's in Asakusa listening to *manzai*. Or this oil seller is just hanging around the stage door. They don't call it oil selling for nothing, you know.

The boat arrives at the Azuma Bridge, and while putting on her round wicker hat, Yumiko says: Now it's even harder to recognize me.

She stands up. Her short blue coat with its white splashes is ripped in the back.

ドナルド
リッチイ様

川端康成

Yasunari Kawabata and Donald Richie, late 1940s. Courtesy Donald Richie.

afterword
donald richie

ONE LATE JANUARY day in 1947, two men were climbing the stairs of the Subway Tower building in Asakusa. The elder, who was forty-eight, wore a kimono and a fedora. The younger, who was twenty-three, was wearing a PX jacket and a civilian shirt. They were climbing the tower so that the Japanese could show the American the old downtown section of Asakusa, or what was left of it.

The reason for this expedition was that the elder, Kawabata, had many years before written *Asakusa kurenaidan* and that the younger, myself, was interested in Asakusa and the as-yet-untranslated book. The younger did not know that the other was a famous writer—the major translations of his work were a whole decade away. The older man knew nothing of the younger except that he seemed well-intentioned and enthusiastic.

Seemed, because there was no way of ascertaining. The Japanese spoke no English, and the American at that time spoke no Japanese. The army interpreter was in bed with a cold, and the English-speaking friend Kawabata had summoned had not shown up. So these two men finally gained the belfried roof of the Subway Tower with everything to say to each other and no way to say it.

The Sumida River, silver in the winter sun, glistened beneath us. We looked out over downtown Tokyo, still in ruins, still showing the conflagration of two years earlier, burned concrete black against the lemon yellow of new wood.

This had been Asakusa. Around the great temple of the Kannon, now a blackened, empty square, had grown a warren of bars, theaters, archery stalls, circus tents, peep shows, places where, I had read, the all-girl opera sang and kicked, where the tattooed gamblers met and bet, where trained dogs walked on their hind legs and Japan's fattest lady sat in state.

Now, two years later, all of this had gone up in flames, after so many of those who worked and played here had burned in the streets or boiled in the canals as the incendiary bombs fell and the B-29's thundered over—now, the empty squares were again turning into lanes, as tents, reed lean-tos, a few frame buildings began appearing. Girls in wedgies were sitting in front of new tearooms, but I saw no sign of the world's fattest lady. Perhaps she had bubbled away in the fire.

Was that what Kawabata was thinking? I wondered, looking at the avian profile of the middle-aged man standing beside me, outlined against the pale winter sky.

"Yumiko," I said, pointing to the silver river beneath us. This was the name of the heroine of the novel he had written when he— twenty years ago, then about the same age I was, and as enraptured of the place as I was now—walked the labyrinth and saw, as he later wrote, the jazz revues, the kiss-dances, the exhibitions of the White Russian girls, and the passing Japanese flappers with their rolled stockings. Where Yumiko had confronted the villain, crushed an arsenic pill between her teeth, and then kissed him full on the lips.

Perhaps he was thinking of this scene from his novel and of the lost Yumiko, tough, muscled, beautiful. Or, looking over that blackened landscape, under this huge white winter sky, perhaps he was feeling a great sorrow. All those lives lost in that blazing, roaring conflagration below.

Imagining a sadness I assumed that I in his place would be feeling, I looked at that birdlike profile. It did not seem sad. Rather, Kawabata smiled, looked over the parapet and indicated the river.

This was where, I knew, the insolent Yumiko, having given the kiss of death to the older man (who, it transpired, was the lover of the local madwoman, who, it turned out, was really our heroine's sister), was taken away by the water police, only to reappear in the final pages of the novel.

I knew all this without knowing any Japanese because, as a member of the Allied Occupation, I had translators at my command and had ordered an English précis of the novel. Now, looking at the author leaning over the edge, as had Left-Handed Hiko and Haruko as they spied the escaping Yumiko, I thought about Kawabata's love for Asakusa.

He had begun his book with the intention of writing a "long, strange novel in which only lowly women would appear." Asakusa had perhaps been for him as it was for me, a place that allowed anonymity, freedom, where life flowed on no matter what, where you could pick up pleasure, and where small rooms with paper flowers were rented by the hour.

Did he, I wonder, find freedom in flesh, as I had learned to? It was here, on the roof of the terminal, that Haruko had permitted herself to be kissed—and more—by members of the gang and had thus earned herself the title Bride of the Eiffel Tower. It was here that the Akaobikai, that group of red-sashed girls who in the daytime worked in respectable department stores, boasted about the

The Subway Restaurant Tower, site of
several pivotal scenes in *The Scarlet Gang of Asakusa*,
ca. 1930. The sign on the side of the building
indicates the entrance to the subway.

bad things they did at night; here that Umekichi disclosed that he
had been molested at the age of six by a forty-year-old woman.

I wondered about all of this but had no way of asking. And now,
chilled by that great sky, we went down the steep stairs, compan-
ionable but inarticulate. I had given him an outing; he had given

me his bird's-eye view of Asakusa. He was also now thoroughly chilled and had begun to cough.

Seeking to warm himself, he suggested coffee. This was a fairly rare and expensive commodity in 1947 Japan. Moreover, as a member of the Occupying Forces, I was not allowed to enter any of the few coffee shops in the city. This was the era when signs were still displayed announcing "Fraternization with the Indigenous Personnel is Forbidden." Naturally, I accepted at once.

The shop is still there, tucked into the street behind what is left of the theater avenue. Here we warmed ourselves over a hibachi and drank bitter Black Arabian and had a conversation. It was a literary conversation. I said, "Gide." He looked thoughtful, nodded, and said, "Mann." I thought, then said, "*Tonio Kröger,*" at which he broke into a smile and said, "*Der Zauberberg.*" In this fashion we talked about Flaubert, Poe, Zweig. I drew a blank on Proust because he had not yet been completely translated into Japanese. Kawabata received nothing for Colette because I did not yet know this admirable writer.

This continued until the coffee was finished and we were warm enough to go out. He was taking the subway. I, not allowed by the Occupation authorities to take it, was to begin my circuitous streetcar route home. With much bowing and shaking of hands (I bowed, he shook hands), we parted.

What struck me then and strikes me now about this literary non-encounter is not how much we couldn't say, but how much we managed to communicate. His patience, his air (habitual, it turned out) of slight sadness, his bemused awareness while surveying the dead ruins of what for him had been alive—all of this was communication. When I now read a Kawabata novel and observe a person silent but aware, knowing an emotion but not partaking of it, I see Kawabata on that cold January afternoon.

I DID NOT SEE Kawabata again for over ten years and then, at the PEN conference, the sun reflecting off the Sukiyabashi Canal just outside the big French windows, I was introduced to the white-haired man who as president had been presiding.

"Oh, but we know each other," he said to the man who was introducing us. "We spent a very chilly afternoon together some ten years or so ago. I caught a cold. Was in bed for a week."

He looked at me, kindly, inquisitively, released my hand: "I imagine he doesn't even remember me."

"But I do," I said.

"He speaks," said the writer, surprised. Then, to the other man: "There we were, stuck up there, the old Subway Tower in Asakusa, and I was wondering what to do about him. He was so terribly enthusiastic and kept pointing things out. And we couldn't talk."

"Tell me," I said, a decade-old curiosity returning: "What were you thinking of that day on the roof when we were looking out over Asakusa?"

"I don't remember."

"But how did you feel about Asakusa all burned? You were seeing it for the first time since the war was over."

"Oh, that. I don't know. Surprise maybe. Sadness probably."

He had gotten over Asakusa. Had he gotten over it ten years before, when we stood there in that cold glare? I wasn't over it, even yet, doubted I ever would be. For me Asakusa had spread to cover the city, the country, maybe even the world.

"And you, did you ever translate *Asakusa kurenaidan?*" he asked.

"I never learned to read."

"Well, at least you learned to speak. We can talk, finally."

And he smiled, his white head cocked toward the flowing glare of the slow canal and the distant clamor of the Tokyo traffic.

But we never did. And now people were pushing, wanting to

speak to the famous novelist. We had already had our talk. And whenever we thereafter met, Kawabata would tilt his head to one side and look at me quizzically, humorously, as though we had something in common.

TEN YEARS LATER, the translation of *The House of the Sleeping Beauties* appeared and I saw that Kawabata had been as true to his vision of Asakusa as I had been to mine. Yumiko, or her daughter, was now in this strange house in Kamakura where old men could find their youth in these sleeping girls, in that firm and dormant flesh.

And after that, one day in 1972, a quarter of a century after he and I had stood on the Asakusa tower and thought of Yumiko, I saw his face flash on the television screen. The avian profile flew past— noted author dead, a suicide.

I did not believe it. Dead, yes, but not a suicide. How could anyone who so loved life, flesh, Asakusa, kill himself? No, it was an accident. The bathroom. The body had been found there, the water running. He had been going to take a bath. He had used the gas hose as a support. He pulled it loose, was overcome. This I wanted to believe. I could hear the water running, and I remembered the silver of the Sumida and the muddy bronze of the Sukiyabashi Canal.

But in time I too came to believe that it was suicide. The gas-filled arsenic kiss had been chosen. Naked, free, Kawabata had stepped into the water just as Yumiko had slipped into the boat.

I turned off the television and closed my eyes. I saw the unwinding Sumida, a molten silver under the great staring sky. I saw him flying off in the motorboat with Yumiko, racing away forever.

glossary

Numbers in parentheses indicate the chapters in which these terms are first mentioned.

Amanoya Rihee: (17) (1662(?)–1727) Osaka salesman who supplied the forty-seven *rōnin* (masterless samurai) with the weapons they needed to storm Lord Kira's mansion and assassinate him on January 31, 1703. The forty-seven *rōnin* served under Asano Naganori, the Lord of Ako, whose death they believed was due to Lord Kira Yoshinaka, a retainer of the Tokugawa shogun. Their deed was celebrated as an example of warrior ethics and loyalty, but it also raised questions among Confucian scholars and the government of the time as to how the forty-seven men should be punished for committing murder. The story of the forty-seven *rōnin* became the subject of theater and literature, including the mid-eighteenth-century puppet play and kabuki drama *Chūshingura*.

Aquarium: (3) Open to the public in October 1899, the Aquarium was located in the fourth district of Asakusa Park. The upper floors of the building were used for the Casino Folies revue.

Arakawa drainage canal: (36) The Arakawa River flows though Saitama and Tokyo prefectures into Tokyo Bay. A drainage canal to prevent flooding and fires was proposed in 1911 and completed by 1930 in the northern part of Tokyo.

Asahi cigarettes: (59) Cigarette brand first sold in 1904.

***Asahi* newspaper:** (14) Popular daily newspaper with Tokyo and Osaka morning and evening editions in which thirty-seven chapters of *The Scarlet Gang of Asakusa* were serialized between December 20, 1929, and February 16, 1930.

Asaji Plain: (27) Area on the west bank of the Ōkawa.

Asakusa Elementary School: (5) Brick school building opened in 1888.

Asakusa Honganji: (40) Temple outside the Sensō Temple complex and one of Tokyo's oldest reinforced-concrete structures.

Asakusa Kannon: (1) Also called the Kannon of Konryūsan-Sensōji and referred to in *The Scarlet Gang of Asakusa* as the Goddess of Mercy; a bodhisattva personifying divine compassion. This deity originated in India as the male god Avalokitesvara. According to legend, the gold statue of the Asakusa Kannon was fished out of the Ōkawa by two fishermen, the brothers Hinokuma Hamanari and Takenari, in 628. Soon after, the head of the riverbank village converted his house into a Buddhist temple, which later became the grounds of the Sensō Temple. The statue of the Asakusa Kannon is hidden from public view in a sealed container kept in the main hall of the Sensō Temple.

Asakusa Kannon Temple: (1) See Sensō Temple.

Asakusa opera: (7) General term for very popular shows in Asakusa theaters from around 1917 that included various kinds of musical performances. This mass entertainment died out with the proliferation of dance revues, movie theaters, and swordfight plays in the years after the 1923 earthquake.

Asakusa Park: (1) One of five parks around large temples formerly connected to the Tokugawa family and opened to the public in 1873 by the Meiji government. Asakusa Park was enlarged in 1876 and 1882, and two artificial ponds were added in 1883. It was divided into the following seven districts in 1884: FIRST DISTRICT: Area around the main hall and other buildings of the Sensō Temple complex. SECOND DISTRICT: Area from the Nio Gate to the site of the old Kaminari Gate; it included the Nakamise. **THIRD DIS-TRICT**: Area around the Denpōin. **FOURTH DISTRICT**: Area that included Gourd Pond, the wooded part of the park, the Aquarium, and the Bug House. **FIFTH DISTRICT**: This area was Asakusa's main entertainment district before many theaters and cinemas opened in the Rokku; it included Okuyama and the Hanayashiki. **SIXTH DISTRICT**: Cinema and theater district also known as the Rokku. **SEVENTH DISTRICT**: Area southeast of the park. Asakusa Park was largely destroyed in the bombing of Tokyo during the Second World War, and the grounds were given back to the Sensō Temple by the Allied Forces. The temple sold much of the land in the early 1950s, and the park no longer exists.

Asakusa phony revue: (38) *(Inochiki rebū)* Playful and self-deprecating nickname for the Casino Folies revue used around 1930 by Kawabata and other authors who wrote scripts for the Casino Folies and by the members of the troupe. The name was a pun on the many sham shops selling imitation goods in Asakusa.

Asakusa Station: (15) Tobu railway line station located close to the site of the Kaminari Gate. The seven-story terminal was opened in 1931 and housed the Asakusa Matsuya Department Store.

Asakusa Street: (28) (Asakusa Hirokoji) Main street of Asakusa, lined with shops, restaurants, and other commercial buildings, that ran in front of the site of the Kaminari Gate from Azuma Bridge in the east to Asakusa Hongonji in the west.

Atami: (38) Resort city known for its hot springs, located in Shizuoka Prefecture in the eastern part of the Ise Peninsula.

Author's Note: Written in old-style language, the author's note is an allusion to and play on the Edo period convention by which an author takes responsibility for his work and any possible consequences it might have at the very beginning of the text. This is the first of many references to the Edo period that permeate the novel.

Azuma Bridge: (30) The iron Azuma Bridge was first constructed in 1882 and then rebuilt in 1931. Wooden bridges had existed at the site from the second half of the eighteenth century and were often depicted in woodblock prints.

Bat cigarettes: (58) Golden Bat cigarettes, a brand first sold in 1906 that was less expensive than Asahi and Shikishima. The words "Golden Bat" were printed in English on the package; the cigarettes were often referred to as just "Bat."

Benzaiten: (28) Originating in India, the only female diety among the seven *Shichifukujin,* or Gods of Good Fortune. Goddess of wisdom, beauty, music, rhetoric, and luck, among other virtues. Benzaiten is said to help secure success in financial matters but to have a reputation for being jealous.

bird catcher: (1) Although not always in the form described here, the bird catcher was a character appearing Edo-period illustrated books. There are several references to birds, or *tori,* in *The Scarlet Gang of Asakusa,* and perhaps the bird catcher is also one incarnation of the narrator, who "hunts out little birds" in his travels through Asakusa Park. In Japanese mythology, birds were also believed to be bearers of the souls of the deceased.

birds of the capital: (31) *(miyakodori)* White and black seagulls with red legs and beaks. A poem containing puns on the name of these birds appears in the tenth-century *Tales of Ise (Ise monogatari)* and *Anthology of Imperial Poetry (Kokin wakashū).* The legendary site of the poem is now in Tokyo's Mukōjima. In the *Tales of Ise,* Lord Narihira asks a *miyakodori* how his lover is faring in Kyoto.

Boat Tokikō: (5) At the time of the novel, boat children had become a social problem. Children of families living on barges on the Ōkawa commuted to elementary school in Asakusa, and, since their parents were often unable to pick them up in the afternoon, they were left behind to pass the time in Asakusa Park, often becoming gang members and delinquents.

Bōshū: (57) Old name for Chiba Prefecture.

bottom of a wooden sandal: (36) At the time of *The Scarlet Gang of Asakusa,* Tokyo did not look like a modern metropolis; it had very few large buildings, and, especially downtown, most of the homes and businesses were shabby wooden structures. Seen from above, Tokyo looked like a worn Japanese wooden sandal or *geta* flipped upside down, its buildings poking up from the expanse of ground like the two platforms on the sole of the sandal.

The Boy Companion: (10) The name of the revue is *Suteku boii,* literally "stick boy," a slang term coined in 1929 to describe young men who accompanied wealthy older women on strolls in the Ginza. There was also a "stick girl," and through the first half of the 1930s these figures often appeared in comics, short stories, essays, and other written and visual media about the erotic and seductive aspects of modern Tokyo and its underworld.

Boy's Day: (51) Also known as the Iris Festival, celebrated on May 5. Traditionally, carp streamers are hung outside homes and warrior dolls are displayed inside. Rice cakes filled with sweet beans and wrapped in oak leaves *(kashiwamochi)* or bamboo leaves *(chimaki)* are eaten.

The Bride of the Eiffel Tower: (34) The play *Les mariés de la Tour Eiffel* by Jean Cocteau was performed at the Casino Folies and other venues in Japan from 1924 on.

Casino Folies: (3) A revue troupe composed mainly of girls between twelve and sixteen years of age. It opened in Asakusa on July 10, 1929, and closed on June 11, 1932. The name came from France's Casino de Paris and Folies-Bergère. Performers included Hanajima Yuko, Umezono Ryūko, Tokugawa Musei, Furukawa Roppa, and Mochizuku Yūko. Patrons ranged from the lower strata of the Asakusa population to Western-style artists and modernist writers. The Casino Folies became popular largely because of *The Scarlet Gang of Asakusa* and a rumor that the dancers dropped their drawers one day a week. A version of *The Scarlet Gang of Asakusa* was performed by the Casino Folies from July 10, 1930. This revue and its dancers were the subject of many stories and drawings of the erotic aspects of late 1920s and early 1930s Tokyo.

charms to protect against thunder: (38) At the July *hōzuki* plant market, ears of corn, said to protect against thunder and lightning, are also sold.

Chiba: (15) Prefecture southeast of Tokyo.

chickens they keep at the Holy Kannon Temple: (1) At the time of the story, many people in Tokyo believed that roosters that crowed at night were harbingers of bad luck, and, as a result, they set these birds free in the Sensō

Temple complex. Kawabata described this custom in a 1930 short story entitled "The Rooster and the Dancing Girl" ("Niwatori to odoriko"), which is included in his *Palm-of-the-Hand Stories (Tenohira no shōsetsu)*.

chitose candy: (4) Long sticks of red and white candy sold at the festivals held in November for children celebrating their third, fifth, and seventh birthdays.

-chō: (2) A block or a street within a larger town or city.

Chōmei Temple: (4) Temple in Mukōjima for the deity Benzaiten; famous for the rice cakes wrapped in cherry blossom leaves sold nearby.

Comparing Heights: (15) See Higuchi Ichiyo.

cropped head: (6) *(zangiri)* Term (already old-fashioned by the time *The Scarlet Gang of Asakusa* was written) for the short hair required for men by a law passed in 1872 but seen as improper for women. This rough-cut style is juxtaposed in the novel to bobbed hair, a fashion among flappers and "modern girls." (See entry for "modern boy, modern girl.")

Danjurō: (42) A statue of kabuki actor Ichikawa Danjurō IX (1838–1903), one of Asakusa's best-known performers, was placed behind the Sensō Temple in 1919.

Denkikan: (39) Japan's first movie theater, opened in 1903, rebuilt in 1927, and closed in 1976.

Denpōin: (21) General term for the large residence of the Sensō Temple's high-ranking priests. The Japanese garden in elegant Edo-period style and Large Pond (Oike), in the shape of the Japanese character for heart and mind *(kokoro)*, were constructed to the left of the front entrance.

Edo: (1) Also known as Tokugawa, the Edo period lasted from 1603 to 1868. Edo is also the old name for the city of Tokyo.

Edo holy sites: (28) Sites of cultural, religious, and historical importance were catalogued and described in Edo-period guidebooks, often for educated but general readers who might not have the chance to see these places with their own eyes. Kawabata playfully uses this convention to refer to areas he believes represent modern Tokyo after the 1923 earthquake. Another example is his mention of the "eight new sights of Asakusa" in chapter 31.

Emperor Kanbun: (1) Edo-period emperor who succeeded Emperor Manji and reigned from April 25, 1661, to September 21, 1673.

Emperor Kazan: (2) Heian-period emperor who lived from 968 to 1008 and reigned from 984 to 986.

Emperor Manji: (1) Edo-period emperor who reigned from July 23, 1658, to April 25, 1661, and was succeeded by Emperor Kanbun.

Emperor Sushun: (28) Emperor who reigned from 587 to 592.

Emperor Yōmei: (27) Emperor who reigned from 585 to 587.

Empress Suiko: (21) Empress who reigned from 592 to 628.

end-of-the-year sales: (35) There are two main sales seasons in Japan, at the end of the year or in January and in the middle of the summer. The narrator indicates the passing of time through these references to Asakusa's commercial culture.

Enoshima: (20) Small island in Kanagawa Prefecture located near the city of Kamakura. Place of worship and a resort area since the Kamakura period (1185–1333).

ero: (41) Taken from the English word "erotic," popular slang for "erotic" or "eroticism" or "sexy" at the time of *The Scarlet Gang of Asakusa.*

festivals celebrating the reconstruction of Tokyo: (21) Three days of parades and other events were held in March 1930 to commemorate the rebuilding of Tokyo after the 1923 earthquake.

film of the popular song: (31) *(koutaeiga)* In 1929 and 1930, several short silent films based on the lyrics of popular songs were shown as parts of longer cinematic programs. The *benshi,* or film narrator, would read (not sing) the lyrics while the movie was being projected.

Five Story Pagoda: (2) Fifty-three-meter-high structure built in 942 where the ashes, stupa, and memorial tablet of the Asakusa Kannon were stored. Destroyed during the war, the pagoda was rebuilt in 1973 out of reinforced concrete.

fortune card: (12) *(omikuji)* A slip of paper on which a fortune is written in old-style Japanese. A fortune card is purchased at a temple or shrine and is obtained by shaking a cylindrical box with a small hole until a numbered stick emerges. The number of the fortune card corresponds to that on the stick. (In chapter 12, the card is number 98.) The fortune is divided into categories, including love, business, and health, and, if the prophecy is inauspicious, the card is folded and tied to a tree or specified rack on the temple or shrine grounds in the hopes that it will not come true.

Foujita Tsuguharu: (10) (1886–1968) Known also as Foujita Tsuguji and Leonard Foujita. Western-style artist famous for his drawings of cats and paintings of nudes and still life. Foujita lived most of his life in Paris and became a French citizen in 1955.

Fukagawa: (11) Tokyo city ward east of the Sumida River, containing a licensed prostitution district. In the late Meiji period, there were more bridges in Fukagawa than anywhere else in Tokyo.

Genroku: (47) Period in the Edo era lasting from 1688 to 1704 seen as the golden age of popular literature.

Genroku *yukata*: (47) *Yukata* with wide, round sleeves from the Genroku period that came back in style after 1905.

gidayū: (45) Narrative songs originally from Osaka named after Takemoto Gidayu (1651–1714) and often accompanied by samisen. From the Meiji period, *gidayū* were often sung by attractive young women.

ginkgo-leaf style: (58) A women's tied hairstyle worn primarily in the earlier part of the Meiji period. The hair was arranged in two loops on top of the head with an ornamental clip in the middle so that it resembled the leaf of the ginkgo tree.

Ginza: (11) Glamorous high-class Tokyo entertainment and commercial district often juxtaposed to Asakusa. Taking leisurely walks in the Ginza was a popular pastime among youth in the late 1920s and early 1930s.

Girl's Day: (30) *(Hinamatsuri)* Celebrated on March 3. Dolls in court dress representing the emperor, empress, and attendants are placed on a tiered stand, and diamond-shaped sweets *(hishimochi)* are traditionally eaten. Girl's Day has been referred to as Doll's Day since the Second World War, when Girl's Day and Boy's Day were combined into Children's Day.

Gon no Sōjō, Vice-Bishop Gon: (21) Abbot who wrote the preface to *A History of the Sensō Temple (Sensō enji)* (Tokyo: Sensōji engi hen sankai, 1927), which is quoted here.

Gourd Pond: (2) Small man-made pond in the fourth district of Asakusa Park constructed in 1883, in part to prevent fires. Gourd Pond was filled in 1952 when the Sensō Temple complex sold the land of Asakusa Park.

Great Kanto Earthquake: (1) Also called the Taisho Earthquake and the Tokyo Earthquake. Magnitude 7.9 earthquake that struck Tokyo at 11:58 A.M. on September 1, 1923, and was followed by forty hours of fires. Most of the eastern part of Tokyo, including 96 percent of Asakusa, was destroyed, and more than 90,000 people were killed, 43,000 were missing, and 100,000 were injured. Many social activists and Korean residents were murdered in the days after the earthquake. Tokyo was rebuilt in the later half of the 1920s into a modern metropolis with many tall buildings, public parks, and modern entertainment areas.

gyudon: (6) Cheap meal of sautéed beef over rice sold at street stalls and Japanese fast-food restaurants.

hagoita: (25) Small wooden paddle decorated on one side with either a zodiac animal or a picture of a kabuki actor. Originally used in a game resembling badminton played on New Year's Day, *hagoita* are also good luck charms.

hakama: (1) Formal skirt worn over the bottom of a kimono so that only the top of the kimono is showing. Dark-colored *hakama* were often worn by male university and female secondary school students.

Hakata sash: (55) Lightweight silk kimono sash characterized by a pattern of woven stripes and named for the region in Kyushu where it originated.

Hanajima: (11) Hanajima Yuko, Casino Folies dancer who starred in the 1930 production of *The Scarlet Gang of Asakusa.*

Hanakawadō no Sukeroku: (13) The hero of the 1713 kabuki play *Sukeroku, the Flower of Edo (Sukeroku yukari no Edo zakura),* set in the Yoshiwara. The part was acted by Danjirō IX in the late 1800s and early 1900s. A section of streets and a small park in Asakusa were named Hanakawadō in the late Edo period. The Subway Restaurant Tower building used to be nicknamed Hanakawadō.

Hanayashiki, Hanayashiki dolls: (1) This popular amusement park in Asakusa opened in 1853. At the time of the novel, the Hanayashiki contained a small zoo, stunt birds, a puppet theater, and other sights and amusements. Life-like dolls were placed outside the entrance and, in the fall, were often decorated with flowers. The park was renamed the Asakusa Hanayashiki in 1947 and still exists today.

handle: (2) This is the first example of Asakusa slang presented through the use of the term followed by a definition in parentheses.

haori coat: (28) Hip-length coat usually worn over kimono.

happi coat: (11) A short cloth coat often worn by workers.

Hashiba: (56) A small, poor district located between the Yoshiwara and the Ōkawa.

Healing Buddha's Temple: (8) The Sensō Temple main hall is referred to here as the temple of the Healing Buddha *(yakushisan)*.

Heian: (35) Japanese historical period that lasted from 794 to 1185.

Higuchi Ichiyo: (15) (1872–1896) Author and poet who often wrote about people living in the neighborhoods around the Yoshiwara licensed prostitution district. One of her most famous stories is *Comparing Heights (Takekurabe)*, which describes the activities and emotions of children coming of age in Shitaya Ryūsenji-machi and vividly depicts the atmosphere of this downtown area.

Hitomaro: (27) (Kakinomoto no Hitomaro) (ca. 660–708) Court poet and one of the four principal poets whose work is collected in the *Man'yōshū*, the influential early anthology of Japanese poetry assumed to have been compiled around 760.

Hokkaido: (8) The northernmost and second largest of Japan's four main islands and the site of labor camps at the time of *The Scarlet Gang of Asakusa*.

Hongō: (20) Area northwest of Asakusa where the Imperial University (now Tokyo University) has been located since the 1880s. Many university students live in Hongō, as did the young Kawabata.

Honjo: (4) Area of northeast Tokyo located across from Asakusa on the east bank of the Ōkawa.

house with two sliding-door entrances: (13) Indicates a house of assignation.

hōzuki plant: (38) Plants with lantern-shaped seedpods sold in Asakusa around July 10. The plants serve as decoration and have medicinal purposes, and the empty seedpods are used as whistles. At the July *hōzuki* plant market, ears of corn, said to protect against thunder and lightning, are also sold.

If infected and not treated immediately: (48) The girl is reading the label for a medication used to treat syphilis.

Imahan: (37) Famous sukiyaki restaurant in Asakusa. Sukiyaki is a main dish of thin slices of beef, vegetables, tofu, and other ingredients cooked quickly in soy sauce, usually at the table.

Imperial Cinema: (48) Cinema that opened in 1910 at the site of Panorama Hall, a former showcase of film, photography, and other visual entertainments considered modern at the time.

Inari shrine: (30) Shrine erected for the Shintō god of the harvest and of success in business and financial matters; this god is often associated with the fox.

"innate Buddha nature": (27) According to Buddhist teaching, everyone has an innate nature as benevolent as that of Buddha, but many people do not realize this until the end of their lives. Through Buddhist enlightenment, it is said that an individual comes to realize that he has always possessed an inner sense of goodness.

Inverness: (34) Western-style men's coat with a cape and snug round collar.

Iojima: (14) Also Iwo Jima. Volcanic island located in the Pacific Ocean, southeast of Japan. Annexed by Japan in 1891, Iojima was the site of prison labor camps. The United States Navy landed on Iojima on February 19, 1945, and won the ensuing bloody battle against the Japanese. Iojima was placed under the control of the U.S. Navy in 1951 but was returned to Japan in 1968 and is now under Tokyo's municipal jurisdiction.

Irifune-chō: (2) Section of the Tokyo Kyobashi commercial area situated southwest of Asakusa.

it: (51) Slang taken from the title of the popular American silent movie by the same name, starring Clara Bow and shown in Japan in 1927. "It" refers to an almost indescribable charm and seductive quality possessed usually by a woman. In this chapter, "it" is written three ways: in katakana (the syllabary primarily used for foreign words), in English, and in hiragana (the cursive symbols often used for indigenous words).

Japanese sweets: (30) The traditional sweets named in this chapter, although often reserved for special occasions, would have seemed less exotic to Kawabata's readers than the Western dishes listed on the Subway Restaurant menu.

JOAK: (14) First Japanese radio station, which began broadcasting in March 1925.

Ka'ei: (52) (1848–1854) Period near the end of the Edo era.

Kagurazaka: (44) Neighborhood in central Tokyo that was a popular entertainment area in the beginning of the twentieth century, especially among male secondary school and university students.

Kaminari Gate: (13) Sensō Temple main gate that burned down in 1865 in a fire that spread from the Yoshiwara. It was rebuilt in 1970, ninety-five years later, at the entrance to the Nakamise.

Kaminari sweets: (37) Candy sold in Asakusa made from sugar pressed into small colored cubes.

Kamiya Bar: (36) Relatively inexpensive bar in Asakusa that opened in 1912 and was frequented by different social classes.

Kanda: (15) Area in central Tokyo west of Asakusa associated with prostitution in the Edo period but home to many schools, publishing companies, and bookstores from the Meiji era.

Kan'ichi and Omiya: (38) Characters from the novel *The Gold Demon (Konjiki yasha)*, by Ozaki Kōyō (1876–1903). The novel was serialized in the *Yomiuri* newspaper, with breaks, from January 1, 1897, until Kōyō's death in 1903. Kan'ichi, a poor student, is rejected by his love interest, Omiya, who would rather marry a wealthy man. In a powerful scene set in Atami, Kan'ichi pushes Omiya aside.

Kannon of Konryūsan-Sensōji: (21) See Asakusa Kannon.

***kantei* style:** (40) Calligraphy style created in 1779 by Okazakiya Kanroku of the Nakamura Theater. These wide, round characters have often been used for programs and advertisements for kabuki and sumo.

Kanto area, Kanto Plain: (54) Highly populated area of central Honshu, the main island of Japan. The Kanto area includes Tokyo, Chiba, Saitama, Kanagawa, Gunma, Ibaraki, and Tochigi prefectures.

kappore: (45) Japanese folk dance, usually accompanied by samisen, first performed at shrines. There are many kinds of local *kappore,* and the dance has also been incorporated into kabuki.

Kawagoe: (13) Castle town and city in Saitama Prefecture, northwest of Tokyo.

Kawai Sumiko: (11) Asakusa opera dancer famous for her many male fans.

Keiō: (52) (1865–1868) The last period of the Edo era.

kimono and a soiled sash . . . tied high and red under her breasts: (16) At the time of *The Scarlet Gang of Asakusa,* it was a style for women who wanted to look promiscuous to wear their kimono sashes high and right under their chests, which emphasized their breasts and hips and made their legs appear longer.

Kinshibori Station: (36) At the time of the novel, a streetcar stop along the old Jōtō route (opened in 1925) that ran southeast of Asakusa.

Kiyomoto style: (14) Developed in the nineteenth century, a form of kabuki recitation accompanied by samisen.

Kiyosu Bridge: (54) A 186-meter-long steel bridge over the Sumida River, completed in 1928.

Kobori Enshū: (31) (1579–1647) Architect of gardens and teahouses who is also said to have designed Nijō Castle in Kyoto. He served as a commissioner of public works under the first and third Tokugawa shoguns and was also renowned as a poet, calligrapher, and master of the Japanese tea ceremony.

koku of rice: (52) A measurement used to calculate wealth in the Edo period. One *koku* is roughly the amount of rice needed to feed one man for a year. The number of *koku* connotes how many people a household can support.

Kokubu tobacco: (1) A high-quality tobacco produced in Kokubu City in Kagoshima Prefecture on Kyushu, the southernmost island of Japan. This tobacco was valued in the Edo period for its fragrance.

Kollontai, Alexandra: (35) (1871–1952) Russian writer and social activist. Kollontai wrote about feminist issues from a Communist perspective, and her book *Red Love,* advocating free choice in love and marriage, was widely read in 1920s Japan.

Komagata Bridge: (14) A 239-meter-long steel bridge constructed in 1927 as part of the Tokyo reconstruction projects after the 1923 earthquake.

Komuro bushi: (1) Popular Edo-period songs, many of which originated in Kyushu.

koto: (1) A thirteen-stringed plucked instrument made mostly from wood.

Kototoi Bridge: (1) A 161-meter-long steel bridge constructed in 1928 connecting both riverbanks in Sumida Park and situated in Mukōjima, near the legendary site of the Miyakodori.

kouta: (10) Popular songs accompanied by samisen. In the 1920s and 1930s, many *kouta* were written for jazz rhythms.

krap: (30) Here, "park." In the slang used by people who passed the time in Asakusa Park, words were inverted, and the first character was pronounced before the second. For example, Haruko also says *enko* instead of *koen* for "park." Other such inversions existed in Tokyo slang; for example, the term *doya* was used instead of *yado* in the poor neighborhood of San'ya, located near Asakusa, to specify a cheap hotel in which beds in shared rooms are rented by the night.

kumade **bamboo rake:** (25) Literally, a "bear paw charm." A small bamboo rake decorated with colorful symbols for luck, wealth, health, and other good things. Sold in Tokyo downtown areas, especially around the Yoshiwara.

Kume no Heinai Shrine: (7) Named for Kume no Heinai, the seventeenth-century samurai who killed nearly one thousand men and then, out of guilt, held a memorial service for them. After his death, he became regarded as a deity of romance, and, according to legend, if a woman visits the statue of Kume no Heinai at the shrine, she will marry the man she loves.

Kuramae: (21) Tokyo neighborhood in the same city ward as Asakusa. The steel Kuramae Bridge was constructed in 1927.

Kurikara-Fudō: (28) God of fire.

left girl: (35) In *The Scarlet Gang of Asakusa,* Kawabata makes many puns using terms (even vulgar ones) for "left-handed," jokes that also refer to the political left. The character Left-Handed Hiko *(Hidari kiki no hiko)* is included in this parody.

"light of the fireflies and the snow by the window": (29) "Light of the Fireflies" was a Meiji-period song set to the tune of "Auld Lang Syne" and often sung in schools. The "snow by the window" is a reference to a legend in which Chinese scholars Che Yin and Sun Kang of the Jin dynasty (265–420) were so poor that they could not afford candles or lanterns and had to study by moonlight.

Literary Arts Chronicle: (50) *(Bungei shunjū)* Literary magazine founded in 1923 by popular writer and influential editor Kikuchi Kan. Kawabata was among the early contributors.

Loose-Hair Oito: (41) Until around the 1930s, most women did not cut their hair and wore it in tied styles. Long, loose hair was considered sexually provocative, as witnessed by the sale of erotic photographs of women emerging from the bath, having just washed their hair.

Lord Kira: (17) See Amanoya Rihee.

Lord Narihira: (31) See Narihira.

-machi: (1) Town or section of a city district.

Makura Bridge: (4) Iron bridge built for the Tobu train line.

mannequin girl: (8) *(manekin gaaru)* Job for women in the late 1920s and early 1930s. Mannequin girls were similar to contemporary fashion models, but they stood still in shop windows, attracting the attention of passersby. Mannequin girls were most prevalent in the Ginza, not Asakusa, and, in mass media, art, and literature, they were often described as erotic icons of Tokyo 1920s consumer culture and as symbols of the more liberal gender interactions envisioned to be part of urban life.

Man'yōshū: (27) See Hitomaro.

manzai: (8) A comic dialogue between two people, originally a pair composed of a drummer and a fan dancer. Before making its way into cabaret theaters in the late nineteenth century, radio in the 1920s, and television after the Second World War, *manzai* was performed on the streets.

-maru: (4) Suffix used for boat names.

Meiji: (9) The Meiji period lasted from 1868 to 1912 and was named for the reign of the Meiji emperor. The Tokugawa (1603–1868) feudal hierarchy was abolished, and the Meiji government instituted educational, political, social, and technological changes, in part to catch up with and surpass the West.

Meiji-brand candy: (40) Western-style sweets manufactured by a Japanese company. Meiji marketed Charlie Chaplin caramels before the 1923 earthquake and chocolate bars from 1926 on.

memorial stone for Master Actor Tsuga: (27) Two-meter-high memorial stone erected behind the Sanja Shrine in 1882 to commemorate Edo-period kabuki actor Takemoto Tsuga. Memorial stones for actors, silent film narrators, and other performers were placed in Asakusa Park.

merry-go-round: (8) Located in the fifth district of Asakusa Park. At the time of *The Scarlet Gang of Asakusa,* a three-minute merry-go-round ride cost five sen per child or adult, approximately the same price as a streetcar ticket.

milk hall: (52) First appearing in Tokyo around 1907, a kind of café in which milk and light snacks were sold.

Mimeguri Shrine: (36) Shrine in Mukōjima devoted to Daikokuten and Ebisu, gods of prosperity in business and commerce and two of the seven *Shichifukujin,* Gods of Good Fortune.

Minowa: (48) Tokyo downtown neighborhood north of Asakusa and close to the Yoshiwara.

Mirror of Virtue: (13) A mirror near the police station at the Kaminari Gate that supposedly reflected not only a person's face but also his or her true character. It was said that when someone with an impure heart looked into the Mirror of Virtue, the surface of the mirror became cloudy and the reflection was distorted, even frightening.

mō: (30) Currency no longer in use. At the time of the novel, it was the smallest denomination. One sen was equal to one hundred mō.

modern boy, modern girl: (12) *(modan boii, modan gaaru)* In common use between around 1927 and the Second World War, these terms were often used in a derogative or satirical way to describe young men and women who strolled the city streets (in Tokyo, mostly Ginza and not Asakusa) in the latest fashions and frequented cafés, movie theaters, department stores, and other modern urban entertainments. The term "modern girl" was more widely used than "modern boy." In literature, the popular press, and visual media, the modern girl was represented by her striking physical appearance—sporting short hair and wearing either Western fashions or Japanese kimono with the sash tied high to emphasize her hips and make her legs look longer—and her perceived licentious behavior. More a media construct than a reality, the dangerous and alluring modern girl came to embody the fears of intellectuals, authors, and social critics that Westernization and capitalist consumer culture had advanced too far in Japan.

momoware: (47) Hairstyle worn by teenaged girls in the early twentieth century in which the hair is tied in back and a ribbon is placed in the middle so that it resembles a halved peach *(momo)*.

Momoyama Castle: (31) Fushimi Castle in the Momoyama district of Kyoto, built from 1592 to 1596 by Toyotomi Hideyoshi, who lived there until his death in 1598.

Morinaga caramels: (51) First marketed in 1899 as a modern American-style candy, these milk caramels were packaged in pocket-sized boxes and sold cheaply at train kiosks and general stores. The now-familiar thin yellow box was first used in 1914. The Morinaga Company also marketed caramels to youth in the Taisho period as a substitute for cigarettes.

Mount Tsukuba: (36) The 876-meter-high mountain in Ibaraki Prefecture to the east of Tokyo. Before many tall buildings were constructed in Tokyo, Mount Fuji could be seen in the west and Mount Tsukuba in the east.

mugitoro: (52) Sweet potato sauce poured over barley and sold at cheap eateries that often doubled as unlicensed prostitution houses.

Mukōjima: (2) Area on the east bank of the Ōkawa near Asakusa once renowned for its temple and plum and cherry blossoms. Mukōjima was waning in popularity as a tourist spot by the beginning of the twentieth century.

municipal barracks: (22) The city sponsored the construction of barracks to temporarily house municipal organizations, families, businesses, and train stations after the 1923 earthquake, and several remained through the 1920s.

Musashino Plain: (27) Plain in southwest Kanto extending from Tokyo to Saitama. This area west of Tokyo often appeared in early-twentieth-century literature, including the stories of Kunikida Doppo (1871–1908), who vividly described the nature and growing suburbs there. At the time of *The Scarlet Gang of Asakusa,* parts of the Musashino Plain were becoming more residential, and in the second half of the 1920s, commuter trains were extended to link these neighborhoods to the center of Tokyo.

Nakamise: (1) Literally, "inner shops." First opened in 1885, the approximately 140-meter-long narrow street lined with shops that runs from the Kaminari Gate to the Nio Gate. Although the Asakusa Nakamise is the most famous, *nakamise* are found near most large temples.

Naniwa bushi: (58) (Also known as *rokyōku.*) Ballad-like songs accompanied by samisen. *Naniwa bushi* originated in Osaka in the Edo period and were mostly performed by street musicians. (Naniwa is the old name for Osaka.) Later they became a main attraction of the Tokyo *yose* vaudeville shows. The songs were often based on historical events and traditional tales and legends.

"Naniwa kouta": (10) Name of a popular song.

Narihira: (31) (Ariwara Narihira) (825–880) Famous courtier, poet, and lover. Long assumed to be the author of the *Tales of Ise.*

Narihira Ferry: (34) The legendary site of the poem about the birds of the capital from the *Tales of Ise* is now in Tokyo's Mukōjima.

newly revised "Showa Map" drawn following the reorganization of the city after the shake-up of the 1923 Great Kanto Earthquake: (1) Plans to rebuild Tokyo after the Great Kanto Earthquake included the construction of parks and wide new roads and reorganization of the fifteen city districts that had been created in 1878. Tokyo was divided into thirty-five wards in 1932, and in March 1947, under the Occupation authorities, the boundaries were redrawn to form twenty-two wards. The current twenty-three wards were established in August 1947.

Nikolai Cathedral: (37) Russian Orthodox cathedral in Tokyo's Kanda area completed in 1891 after eight years of construction work. The cathedral was destroyed in the Great Kanto Earthquake, and a smaller structure was built in its place.

Nio Gate: (2) At the time of *The Scarlet Gang of Asakusa,* the main gate entrance to the Sensō Temple complex containing the Niō protector statue.

Niten Gate: (12) East gate of the Sensō Temple, built in 1618; it survived the 1923 earthquake but burned in the Second World War.

O-: (6) Prefix for female first names, especially those of prostitutes and servants.

Obon: (42) Festival of the dead held in the middle of August, when the deceased are said to return to their former homes.

Ohara bushi: (16) Folk songs originally from Kagoshima in Kyushu.

Ōkawa: (2) (Also called Asakusagawa.) The name used to connote the lower reaches of the Sumida River until the first decades of the twentieth century. The Ōkawa was the subject of songs and poems, especially during the Edo period. In *The Scarlet Gang of Asakusa,* Kawabata mostly uses Ōkawa but occasionally refers to this section of the river as Sumida. This usage has been maintained in the translation.

"Okesa Song," "Okesa Dance": (43) Folk dances and songs originating from Niigata Prefecture, northwest of Tokyo; there are many local varieties.

Okichi: (45) Courtesan who was in the service of American General Counsel Townsend Harris (1804–1878) and was the model for Giacomo Puccini's 1904 opera *Madama Butterfly.*

Okuyama: (14) Established after the great fire of 1657 in what became the fifth district of Asakusa Park, Okuyama was a popular amusement area filled with shooting stalls, archery stands, circus tents, show booths, and other forms of entertainment. The area was also known for prostitution. Okuyama faded in popularity with the growth of the Rokku. Now it only remains in the form of a small park.

one-yen taxi: (1) One-yen taxi *(entaku)* service began in Tokyo in 1927. As the name indicates, a passenger could travel anywhere in the Tokyo metropolitan area for one yen. Compared to trains, streetcars, and buses, one-yen taxies were expensive modes of urban transportation. Fares were usually negotiable, however, and as the number of cabs increased and competition intensified, people often paid less.

opera nuts: (11) *(peraguro)* Common slang for avid male fans of Asakusa opera.

Oshiage Station: (36) Station on the old Keijō streetcar route that ran east of Asakusa.

Oshichi: (14) Daughter of a vegetable dealer who was said to have set a fire in order to see her lover again. Oshichi and her family lost their home in the fire of December 1682 that destroyed much of the city (then Edo). They took shelter at a local temple, where Oshichi fell in love with a young monk. In March 1863, Oshichi set her new home on fire in hopes of seeing the young monk again. However, her plan failed; the fire spread and she was executed for arson. Oshichi's story became the subject of puppet theater, kabuki plays, and a story by Ihara Saikaku.

Ōta Nanpo: (52) (1749–1823) Born Ōta Tan and also known as Shokusanjin, Yomo no Akara, and Kyōkaen. Member of a lower-ranking samurai family who served the Tokugawa shogunate. He was a central figure in the literary scene and was known for writing *kyōka,* humorous *waka* poems that satirized eighteenth-century society.

Otori shrine: (25) Shrines erected for the bird sign of the Chinese zodiac. Most Otori shrines are located near the Yoshiwara. *Otori* is also a pun for receiving wealth and other wishes, and, at the Otori festivals held mainly in November at the Yoshiwara, rake-shaped *kumade* charms, *hagoita* paddles, and New Year's decorations are sold.

people beaten to death with iron bars: (21) There was widespread violence against Koreans in Tokyo after the 1923 earthquake, due to rumors that Koreans had caused the earthquake and the forty hours of fires that followed, and to a long history of discrimination in Japan against foreigners, especially from other Asian nations. The police did not stop and even encouraged the killing of Koreans, and the number of casualties reached perhaps as high as two thousand. Several social activists, including anarchists Ōsugi Sakae and Ito Noe, were also murdered.

pigeon ladies: (7) Usually older women who earned money selling beans to feed the many pigeons in Asakusa Park. They could frequently be seen sitting along the roads leading into the Sensō Temple complex.

"poison woman": (34) *(dokufu)* Term in common use in the 1870s and 1880s for femmes fatales or women who had illicit love affairs and committed crimes of passion. Articles about "poison women" appeared in early Meiji-period newspapers. The story of Takahashi Den (commonly called Oden) (1847–1879), who allegedly murdered her husband, was widely published.

police box: (13) Most Tokyo police stations are small booths *(koban)* often found at street corners, park entrances, train stations, and other public places. Today, the words "Police Box" are written in English above the doorways.

Prince Genji: (31) Protagonist of the *Tale of Genji (Genji monogatari)*, said to have been written by Murasaki Shikibu, lady of the court in the service of the empress, around 1000. Genji was described as extremely attractive to the women of the Heian court, which whom he had many love affairs.

pro: (34) I'm a pro, in my overalls: Here, "pro" is short for "proletarian."

recession: (14) The Japanese economy suffered a recession after the First World War, culminating in the financial panic of 1927. Japan was affected by the worldwide depression beginning in 1929, in part because of dependence on American markets. The late 1920s and 1930s were also a time of labor strife and activism, although the government took strict, even violent, measures to prevent social protest.

Red Sashes, Purple Sashes: (40) Unlike the Scarlet Gang, these bands of girls actually existed at the time the novel was written.

rin: (30) Currency no longer in use. One yen was equal to one thousand rin.

Rokku: (2) Popular name for the bustling sixth district of Asakusa Park, where cinemas, opera houses, and theaters were constructed from around 1886. The first movie theater in Japan, the Denkikan, opened in the Rokku in October 1903. The area began to lose popularity in the years after the Second World War and died out by the end of the 1950s.

rubber-soled cloth boots: (1) Close-fitting footwear often worn by laborers. Like *tabi* socks, these have a gap between the big toe and the other toes.

Russo-Japanese War: (52) War fought between Japan and Russia from 1904 to 1905, and the first time in modern history that Japan militarily defeated a Western nation.

samisen: (15) A three-stringed, plucked lute associated with the Edo pleasure quarters and theaters. The front and back of the wooden body of the samisen were traditionally covered with cat or dog skin.

Sanja Shrine: (27) Also known as the Asakusa Shrine. Shrine within the Sensō Temple complex constructed in 1649 where the brothers Hinokuma Hamanari and Takenaro and their lord Haji no Nakatomo, integral to the founding of the Sensō Temple, are enshrined. The Hinokuma brothers were said to have fished the small gold statue of the Asakusa Kannon from the Sumida River in 682, an event that led to the construction of the temple.

Sanja Shrine Festival: (52) Festival of the Sanja Shrine held on the Saturday and Sunday closest to May 17 and 18.

Satō Hachirō: (55) (1903–1973) Born and raised in Asakusa, this writer and poet colorfully described the lives of the lower classes in Tokyo's downtown. He also detailed his own experiences as a youth who passed the time in Asakusa Park. Kawabata referred to Satō's writings about Asakusa while creating *The Scarlet Gang of Asakusa*. Satō also wrote popular songs and children's books and was active in radio and television after the Second World War. Satō's passage quoted in chapter 55 is found in "The Essence of Strange Stories" ("Kidan essensu"), published in the December 1929 issue of the journal *New Currents (Shinchō)*.

selling oil: (61) As Donald Richie explains in the foreword, "selling oil" *(abura o uru)* is a pun for "pulling a fast one and getting away with it"; it also means "loitering."

sen: (1) Currency no longer in use but widely circulating in 1930. One hundred sen equaled one yen.

senryū: (34) Humorous, even bawdy, seventeen-syllable verses about the everyday life of ordinary people at the end of the Edo period, usually by anonymous poets. In the Meiji period, efforts were made to make *senryū* poetry less obscene and to revive it as a satirical literary form. THE FERRY-

MAN CUTS THE NAME OF THE BIRD IN TWO: (34) *Miyakodori* (birds of the capital) is composed of two kanji characters, the one for *miyako* (capital) and the one for *dori* (birds). The joke and social statement in this *senryū* poem are based on reading these two characters separately.

Sensō Temple: (1) Also referred to as the Asakusa Kannon Temple. Large temple in Asakusa that has, for centuries, drawn crowds of visitors for reasons ranging from religious observances to commercial ventures. The main object of worship at the temple is the small gold statue of the Asakusa Kannon, housed in a sealed container in the main hall. The number of visitors to the Sensō Temple increased from around the beginning of the seventeen century as the legend of the Asakusa Kannon's discovery became popularized through help from the government and as travelers passed the complex on their way to the Yoshiwara licensed prostitution quarter.

sheet of writing paper: (23) Packs of Japanese-style writing paper *(hanshi)*, whose standard size was twenty-four by twenty-four centimeters, were given as small presents or tokens of appreciation. Since this kind of writing paper is no longer in common use, this custom has died out.

Shibuya's Dōgenzaka: (34) An area southwest of Asakusa that was growing into a commercial and entertainment district at the time of *The Scarlet Gang of Asakusa,* mostly because of the growth of surrounding suburbs and the extension of commuter train networks. Shibuya reached its heyday as a place popular among youth in the postwar period, and since the time of this novel has been associated with illicit love affairs.

Shikishima: (58) High-class cigarette brand first marketed in 1904.

shimada: (7) A Japanese hairstyle in fashion among unmarried young women in the early twentieth century. The style was first worn in the Yoshiwara and is said to be named after the courtesan from Shimada in Shizuoka Prefecture who made it popular.

Shinjuku: (10) Entertainment area in the western part of Tokyo that attracted various kinds of people, including bad boys and girls, writers and artists, and suburban housewives and businessmen. Reporters and literary writers of the late 1920s and 1930s described Shinjuku as more middle-class than, and lacking the Edo mystique of, Asakusa. Shinjuku Station became Tokyo's most-used train terminal soon after it was constructed in 1925.

Shinshū silk-factory girls: (41) From the latter part of the nineteenth century, girls, mainly from poor, rural areas, were sent or sold by their families to work at silk and cotton factories, many of which were located in the mountainous northern regions. These factories were hard hit by the recession of the late 1920s. (Shinshū is the old name for Nagano Prefecture in northern Japan.)

Shizuoka: (42) Prefecture bordering Yamanashi, Nagano, and Kanagawa prefectures and the Pacific Ocean and containing part of Mount Fuji and the eastern section of the Ise Peninsula.

Shokusanjin: (52) See Ōta Nanpo.

Showa: (1) The Showa period was named for the reign of the Showa Emperor and lasted from 1926 to 1989.

Sino-Japanese War: (7) War that lasted from 1894 to 1895 and ended with Japan's defeat of China and the signing of the Treaty of Shimonoseki.

Soeda Azenbō: (10) (1872–1944) Writer of prose sketches of Asakusa and popular songs, the lyrics of which often depicted social problems with humor. His memorial stone is located on the grounds of the Sensō Temple. While writing this novel, Kawabata consulted Soeda's descriptions of Asakusa.

"Southern Evening," designed by Yosano Akiko: (51) As a joke on the value of literature and novels as commodities, Kawabata calls the different *yukata* fabrics by the names of literary works.

Subway Restaurant, Subway Restaurant Tower: (4) Tall building above the Asakusa subway station. The first subway in Tokyo opened on December 30, 1927, and extended for 2.2 kilometers between Ueno and Asakusa. The subway company constructed tall buildings at both of these stations. The Subway Restaurant Tower is now the site of the Ginza subway line lost-and-found office.

Sumida Park: (4) As part of then-mayor Gotō Shimpei's Tokyo reconstruction plan after the 1923 earthquake, iron and steel bridges were built on the Ōkawa and three large parks were constructed near Asakusa. These included Sumida and Hama-chō parks, situated along the riverbanks. The large bridges constructed on the Ōkawa include the Kototoi Bridge (1928), the Azuma Bridge (1931), the Komagata Bridge (1927), the Kiyosu Bridge (1928), and the Kuramae Bridge (1927).

Sumida River: (21) See Ōkawa.

tabi: (29) Usually white socks with a gap between the big toe and the other toes and worn with sandals and kimono.

Taisho: (1) The Taisho period was named for the reign of the Taisho Emperor and lasted from 1912 to 1926.

Tale of the Scarlet Gang: (38) In chapter 38, the narrator refers to the novel as *The Tale of the Scarlet Gang (Kurenaidan monogatari)*. Chapter 37 was the last chapter serialized in *Tokyo Asahi,* on February 16, 1930. Chapters 38–51 were published in two literary journals (see the translator's preface).

Tanizaki Jun'ichirō: (14) (1886–1965) Novelist who wrote many stories set in Asakusa during the 1910s and 1920s, including *The Mermaid (Kōjin),* which is quoted in chapter 14.

tatami: (20) Rectangular floor mat comprised of a straw base covered in woven rush and used in Japanese houses. Rooms are measured by how many tatami mats they contain. Tatami are different from the flimsy straw mats used by street vendors and by the character Yumiko after the earthquake.

Tawaramachi: (41) Area in west Asakusa.

tekiya: (56) Itinerant peddlers who sold their wares on the streets. *Tekiya* were often low-level *yakuza* or gangsters.

torii: (30) Symbolic gate with two horizontal bars that indicates the entrance to a Shintō place of worship.

Twelve Stories, Twelve Story Tower: (13) Nickname for Ryōunkaku, literally the "cloud-surpassing pavilion." A fifty-meter octagonal red-brick building constructed in 1890, the Twelve Stories was the tallest building in Tokyo and the only structure with a passenger elevator before the 1923 earthquake (although the elevator had been closed by the police in 1891). There were shops selling wares from around the world on the second through seventh floors, restaurants, and an observation deck with telescopes on the tenth floor. The building was lit by electric arc lights at night. Many unlicensed prostitution houses were located around the Twelve Stories until the years after the earthquake, when they were relocated east of the Ōkawa.

two bells under her pillow: (22) There was a superstition that sleeping with two little bells purchased at a temple under one's pillow would help prevent disasters during the night.

Ubamiya and Himemiya: (27) Old legend also described by other twentieth-century writers, including Akutagawa Ryūnosuke. The stone pillow is kept in the Sensō Temple. In *The Scarlet Gang of Asakusa*, the legend is told using both the narrator's voice and a quotation from an unspecified source, indicated by the use of dashes.

Ueno Park: (13) The site of a former nobleman's residence that was turned into a public park in 1873. Tokyo's first art museum (Tokyo Metropolitan Museum of Art), zoo, and other cultural and entertainment facilities were constructed in Ueno Park, and international expositions were held there in the early decades of the twentieth century.

Umekichi's confessions of love: (13) Such a listing of confessions and revelations was an Edo-period literary convention.

Umezono Ryūko: (11) Popular Casino Folies dancer who was the granddaughter of a famous dancer and who, with the help of Kawabata, studied ballet with a Russian teacher. Umezono acted in the 1935 movie version of Kawabata's story "Asakusa Sisters" ("Asakusa no shimei") and appears in stories by Satō Hachirō, Ryūtanji Yū, and other writers who described Tokyo and its erotic appeal at the time.

Ushigome: (52) Old name for the eastern part of Tokyo's Shinjuku ward.

Ushijima Shrine: (2) With a history dating back to around 860, the Ushijima Shrine was moved from Mukōjima to the newly constructed Sumida Park after the earthquake. Visitors to the shrine touch areas of the cow statue that correspond to their own ailing body parts.

Utagawa Toyokuni: (2) (1769–1825) Ukiyoe artist, printmaker, book illustrator, and painter who developed an influential style of portraiture of actors.

Utamaro: (52) Kitagawa Utamaro (1753–1803), Ukiyoe artist and book illustrator known for his portraits of women of the Yoshiwara.

virgin in a box: (34) *(hako iri musume)* Slang used from the 1880s for a treasured daughter whose family tries to protect her from the bad influences of the outside world. Haruko uses this term sarcastically in a play on words with the phrase "to enter into marriage" *(yome iri)*.

votive stickers: (1) *(senjafuda)* Literally, "one thousand blessings." Seals stuck on shrines and other places of worship by individuals or groups to show that they prayed there.

votive tablets: (40) *(ema)* Small flat wooden boards hung by visitors to shrines. Many votive tablets feature pictures of animals, particularly horses. These serve as substitutes for real horses once presented to the gods, especially during times of droughts and floods.

waitress in a white apron: (9) At the time of the novel, it was a fashion for Japanese café waitresses *(jokyū)* to wear white Western-style aprons. Early Showa-period café waitresses were similar to contemporary bar hostesses and served alcoholic beverages, catered to predominantly male customers, and earned a living mostly through tips.

Women's Club: (46) *(Fujin kurabu)*. Founded in 1920, a women's magazine that targeted a broad readership and included articles on fashion and domestic living, along with fiction. Supplementary pamphlets, like those sold in Asakusa sham shops (see chapter 38), were included from 1923 on.

Yamanashi: (41) Mountainous prefecture that borders Tokyo, Kanagawa, Shizuoka, Nagano, and Saitama prefectures.

Yasuki bushi: (5) Fishermen's songs and dances accompanied by drum and flute music; originally from the harbor city Yasugi in western Japan. *Yasuki bushi* were first performed in Osaka in 1914 and Tokyo in 1917 and became extremely popular with audiences in those cities.

Yasukuni Shrine: (37) Shrine dedicated to the memory of soldiers who died in battle. The shrine was named the Shōkon Shrine when it was constructed in 1869 and was renamed the Yasukuni Shrine in 1879.

yen: (1) Introduced as the national currency in 1871. At the time of the novel, one yen equaled one hundred sen.

Yosano Akiko: (50) (1878–1942) Female poet who wrote in both classical Japanese and free verse styles and often described themes of love and passion. She became famous with the publication of her poetry collection *Tangled Hair (Midaregami)* in 1901.

yose: (58) Japanese form of witty comic monologue that originated in the twelfth century. It flourished in the late nineteenth and early twentieth centuries as a popular form of inexpensive vaudeville-style entertainment and was often broadcast on the radio in the 1920s.

Yoshiwara: (1) Licensed prostitution quarter and an important area for the production of art and culture and fashion trends during the Edo period. Established by the Tokugawa military government in 1617, the Yoshiwara was first located on a reclaimed marsh closer to the center of the city of Edo, but it was moved to its present location in 1657 when government officials decided that the old site was needed for urban expansion. A tall gate was placed at the entrance and a large moat was dug around Yoshiwara, mostly to prevent the escape of the women confined there, many of whom were sold into prostitution and were not free by law to leave until 1900. The Yoshiwara had passed its heyday by the turn of the twentieth century and was officially closed in 1958.

Take this road: (1) Asakusa developed into a pleasure area because of its location on the circuitous, mostly land route that led to the Yoshiwara.

displaying the girls' pictures forbidden even in the Yoshiwara: (1) Before the twentieth century, Yoshiwara courtesans often sat, fully adorned in lavish kimono and makeup, in front of their establishments in cage-like structures with bars, facing the public thoroughfares. This practice of displaying women for sale had changed by the time of the novel.

Young Girls' Club: (47) *(Shōjo kurabu)* Magazine for girls begun in 1922. At the time of the novel, photographs of wealthy young women appeared as frontispieces in the magazine.

yukata: (22) Summer kimono, the printed fabric for which was often sold in rolls to be sewn at home.

zubu: (2) One rung in the hierarchy of vagabonds who made their homes in Asakusa Park. Here, Asakusa slang is defined through dialogue between the narrator and one of the members of the Scarlet Gang.

selected bibliography

Unless otherwise noted, the Japanese sources listed here and in the notes were published in Tokyo.

Japanese-Language Sources

Asahara Rokurō. "Shinkō geijutsu ha ni tsuite" (About the New Art School). *Bungei jidai* (July 1930): 48–51.

Asakura Haruhiko. *Shinsōban Meiji sesō hennen jiten* (Chronological Dictionary of Everyday Life in the Meiji Period: New Edition). Tokyodō shuppan, 1998.

Asakusa Rokku kōgyōshi (History of Asakusa Sixth District Entertainments). Shitamachi Shiryōkan, 1983.

Asakusa Sōshi. *Asakusa no kai: 200-kai kinen tokushū* (The Asakusa Society Journal: Special Edition to Commemorate the Two-Hundredth Issue). Miōsha, 1978.

Gon no Sōjō. *Sensō enji* (A History of the Sensō Temple). Sensōji engi hen sankai, 1927.

Hamamoto Komei. *Asakusa fūzoku nijyū jyō* (Twenty Notes on Asakusa Customs). Engeki shuppansha, 1997.

Hatsuda Tohru. *Modan toshi no kūkan hakubutsugaku—Tokyo* (The Natural History of Modern Urban Space: Tokyo). Shokokusha, 1995.

———. *Tokyo: Toshi no Meiji* (Tokyo: The Meiji City). Chikuma shobō, 1994.

Hayashi Junshin and Yoshikawa Fumio. *Tokyo shiden meishozue* (Maps and Pictures of Tokyo Streetcars and the Famous Places They Traversed). JTB kyan bukkusu, 2000.

Hosoma Hiromichi. *Asakusa Jyūnikai—Tō no nagame to 'kindai' no mana- zashi* (Asakusa's Twelve Stories: Viewing the "Modern" from Atop the Tower). Seitōsha, 2001.

Ishiguro Keisho. *Natsukashiki Tokyo* (Tokyo of Days Gone By). Kōdansha, 1992.

Ishikawa Kiyoko. *Anokoro no machi to fūzoku* (The City Streets and Customs of the Time). Morita Photo Laboratory, 1987.

Ishizuka Hiromichi and Narita Ryūichi. *Tokyo no hyakunen* (One Hundred Years of Tokyo History). Yamakawa shuppansha, 1986.

Ishizumi Harunosuke. *Asakusa ritan* (Little-Known Asakusa Stories). Bungeishijō, 1927.

Jinnai Hidenobu. *Tokyo: Sekai no toshi no monogatari* (Tokyo: The Story of a World City). Bungei shunju, 1999.

Kawabata Yasunari. *Asakusa kurenaidan* (The Scarlet Gang of Asakusa). Sen-shinsha, 1930. Facsimile ed., Nihon kindai bungakukan, 1971.

———. *Asakusa kurenaidan* (The Scarlet Gang of Asakusa). In *Kawabata Yasunari zenshū* (Collected Works of Kawabata Yasunari). Vol. 4. Shin-chōsha, 1982.

———. *Asakusa kurenaidan* (The Scarlet Gang of Asakusa). Kōdansha, 1996.

———. *Asakusa kurenaidan ni tsuite* (About *The Scarlet Gang of Asakusa*). In *Isso ikka—Gendai Nihon no essai* (Collected Essays on Modern Japan). Kōdansha, 1991.

———. *Asakusa kurenaidan no koto* (On *The Scarlet Gang of Asakusa*). In *Kawabata Yasunari zenshū* (Collected Works of Kawabata Yasunari). Vol. 33. Shinchōsha, 1982.

————. *Asakusa kurenaidan zokkō* (On the Sequel to *The Scarlet Gang of Asakusa*). In *Kawabata Yasunari zenshū* (Collected Works of Kawabata Yasunari). Vol. 33. Shinchōsha, 1982.

————. *Asakusa matsuri* (Asakusa Festival). In *Kawabata Yasunari zenshū* (Collected Works of Kawabata Yasunari). Vol. 4. Shinchōsha, 1982.

————. *Asakusa matsuri* (Asakusa Festival). Kōdansha, 1996.

————. *Kawabata Yasunari zenshū* (Collected Works of Kawabata Yasunari). 37 vols. Shinchōsha, 1982.

————. *Kon Wajirō, Yoshida Kenkichi ryōshi henchō no Moderunorojio* (On *Modernologio*, edited by Kon Wajirō and Yoshida Kenkichi). In *Kawabata Yasunari zenshū* (Collected Works of Kawabata Yasunari). Vol. 20. Shinchōsha, 1982.

Koga Harue sōsaku no genten: Sakuhin to shiryō de saguru (Koga Harue: Exploring the Origins of His Art through His Works and Materials). Special Exhibition Catalogue. Bridgestone Museum of Art, Ishibashi Foundation Tokyo and Kurume, and Ishibashi Museum of Art, 2001.

Kon Wajirō. *Shinpan dai Tokyo annai* (New Edition of the Guide to Greater Tokyo). Chūō kōronsha, 1929.

Kuno Toyohiko, ed. *Modan TOKIO Rondo: Shinkōgeijutsuha jūninin.* (Modern Tokyo Rondo: Works by Twelve New Art School Authors). Sekai daitokai sentan jazu bungaku shiriizu (Vanguard Jazz Literature of the World's Biggest Cities). Shun'yōdō, 1930.

Maeda Ai. *Bungaku no machi* (The City in Literature). Shogakkan raiburari, 1991.

————. *Toshi kūkan no naka no bungaku* (Literature and Urban Space). Chikuma shobō, 1989.

Masai Yasuo. *Kono issatsu de Tokyo no chiri ga wakaru!* (All You Need to Know about Tokyo Geography in One Book). Mikasa shobō, 2000.

Masaoka Iruru. *Meiji Tokyo fūzokugo jiten* (Dictionary of Tokyo Customs of the Meiji Period). Chikuma shobō, 2001.

Matsumoto Kazuya. *Tokyo shiseki gaido—Taito ku shiseki sanpo* (A Guide to Tokyo Historical Landmarks: A Walk through the Taito Ward). Gakuseisha, 1992.

Mochizuki Yūko. "*Kurenaidan* no ano koro" (About the Time of *The Scarlet Gang*). In Takami Jun, ed., *Asakusa*. Eihōsha, 1955.

Odagairi Susumu. *Nihon kindai bungaku nenpyō* (An Annotated Chronology of Modern Japanese Literature). Shogakkan, 1993.

Okuyama Masurō. *Wagashi no jiten* (Dictionary of Japanese Sweets). Tokyodō shuppan, 1989.

Satō Hachirō. *Asakusa*. Shirotosha, 1931.

———. "Kidan essensu" (Essence of Strange Stories). *Shinchō* (December 1929): 58–62.

Shigenobu Yukihiko. *Takushii/Modan Tokyo minzokushi* (Taxi: Journal of Modern Tokyo Folk Customs). Nihon editaa sukuru, 1999.

Shimokawa Akishi, ed. *Taisho kateishi nenpyō* (A Chronological Listing of the History of the Family in the Meiji and Taisho Periods). Kawade shobō shinsha, 2000.

Shinchōsha Nihon bungaku arubamu bekkan: Showa bungaku arubamu I (Shinchō Publishing Company Albums of Japanese Literature Supplementary Volume: Showa Literature Album I). Shinchōsha, 1986.

Shirahama Ken'ichirō. *Asakusa no techō: Tokyo no furusato* (Asakusa Notebook: On Tokyo's Hometown). Kyōei shobō, 1978.

Shitamachi hajimete monogatari (Introduction to Downtown Tokyo). Shitamachi Shiryōkan, 2001.

Showa hayariutashi (History of Popular Songs of the Showa Era). Mainichi shimbunsha, 1985.

Shūkan Asahi, ed. *Nedan no Meiji, Taisho, Showa fūzoku shi* (A Cultural History of the Prices of Objects and Practices in the Meiji, Taisho, and Showa Periods). Vol. 1. Asahi shimbunsha, 1981.

———. *Nedan no Meiji, Taisho, Showa fūzoku shi* (A Cultural History of the Prices of Objects and Practices in the Meiji, Taisho, and Showa Periods). Vol. 2. Asahi shimbunsha, 1981.

———. *Nedan no Meiji, Taisho, Showa fūzoku shi* (A Cultural History of the Prices of Objects and Practices in the Meiji, Taisho, and Showa Periods). Vol. 3. Asahi shimbunsha, 1981.

Shūkan Yearbook: Nichiroku 20 seiki—1927 (Weekly Yearbook: Journal of the Twentieth Century—1927). Kōdansha, 1998.

Shūkan Yearbook: Nichiroku 20 seiki—1929 (Weekly Yearbook: Journal of the Twentieth Century—1929). Kōdansha, 1998.

Shūkan Yearbook: Nichiroku 20 seiki—1931 (Weekly Yearbook: Journal of the Twentieth Century—1931). Kōdansha, 1998.

Shūkan Yearbook: Nichiroku 20 seiki—20 seiki nito monogatari—Tokyo to Osaka (Weekly Yearbook: Journal of the Twentieth Century—A Tale of Two Twentieth-Century Cities: Tokyo and Osaka). Kōdansha, 1999.

Soeda Azenbō. *Asakusa teiryūki* (Record of the Asakusa Underworld). Kindai seikatsusha, 1930.

Suzuki Masao. *Tokyo no chiri ga wakaru jiten* (Guide to Understanding Tokyo Geography). Nihon jigyō shuppansha, 1999.

Takami Jun, ed. *Asakusa.* Eihōsha, 1955.

Takeuchi Makoto. *Edo no sakariba ko—Asakusa Ryōgoku no sei to zoku* (Considering Edo Entertainment Districts: The Holy and Profane of Asakusa and Ryogoku). Kyōiku shuppansha, 2000.

Takeuchi shōten shinsha, ed. *Chōronguseraa daizukan: Kao sekken kara kappu nuudoru made* (Big Illustrated Book of Longtime Bestsellers: From Kao Soap to Cup Noodles). Takeuchi shōten shinsha, 2000.

Tanaka Satoshi. *Chizu kara kieta Tokyo isan: Jinbutsu tanbō* (Tokyo Landmarks That Have Disappeared from the Map: Inquiring about Great Men). Shōdensha, 2000.

———. *Chizu kara kieta Tokyo isan: Meisho tanbō* (Tokyo Landmarks That Have Disappeared from the Map: Inquiring about Famous Places). Shōdensha, 1999.

Tanizaki Jun'ichirō. *Kōjin* (The Mermaid). In Chiba Junji, ed., *Jun'ichirō rabirinsu* (Jun'ichirō's Labyrinth), vol. 9. Chūō kōronsha, 1998.

Tokyo Taito-ku. *Taito fūzoku bunka shi* (The History of Taito Ward Customs and Culture). Taito-kuyakushō, 1957.

Tokyo toshizu (Tokyo City Map). Shobunsha, 2001.

Tokyo-to, ed. *Tokyo hyakunenshi* (One Hundred Years of Tokyo History). Vol. 5. Gyōsei, 1979.

Tsuda Kiyo and Murata Koko. *Modan keshō shi—yosoi no hachijyūnen* (The History of Modern Cosmetics: One Hundred and Ten Years of Makeup). Pola bunka kenkyūjo, 1986.

Tutida Mituhumi. *Tokyo bungaku chime jiten* (Dictionary of Place-names in Tokyo Literature). Tokyodō shuppan, 1978.

Unno Hiroshi. "Bohemian ga toshi sakariba o tsukuru" (Bohemians Create City Entertainment Districts). In *Tokyo Jin. Tokushu: Modan Tokyo sakariba annai* (Special Issue: Guide to Modern Tokyo Entertainment Districts). Vol. 1 (November 1992): 44–47.

———. *Modan Toshi Tokyo: Nihon no 1920 nendai* (Modern City Tokyo: The 1920s in Japan). Chūō kōronsha, 1988.

———. *Shinhen Tokyo no sakariba* (Tokyo Entertainment Districts: New Edition). Attsu ando kurafutsu, 2000.

Wada Hirofumi. *Tekutsuto no modan toshi* (The Modern City in Literature). Nagoya: Fubaisha, 1999.

Yamada Taichi. *Asakusa: Dochi no kioku* (Asakusa: Local Memories). Iwanami shōten, 2000.

Yonekawa Akihiko. *Yonde ninmari: otoko to onna no hayari kotoba* (Popular Words for Men and Women: Read Them and Smile). Shogakkan, 1998.

Yoshimi Shun'ya. *Toshi no doramaturugi: Tokyo sakariba no shakaishi* (The Dramaturgy of the City: The Social History of Tokyo Entertainment Districts). Kobundō, 1987.

Yoshiyuki Eisuke. *Yoshiyuki Eisuke to sono jidai—Modan toshi no hikari to kage* (Yoshiyuki Eisuke and His Times: The Light and Shadows of the Modern City). Ed. Yoshiyuki Kazuko and Saito Shunji. Tokyo shiki shuppan, 1997.

English-Language Sources

Benjamin, Walter. "The Task of the Translator: An Introduction to the Translation of Baudelaire's *Tableaux parisiens*." In *Illuminations*. Trans. Harry Zohn, ed. and intro. Hannah Arendt. New York: Schocken, 1968.

Bradbury, Malcolm. "Modernism." In *A Dictionary of Modern Critical Terms.* Ed. Roger Fowler. London: Routledge & Kegan Paul, 1987.

Chapman, Robert, ed. *American Slang.* 2d ed. New York: HarperCollins, 1998.

Danly, Robert Lyons. *In the Shade of Spring Leaves: The Life and Writing of Higuchi Ichiyo, a Woman of Letters in Meiji Japan.* New York: W. W. Norton, 1992.

Fowler, Edward. *San'ya Blues: Laboring Life in Contemporary Tokyo.* Ithaca, NY: Cornell University Press, 1996.

Freedman, Alisa. "Tracking Japanese Modernity: Commuter Trains, Streetcars, and Passengers in Tokyo Literature, 1905–1935." PhD diss., University of Chicago, 2002.

Gessel, Van C. *Three Modern Novelists: Sōseki, Tanizaki, Kawabata.* Tokyo: Kodansha International, 1993.

Hur, Nam-lin. *Prayer and Play in Late Tokugawa Japan: Asakusa Sensōji and Edo Society.* Cambridge, MA: Harvard University Press, 2000.

Ito, Ken K. *Visions of Desire: Tanizaki's Fictional Worlds.* Stanford, CA: Stanford University Press, 1991.

Jinnai, Hidenobu. *Tokyo: A Spatial Anthropology.* Trans. Kimiko Nishimura. Berkeley: University of California Press, 1995.

Kataoka, Yoshikazu. "*Asakusa kurenaidan.*" In *Introduction to Contemporary Japanese Literature.* Tokyo: Kokusai Bunka Shinkokai, 1939.

Kawabata, Yasunari. *Beauty and Sadness.* Trans. Howard Hibbett. New York: Alfred A. Knopf, 1975.

———. *First Snow on Fuji.* Trans. Michael Emmerich. Washington, DC: Counterpoint Press, 1999.

———. *"House of Sleeping Beauties" and Other Stories.* Trans. Edward Seidensticker. Intro. Mishima Yukio. Tokyo: Kodansha International, 1969.

———. *The Izu Dancer.* Trans. J. Martin Holman. Washington, DC: Counterpoint Press, 1998.

———. *"The Izu Dancer" and "Snow Country."* Trans. Edward Seidensticker. New York: Alfred A. Knopf, 1969.

———. *Japan, the Beautiful, and Myself.* Trans. Edward Seidensticker. Tokyo: Kodansha International, 1969.

―――. *The Lake*. Trans. Reiko Tsukimura. Tokyo: Kodansha International, 1974.

―――. *The Master of Go*. Trans. Edward Seidensticker. New York: Alfred A. Knopf, 1972.

―――. *The Old Capital*. Trans. J. Martin Holman. San Francisco: North Point Press, 1987.

―――. *Palm-of-the-Hand Stories*. Trans. Lane Dunlop and J. Martin Holman. San Francisco: North Point Press, 1988.

―――. *The Sound of the Mountain*. Trans. Edward Seidensticker. New York: Alfred A. Knopf, 1970.

―――. *Thousand Cranes*. Trans. Edward Seidensticker. New York: Alfred A. Knopf, 1959.

Keene, Donald. *Dawn to the West: Japanese Literature of the Modern Era*. Vol. 3. New York: Holt, Rinehart, and Winston, 1984.

Kodansha Encyclopedia of Japan. Tokyo: Kodansha International, 1983.

Lippit, Seiji Mizuta. "Japanese Modernism and the Destruction of Literary Form: The Writings of Akutagawa, Yokomitsu, and Kawabata." PhD diss., Columbia University, 1997.

―――. *Topographies of Japanese Modernism*. New York: Columbia University Press, 2002.

McCullough, Helen Craig. *Kokin Wakashū: The First Imperial Anthology of Japanese Poetry*. Stanford, CA: Stanford University Press, 1985.

―――. *Tales of Ise: Lyrical Episodes from Tenth-Century Japan*. Stanford, CA: Stanford University Press, 1968.

Menzies, Jackie. *Modern Boy, Modern Girl: Modernity in Japanese Art, 1910–1935*. Sydney: Art Gallery of New South Wales, 1998.

The New Tokyo Bilingual Atlas. Tokyo: Kodansha International, 1993.

Richie, Donald. *Japanese Literature Reviewed*. Tokyo: I.C.G. Muse, 2003.

―――, ed. *Words, Ideas, and Ambiguities: Four Perspectives on Translating from the Japanese*. Chicago: Imprint Publications, 2000.

Rubin, Jay. *Haruki Murakami and the Music of Words*. London: Harvill Press, 2002.

Sawamura, Sadako. *My Asakusa: Coming of Age in Pre-War Tokyo.* Trans. Norman E. Stafford and Yasuhiro Kawamura. Boston: Charles E. Tuttle, 2000.

Seidensticker, Edward. "Edward Seidensticker on Nagai Kafū and Kawabata Yasunari." In Donald Richie, ed., *Words, Ideas, and Ambiguities: Four Perspectives on Translating from the Japanese.* Chicago: Imprint Publications, 2000.

———. *Kafū the Scribbler: The Life and Writings of Nagai Kafū.* Stanford, CA: Stanford University Press, 1965.

———. "Kawabata Yasunari." In *Kodansha Encyclopedia of Japan.* Vol. 4. Tokyo: Kodansha International, 1983.

———. *Low City, High City: Tokyo from Edo to the Earthquake.* Cambridge, MA: Harvard University Press, 1983.

———. "On Trying to Translate Japanese." In John Biguenet and Rainer Schulte, eds., *The Craft of Translation.* Chicago: University of Chicago Press, 1989.

———. *Tokyo Rising: The City Since the Great Earthquake.* Cambridge, MA: Harvard University Press, 1990.

Shea, G. T. *Leftwing Literature in Japan: A Brief History of the Proletarian Literary Movement.* Tokyo: Hosei University Press, 1964.

Silverberg, Miriam. "Constructing the Japanese Ethnography of Modernity." *Journal of Japanese Studies* 51, no. 1 (February 1992): 30–54.

Smith, Henry Dewitt, II. "Tokyo as an Idea: An Exploration of Japanese Urban Thought until 1945." *Journal of Japanese Studies* 4 (Winter 1978): 45–80.

Snyder, Stephen. *Fictions of Desire: Narrative Form in the Novels of Nagai Kafū.* Honolulu: University of Hawaii Press, 2000.

Tanizaki, Jun'ichirō. "The Secret." Trans. Anthony Hood Chambers. In Aileen Gatten and Anthony Hood Chambers, eds., *New Leaves: Studies and Translations of Japanese Literature in Honor of Edward Seidensticker.* Ann Arbor: Center for Japanese Studies, University of Michigan, 1993.

Waley, Paul. *Tokyo: City of Stories*. New York: Weatherhill, 1991.

———. *Tokyo Now and Then: An Explorer's Guide*. New York: Weatherhill, 1984.

Weisenfeld, Gennifer. *MAVO: Japanese Artists and the Avant-Garde, 1905–1931*. Berkeley: University of California Press, 2001.

illustration credits

All drawings are by Ōta Saburō and appear courtesy of his estate.
Frontispiece: Cover illustration of *Asakusa kurenaidan* (Senshinsha, 1930).

Photographs

Page xii: Visitors to the Sensō Temple in the 1920s. Courtesy of the Edo-Tokyo Museum.

Page xii: The Nakamise and the Nio Gate, 1924. Courtesy of the Shitamachi Museum.

Page xv: The Rokku in the late 1920s. Courtesy of the Shitamachi Museum.

Page xv: The Rokku and its cinemas and revue halls, 1933. Courtesy of the Shitamachi Museum.

Page xvi: Movie theaters in Asakusa Park around 1930. Courtesy of the Shitamachi Museum.

Page xvi: Movie theaters in the Rokku in the second half of the 1920s. Courtesy of the Edo-Tokyo Museum.

Page xx: The Twelve Story Tower, sometime between 1910 and 1923. Courtesy of the Shitamachi Museum.

Page xxii: Poster for the Casino Folies revue, June 9, 1930. Courtesy of the Shitamachi Museum.

Page 182: Yasunari Kawabata and Donald Richie. Courtesy Donald Richie.
Page 186: The Subway Restaurant Tower, ca. 1930. Courtesy of the Shitamachi Museum.

Drawings

Page 3: From "The Piano Girl," *Tokyo Asahi,* December 12, 1929.
Page 6: From "The Piano Girl," *Tokyo Asahi,* December 13, 1929.
Page 7: From "The Piano Girl," from *Asakusa kurenaidan* (Tokyo: Senshinsha, 1930).
Page 9: From "The Piano Girl," *Tokyo Asahi,* December 14, 1929.
Page 12: From "Sumida Park," *Tokyo Asahi,* December 15, 1929.
Page 15: From "Sumida Park," *Tokyo Asahi,* December 17, 1929.
Page 18: From "Cropped-Head O-So-and-So," *Tokyo Asahi,* December 19, 1929.
Page 21: From "Cropped-Head O-So-and-So," *Tokyo Asahi,* December 20, 1929.
Page 24: From "The Bug House," *Tokyo Asahi,* December 21, 1929.
Page 27: From "The Bug House," *Tokyo Asahi,* December 22, 1929.
Page 30: From "The Aquarium," *Tokyo Asahi,* December 25, 1929.
Page 33: From "The Aquarium," *Tokyo Asahi,* December 26, 1929.
Page 34: From "The Aquarium," from *Asakusa kurenaidan* (Tokyo: Senshinsha, 1930).
Page 36: From "The Aquarium," *Tokyo Asahi,* December 29, 1929.
Page 40: From "Silver Cat Umekō," *Tokyo Asahi,* January 5, 1930.
Page 43: From "Silver Cat Umekō," *Tokyo Asahi,* January 8, 1930.
Page 46: From "Silver Cat Umekō," *Tokyo Asahi,* January 10, 1930.
Page 48: From "Silver Cat Umekō," *Tokyo Asahi,* January 11, 1930.
Page 51: From "Silver Cat Umekō," *Tokyo Asahi,* January 14, 1930.
Page 54: From "The Dirigible and the Twelve Stories," *Tokyo Asahi,* January 16, 1930.
Page 56: From "The Dirigible and the Twelve Stories," *Tokyo Asahi,* January 17, 1930.

Page 58: From "The Dirigible and the Twelve Stories," from *Asakusa kurenaidan* (Tokyo: Senshinsha, 1930).

Page 59: From "The Dirigible and the Twelve Stories," *Tokyo Asahi,* January 19, 1930.

Page 62: From "The Great Kanto Earthquake," *Tokyo Asahi,* January 24, 1930.

Page 65: From "The Great Kanto Earthquake," *Tokyo Asahi,* January 25, 1930.

Page 67: From "The Great Kanto Earthquake," *Tokyo Asahi,* January 28, 1930.

Page 68: From "The Great Kanto Earthquake," from *Asakusa kurenaidan* (Tokyo: Senshinsha, 1930).

Page 71: From "The Great Kanto Earthquake," *Tokyo Asahi,* January 29, 1930.

Page 74: From "The Arsenic Kiss," *Tokyo Asahi,* January 31, 1930.

Page 76: From "The Arsenic Kiss," *Tokyo Asahi,* February 1, 1930.

Page 80: From "Ubamiya and Himemiya," *Tokyo Asahi,* February 2, 1930.

Page 83: From "Ubamiya and Himemiya," *Tokyo Asahi,* February 4, 1930.

Page 87: From "The New 'Light of the Fireflies' Song," *Tokyo Asahi,* February 6, 1930.

Page 89: From "The New 'Light of the Fireflies' Song," *Tokyo Asahi,* February 7, 1930.

Page 93: From "Concrete," *Tokyo Asahi,* February 8, 1930.

Page 96: From "Concrete," *Tokyo Asahi,* February 9, 1930.

Page 99: From "Birds of the Capital," *Tokyo Asahi,* February 11, 1930.

Page 101: From "Birds of the Capital," *Tokyo Asahi,* February 13, 1930.

Page 104: From "Birds of the Capital," *Tokyo Asahi,* February 14, 1930.

Page 107: From "The Bride of the Tower," *Tokyo Asahi,* February 15, 1930.

Page 108: From "The Bride of the Tower," from *Asakusa kurenaidan* (Tokyo: Senshinsha, 1930).

Page 111: From "The Bride of the Tower," *Tokyo Asahi,* February 16, 1930.

Designer Nicole Hayward | **Text** 10/15 Scala | **Display** Trade Gothic Condensed
Compositor Integrated Composition Systems | **Printer and binder** Friesens Corporation